Stop being foolish, Miranda, she said to herself. You didn't come to London for romantic adventures. You came for the sake of Amanda. You must act like a well-brought-up young lady, not a flighty rustic. Ladies aren't allowed to be foolish. Only poor peasant girls can afford the luxury of falling in love.

A poor peasant girl . . . A sudden wave of fatigue made her shoulders droop. She squared them resolutely. Just a few more weeks to keep up this stupid pretense. But, dear God, she thought, I'm growing so weary. Let it end, let it end soon. Soon, God, but not too soon. I must have one more chance to see Theo Moreland!

THE

COUNTERFEIT BRIDE

a novel by

Vivian Connolly

FAWCETT COVENTRY • NEW YORK

THE COUNTERFEIT BRIDE

Published by Fawcett Coventry Books, a unit of CBS Publications, the Consumer Publishing Division of CBS Inc.

ISBN: 0-449-50099-3

Printed in the United States of America

First Fawcett Coventry Printing: September 1980

10 9 8 7 6 5 4 3 2 1

Chapter One

"Miranda! Miranda! I've had the most frightful news!"

With a sigh of regret, Miranda Testa laid aside her book. Stretching like a cat in the warmth of the August sunshine, she slipped her calloused feet back into the goatskin sandals, then jumped up and leaned her lithe, young body over the wrought iron balcony railing. The gilded coach on the carriageway below had just discharged its cargo. Miranda caught a glimpse of a flurry of blue and white chintz, whisking through the great bronze front doors of the Villa Bertolini.

What could have happened in Florence to send the *signorina* home in so frantic a state? Miranda turned and ran back into the villa and down toward the entrance hall. She met Amanda Fitton halfway up the broad marble staircase. "Oh, Miranda, my dearest comrade! I shall die, I shall certainly die! Oh my darling Charles, what's to become of us! This frightful predicament! I shall never survive it!"

"*Calmati, mia cara.* Take time to catch your breath." Miranda put a comforting arm around the girl's fragile shoulders, urged her up the staircase and into her bedroom, settled her on a sofa, took off her wide-brimmed Leghorn hat and stroked the golden hair with a soothing hand. "What is this terrible news? Has the milliner's shop run out of your favorite ribbons?"

"Please don't jest with me, little Miranda. You know me better than that. This is no frivolous whim. It's a major catastrophe. Mr. Armour, my guardian in London, has sent a most urgent letter. He says I must go there at once, or risk losing all my fortune."

Miranda frowned doubtfully. "Perhaps he's exaggerating? Your dear *papa* was so certain of his arrangements. Long before he was carried off by that miserable fever, he'd contrived to make you secure against any hazard."

Amanda shrugged impatiently. "Who knows what those pestilent Whigs may be up to now? You know how they made *papa* suffer all through his life, just because he was honorable enough to keep his oath to King James."

Miranda nodded. "They drove the *signore* from his homeland. But some friends remained loyal to him. They managed to save his estates—"

"Which now are threatened with seizure. I don't know the details. Mr. Armour says he can save them, but I must appear in person. I read the letter to Mr. Faldini, my banker in Florence. He looked very grave, and said I must go at once."

"Then what's all this talk of dying and frightful predicaments? You have nothing to worry about. You will go to London; this Mr. Armour of yours will help you to save your estates. How can you cavil at that? If I were in your shoes, I'd be giddy with pleasure. To spend a month or two in that wonderful London, see all those marvelous shops, meet those paragons of wit and fashion whom *Maestro* MacCrae told us so much about—"

"If only it were that simple. But I don't trust this Mr. Armour."

Miranda felt a chill that traveled the length of her spine. Amanda left poor and in want? Surely that couldn't happen! "You don't think it's true what he writes, that your coming will save the estates?"

"Oh, that part is probably true. Mr. Faldini says Mr. Armour has powerful friends at court. But it still rankles in my mind that he was strangely importunate in pressing Lord Fortescue's suit. Surely it isn't part of a guardian's duties to push his ward into marriage?"

"Lord Fortescue? But surely that matter is closed. A preposterous idea, to expect you to promise your hand to a man you had never met. A man so cold-blooded that he sent his cousin to woo his bride for him! When you sent your rejection—"

"That's part of the trouble. I didn't send it."

"But you wrote him! I saw you! You and Lieutenant Charles took hours composing the letter, and it went off by special post."

Amanda waved her hand in an airy gesture. "Mere procrastination. I asked for more time to consider Lord Fortescue's offer."

"But you'd already pledged your hand to his cousin Charles! You'd promised to marry him the moment you came of age. Surely if Lord Fortescue knew—"

"If Lord Fortescue knew, God knows what might happen to Charles. Lord Fortescue wields great power in the Admiralty. You know what an unfeeling kinsman he's always been. In his rage at being thwarted, he could have Charles stationed permanently at the ends of the earth—East India, perhaps, or even New York! How could I follow him there?"

"Surely if you love him enough—"

"My dear Miranda, you've been reading too many sentimental English novels. I love Charles very much here at Villa Bertolini. One day's acquaintance was enough to convince me of that. But out in some jungle, surrounded by savages? Love *might* survive, but I'd rather not take the risk."

"Mr. MacCrae used to say that some people in England considered *us* savages, here in Italy."

"I'm inclined to believe that is true. Certainly Lord Fortescue thinks so. That's why he refused to come here. He calls this a decadent country, lacking in civilization."

Miranda's cheeks grew flushed with indignation. "How dare he say that! With all our magnificent churches and paintings and statues? He can't be much of a scholar, to dismiss us like that."

"A scholar? Of course not. Don't be misled by our dear old *maestro*'s nonsense. No English *milord* has time to dabble in scholarship. He's much too busy with higher pursuits like gambling and racing."

Miranda bit her tongue to check an impulsive retort. What did Amanda know of that life in London, where learned men like the great Dr. Johnson were the toast of the town? Where men of fashion vied with each other to surpass Mr. Walpole's collection of *objets d'art*? Where Mr. Garrick held the town enthralled with each new production of the great Shakespeare's plays? "You've never seen London," she said. "Shouldn't you pay your father's homeland a visit, before you settle down to marriage and children?" In the back of her mind a timid hope burgeoned: perhaps Amanda would take her along.

"No," said Amanda flatly. "What do I want with London, that immoral city? You should know that yourself from Mr. Fielding's novels, and Mr. Smollett's. When they aren't gambling their money away or killing each other in duels, they're plotting ingenious ways to dishonor women. Don't protest; I'm determined. I've made a vow to my mother's memory to live in her country forever, surrounded by civilized people who believe in enjoying life, not making it hideous."

"Then why not tell Lord Fortescue that? Write him that you've sworn not to leave your mother's country.

8

Even an Englishman must have *some* religion. Your vow will touch his heart, he'll desist in his suit—and the name of Charles needn't come into it."

"Do you think that would end it? You don't know Lord Fortescue. Charles has told me about him. He inherited great estates, but he's always short of money. That's why he made his proposal, to secure my fortune. I'm sure once the wedding was over, he wouldn't give a hang where I lived, so long as he held my estates."

"If he wants your fortune so badly, why won't he come courting himself?"

"I've already told you. He hates this country. He won't set foot here, no matter how urgent his business. That's why I fear this summons from Mr. Armour. I'm afraid Lord Fortescue's induced him to lure me into a trap."

"This summons to London—you think it's a trap? But surely you can't be forced to marry against your will?"

Amanda's green eyes rolled up in despair. "What do I know of the power of these English lawyers? Until I'm twenty-one, I depend upon Mr. Armour for every penny. *Papa*'s will named me his ward. Perhaps he could order me into a marriage. I'd be there in London, one poor weak girl among all his powerful friends—"

"Why not pretend a delay? Tell him you'll come in November, after you're twenty-one! According to Charles's last letter, he'll be back from Jamaica by then. You can go directly to Portsmouth, marry your dear lieutenant, and arrive in London as a married woman."

"That was my first thought also. But it seems I can't wait that long. Mr. Armour's letter says the risk increases hourly."

"Then you mustn't go!" cried Miranda. "Forget your English estates. Marry your Charles and content yourself here at Villa Bertolini, your mother's birthright."

Amanda shook her head dolefully. "Would to God it were all that simple. But you know my mother's farm won't support itself. We depend on money from England to make up our losses. If my English estates were seized, it wouldn't be long before we'd be forced to sell some of *this* land. Our neighbor, Conte Lorenzi, is eager to buy." Overcome by the prospect, she burst into racking sobs.

"That tyrannical old skinflint!" Miranda was aghast. Here indeed was a *major catastrophe*. "No, Amanda! That mustn't happen! Your *papa* was truly a father to all his peasants, reducing their rents, helping them through the years of famine. But this stingy count thinks of nothing but money. He's already turned some of his people out of their holdings. My dear mama's uncle, a sick man of fifty-eight—"

Amanda's tears stopped abruptly. She raised her head and looked meaningfully at Miranda. "Would you help me to ward off that fate, if it lay in your power?"

"Anything, my dear comrade. You have but to name it. Surely you know I would give my life for you. I swear on my grandmother's soul to do anything in my power to save your estates."

Amanda hopped up from the sofa, seized Miranda around the waist and swung her around in a joyful dance. "I knew you would help me! It's all settled, then. *You* shall go visit London. *You* shall become Amanda Fitton!"

"You've gone mad!" exclaimed Miranda, stumbling over her feet in her haste to withdraw herself from Amanda's wild careening. "How can I be Amanda Fitton? We look nothing alike. With your golden hair and alabaster complexion—"

"And your perfect English accent, your impeccable education? Who in London will know the difference? Mr. Armour has never seen me. And *papa* had grown so cold toward his countrymen that he received no English visitors."

"There was one, remember? A long time ago? That young friend of *Maestro* MacCrae's."

"Oh, that strange Mr. Boswell, the one who upset

all the maids. Don't worry; he doesn't count. He's a Scotsman, like *Maestro* MacCrae. You'll never meet him in London. You'll fool them all, never fear. They know my *mama* was Italian. That will explain your darker complexion. And you know how everyone says our eyes are the same."

Miranda knew that all too well. She also knew all the reasons she must quickly skip over that threatening topic. "But this business about your estates," she broke in quickly, "how can I deal with that? I know nothing of money and banking."

"That's just what they'll be expecting. No English lady knows the slightest thing about money, except how to spend it. They leave all the rest to their men. Mr. Armour will handle the business. You will simply sign my name on the proper occasions."

Miranda shook her head doubtfully. "Someone will find me out. I can't go on playing Amanda Fitton the rest of my life."

Amanda's smile was brilliant. "Of course you can't. You won't need to. I shall travel with you as far as Portsmouth and wait there till darling Charles comes back from Jamaica. As soon as I turn twenty-one, we'll be married. Then we'll drive up posthaste to London, and we'll all have a lovely time laughing at how we've fooled them."

Miranda considered the prospect. Lawyers, in her experience, were not easily moved to laughter. She doubted that this Mr. Armour would prove an exception. "And what about this Lord Fortescue?" she said with a sinking heart. "If you've read Mr. Armour aright, if he's really trying to force you into that match—"

"Oh, my dear Miranda, you can surely delay things awhile. They won't expect a direct answer, the simple *yes* or *no* an Italian lady would give them. You can simper and flirt and go into vapors, like the girls in those English novels. And if worst comes to worst—

well, it wouldn't be a real marriage, would it? Since you're really Miranda Testa, not Amanda Fitton."

Miranda's blood turned cold. She gave Amanda a long, level look. She was alarmed to find the golden-haired girl refusing to meet her eyes. "Might that not be a trifle awkward? Beginning my wedding night with your snobbish Lord Fortescue by explaining we're not really married?"

A wave of color swept up from Amanda's neck suffusing her face. Miranda bit back the words she'd intended to say. The delicate sensibilities of a well-brought-up English lady! How dangerously close she'd come to offending Amanda's innocence!

Amanda was rattling on, still not daring to meet her eyes. "All this nonsense about wedding nights! I tell you, it won't come to that. It will take us a month, at least, to journey to England. Two months in Portsmouth, then, till I'm safely married to Charles. Then we'll drive straight up to London, tell Mr. Armour the truth."

"Meanwhile, *I'll* be the one alone and friendless in London for months, masquerading and dreading exposure each moment, continually at the mercy of this stranger's hateful advances—"

"Oh, tush," said Amanda sharply. "You know you're much better than I at warding off men's advances. The time will pass like a fleeting dream. Besides you've already promised. You swore on your grandmother's soul."

A shiver passed through Miranda's body. It was true; she had already sworn. She wouldn't dare to transgress that binding vow. And Amanda knew it, the minx. Sometimes that frivolous brain was uncannily shrewd.

Amanda's eyes lit up. She saw she had won. She dashed to the heavy armoire, started pulling out all its contents, flinging the gowns on the bed and sofa. "Just picture yourself at the Opera, in this pomona green brocade. Or in some Portman Square ballroom in this dove-color paduasoy. Or a Drury Lane box in this *crème de noisette* satin."

Drury Lane! The name chimed like a bell deep in Miranda's soul. To see those marvelous plays she'd reread so often. To watch the fabulous Mrs. Yates and Mrs. Abington. And Mr. Garrick himself, playing Lear or Hamlet. She remembered the way the *maestro*'s voice used to tremble, describing the scene with Cordelia . . .

Miranda was slipping the satin gown over her shoulders. She gazed at herself in the long narrow pier glass. The color suited her better than it did Amanda. And this time *mama* wouldn't be altering it as she did with the usual cast-me-downs, filling in the low decolletage, trimming down the voluminous petticoat. She glanced at herself again. She could do it. She could play at being Amanda. Just for a little while, she'd be one of those lucky Londoners *Maestro* MacCrae had told them about. *The most civilized folk in the world—never a cruel word of gossip, or lapses into coarse language— that brilliant conversation on only the noblest of topics—* She caught her breath in wonder, already seeing herself in some glittering drawing room. What a lark it would be, pretending to be a fine lady! And besides, it was only fair, her proper birthright . . .

She cut the thought short. As *mama,* God rest her soul, had always said, *Moonbeams make scanty eating.* The world was the way it was. Miranda would never let fall the slightest hint of that hidden subject, to shatter the innocent bliss of Miranda, her dearest comrade.

Amanda was standing behind her, eyes grown a little rueful. "Perhaps I'm asking too much? I know it will be an ordeal. But I must have my Charles! I must! I'd do the same for you, if you were in love."

Compared with Miranda's new splendor, the girl in the blue and white chintz looked like a waif, small and

13

orphaned and lost. A rush of protective compassion flooded Miranda's heart. "I'd go to the ends of the earth for you, my dearest Amanda. Surely a trip to London is little enough to ask."

Chapter Two

Miranda touched her cheek lightly with rouge, then laid down the Spanish wool and gazed at herself in the glass as La Sogghignatora finished pinning the sidecurls to balance her high toupee. Mrs. Armour assessed the effect with a critical eye. "I wonder that you take the trouble to dress when you refuse to meet any people of fashion."

"My dear Mrs. Armour, you have overwhelmed me with people of fashion. The assembly last Tuesday, Wednesday's drum at Lady Pembroke's, last night at the Opera! And all those ladies who've been so kind as to call."

"Oh, yes, you've quite charmed the ladies. But what does that signify? The time to cultivate *ladies* is after you're married."

Miranda waved her maid's further attentions away with an impatient hand. "That's enough, La Soggh— Lucy." She caught herself just in time. *La Sogghignatora*, the Sneerer, was a perfect name for the supercilious servant Amanda had chosen for her in Dover. But it wouldn't do to call her that in public. Too many of the vapid idlers in Mrs. Armour's set spoke a smattering of Italian.

Over her mirrored shoulder, she saw the petulant frown on her hostess's plump round face. With a sigh of exasperation she turned to confront her. "So we're back to Lord Fortescue? I thought we'd abandoned that topic. I assure you I won't be at home when he calls here this noon. You might have told him as much, and saved him a visit."

"My dear Miss Fitton, these excuses grow very thin. I can't keep putting him off. He insists that your first encounter should be in private, not at some public gathering. One doesn't risk insulting a man in Lord Fortescue's position."

"Why trouble to make excuses? Tell him the truth—that I'm firmly resolved not to meet him so long as he persists in his impossible suit."

"Impossible suit!" The plump little face turned pink with indignation. "I vow, Miss Fitton, your attitude's most provoking. You'd think we were talking about some shabby bank clerk, not the most glittering catch in London."

Miranda assumed her well-rehearsed pious look, gazing with dreamy eyes at the bedroom's garlanded ceiling. "My dear Mrs. Armour, I know you've the best intentions. But I promised my sainted mother—"

"That ridiculous promise, made at the age of five. No one with any sense would consider that binding. Besides, a generous man like Lord Fortescue would surely accede to your wishes and spend at least part of the year on your Italian estate."

"You don't really believe that! A man who protests such disdain for anything outside England?"

"Ah, my dear, but he hasn't met *you*." Mrs. Armour's strident voice was replaced by a guileful coo. "One sight of that pretty face will dispel his cranky notions. He'll be your abject slave, subject to every whim. It confounds all reason, this refusal even to meet him. No girl reared in England would dare be so rude."

Miranda summoned up the dregs of her waning patience. "It is true our customs are different. The girls in my country do not begin games they do not intend to finish."

Mrs. Armour turned even pinker. "A most indelicate way to speak of so serious a matter. Games indeed! When your whole future hangs in the balance..."

Miranda let her sputter on. She knew it was useless to argue. They'd gone over this ground many times. And she had the gall to call Miranda *indelicate*—this woman who went at the task of pairing her off with a single-minded gusto that would have shamed old Serafina, the village marriage-broker.

She stood up abruptly. "My dear Mrs. Armour, please forgive my rudeness, but I'm already late for my shopping. You're sure you don't wish to come with me?"

Mrs. Armour cut short her tirade and glared at her guest in frustration. "You really plan to be out when Lord Fortescue calls? He's very punctual. He'll be here on the stroke of noon."

"And I will be far from here, in that little Russell Street bookshop. My cloak, please, Lucy."

"But what excuse shall I give?" *Dio mio,* the woman was frantic.

"You may plead a prior appointment," called Miranda over her shoulder as she hurried out the door and down the stairs. "Tell him I'd already promised to spend these hours with his distinguished old countryman, Mr. William Shakespeare."

Miranda breathed a sigh of relief as she settled her skirts in the sedan chair. Lucy would follow behind her. What a relief to be out from under her eagle eyes! And what a delight to escape from Mrs. Armour, for a few hours at least. That devious old schemer! How right Amanda had been! This panic abut the estates was all a pretext. She'd been in London a month now, and seen no real sign of legal proceedings. Mr. Armour was infuriatingly vague when she pressed him about the supposed threat of seizure. Miranda was willing to bet it didn't exist. But each time she suggested a return to Florence, he'd produce some impressive parchments, tell her the hearing had been postponed but would surely come up next week, insist on her utter ruin if she failed to appear. Miranda was sure it was nonsense, dust to dazzle her eyes, but the need to protect Amanda's interests forbade her to take the risk of leaving.

There was no doubt about it, the match with Lord Fortescue was the business that really concerned her guardian. She was sure her instinct was right in refusing even to meet him. Who knew what trap she might fall into if she let him make his addresses in person? She knew nothing of English betrothal customs. Indeed, most English manners seemed to her full of riddles. Lucy's raised eyebrows had already informed her of her myriad lapses from obscure rules of conduct. It was like groping her way through a tangled thicket, trying to understand what went on among these people. All those cold masklike faces concealing devious minds!

The Armours, for instance. What was their motive in pushing her toward this marriage? Lord Fortescue's intrest was clear. He wanted her fortune—or rather, Amanda's fortune. But this man whom her father had trusted to be her guardian—what was his stake in the matter? Had Lord Fortescue pledged some reward to encourage his efforts? Did these English buy and sell their wives like Turkish sultans?

T. DAVIES, BOOKSELLER. The sign was a welcome distraction from her circling thoughts. The next hour sped by unnoticed as a middle-aged man in a green baize apron pulled out volume after volume for her inspection, while Lucy waited by the street door in ostentatious boredom. Miranda piled up a sizable parcel, smiling at the thought of the drowsy afternoons back in the Villa Bertolini when she'd have a chance to read them at leisure. How pleasant it was not to worry about the bill. At least Mr. Armour didn't stint her for money. She'd already spent a small fortune, at Mrs. Armour's direction, in replacing Amanda's wardrobe with more fashionable array—petticoats baring the ankle, waistcoats instead of stomachers, gowns looped up at the back in the *polonese* style. She enjoyed the new gowns, of course, though some seemed a trifle immodest. But she knew they were borrowed feathers, hers for a season only. The books would be hers to cherish forever. She knew Amanda wouldn't begrudge her this single pleasure. It was only fair, a reward for the hours of boredom this trip to London had cost her.

Mr. Davies, she found, had all but one of the books on her list. The single exception was Shakespeare's *Sonnets*. He suggested she try a shop on the other side of the little street. She thanked him and gave directions for sending the parcel, all except one special volume bound in gilded red morocco. *Romeo and Juliet*, her favorite play. That pretty thing she couldn't bear to let out of her sight.

She stepped out into the street and paused there a moment, pierced by the gust of excitement she always felt at the sight of the bustling London traffic. A lordly city indeed, the capital of the world. *Maestro* MacCrae had been right. And somewhere out there, all those fabulous people were thinking their marvelous thoughts, writing their wonderful books, conducting their brilliant conversations—Dr. Johnson, Mr. Burke, Mr. Walpole . . . She'd been silly to think she could hope to meet them in this teeming city. They moved in another orbit—an exalted one, far removed from these boring idlers Mrs. Armour called *people of fashion*.

"Have a care, miss!" Lucy grasped her arm, pulling her back toward the shop as a pair of prancing white horses hurtled past the spot where she had been standing. She trembled with shock as the shiny black landau lurched to a creaking stop a few hundred feet up the narrow street. A man in a blue frock coat and buckskin breeches had leapt out of the carriage and was already hastening toward her.

"A thousand apologies, madam," he said as he reached her side. "My coachman was woefully careless. I sincerely hope you're not injured."

Miranda stared at him for a moment, struggling to collect her wits. His high, powdered toupee, his snug-fitting buckskins, his red-heeled, narrow-toed shoes were the sort of thing worn by all the vapid drones in Mrs. Armour's set. But his manner was different—no rigid, expressionless mask, but a bright-eyed, good-humored face alive with concern. "No, thank you, I'm quite unharmed." She raised one hand to steady the little chip hat precariously perched over her forehead. Then she realized her hand shouldn't be empty. "My book!" she cried. "My lovely new book! I must have dropped it."

She gazed dejectedly out at the morass of mud churned up by the busy traffic. A few feet from where they stood, a bit of red leather peeked forlornly up from its squishy hiding place. "Allow me." With complete disregard for the threat to his pale blue silk hose, he waded out to retrieve the buried book. He picked it up and examined it, brushing off the worst of the mud, then opened it to assess the damage done to its pages. His intent concern changed to a smile of delight. *"Romeo and Juliet!* A fortunate omen." Then the mobile face clouded over with a rueful look. "But this only heightens the crime. To thus profane this shrine of the poet—" The smile came back again, a mischievous one this time, as he thrust his hand out, intoning in a musical voice:

> *"If I profane with my unworthiest hand*
> *This holy shrine, the gentle sin is this;*
> *My lips, two blushing pilgrims, ready stand*
> *To smooth that rough touch with a tender kiss."*

With a graceful gesture, he raised the book to his lips. Miranda reached out to snatch it from him before it could muddy his gleaming throat ruffles. She was on the verge of laughing with the pleasure of recognition, replying:

"Good pilgrim, you do wrong your hand too much,
Which mannerly devotion shows in this;
For saints have hands that pilgrims' hands do touch,
And palm to palm is holy palmers' kiss."

Impulsively, she reached out to grasp his hand, remembering the hundreds of times she and Amanda had acted the scene under *Maestro* MacCrae's direction. Just in time, Lucy's shocked gaze reminded her that this was no schoolgirl, but a man—and a stranger.

She snatched back her hand, clasped it with her other hand around the rescued book. "You admire Mr. Shakespeare's works?" she said, trying to make her voice cool and proper.

"Above all others. You're an admirer too? I presume so, from the way his words spring to your lips."

"I think he's the greatest poet who ever lived." How delightful it was at last to find one man in London who could talk about something other than horses.

His eyes were dancing with shared enthusiasm. "I think the same. It seems a pity that so fair a Juliet must read his words from that bedraggled volume. I have a fine copy myself, the personal gift of Mr. David Garrick. If you'll permit me to send it to you in humble atonement—"

"Why don't you bring it yourself?" The impulsive words were out before she could stop them. "We could continue our conversation about Mr. Shakespeare." Deliberately ignoring Lucy's meaningful glare, she reached into her purse and handed him one of her cards. "I'm staying with Mr. Armour in Argyll Street."

With a shock of dismay, she saw the lively blue eyes turn to colorless ice. He'd barely glanced at the card.

Now he handed it back. "I fear I've presumed too far," he said in the cold, dead drawl of the man of fashion. "I'll see you and your maid into chairs, before you risk further embarrassments."

Miranda felt her cheeks flame. Another lapse in manners, this time clearly a grave one. Even so, had she given him cause to look quite so forbidding? Really, he was worse than La Sogghignatora!

The surge of resentment gave way to sudden remorse. The first man of good sense in London, and she'd spoiled things between them forever! "Please don't trouble yourself," she said in a haughty voice. "I've just remembered another book I must order." Before he could protest, she had turned back into the shop.

The bookseller came to meet her, looking worried. "I hope you're not harmed, Miss Fitton. A most distressing occurrence. I fear Lord Fortescue's horses have far too much spirit for our humdrum London traffic."

Miranda stood stock-still, bereft of motion. "Lord Fortescue? That was Lord Fortescue's carriage?"

"Of course, my lady." The bookseller rattled on, pleased to be able to give her the information. "He's a fine judge of horseflesh, Lord Fortescue. He insists on purebred stock, even to draw his carriage." His eyes shifted to the muddy object clutched against her breast. "Is that pretty binding ruined? What a miserable shame! I have one other copy, but it's in plain buckram. Would you like me to show you?"

Miranda broke out of her trance into a flurry of action. "So kind of you, Mr. Davies, but I haven't the time. Would you find me a hackney coach—quickly, please. I must hurry back to Argyll Street as fast as I can. I fear I'll be late for a very important caller."

"Well! Here's a quick about-face!"

Miranda bent toward the glass, ignoring her hostess's blatant curiosity. She didn't care to explain her sudden eagerness to be introduced to Lord Fortescue. If she'd known the woman better, or liked her more, she might have asked her how grave a lapse of good manners her *faux pas* with the card had been. As things were, it seemed just too awkward. She'd have to trust that this second, proper introduction would wipe out the stain of that first impropriety.

When she heard the rap of the heavy brass knocker on the street door downstairs, her pulse started racing. In a moment she would see him again—smile into those dancing blue eyes, listen to that expressive voice. *To smooth that rough touch with a tender kiss....* The remembered words brought a heightened flush to her cheeks. To think she'd wasted all those precious days when she could have spent them reading the plays with him, discussing Shakespeare and her other favorite authors. Would he like Mr. Pope's work too? She was sure he would. And perhaps Mrs. Sheridan's novels, for less exalted amusement.

How should she greet him? Should she mention their previous meeting? It might seem strange to him if she didn't. But surely he'd understand her reasons for wanting to keep that embarrassing incident secret. Still, the choice wasn't really hers. He was the one who would set the tone of this meeting. She'd simply have to wait and follow his lead.

A footman appeared with a card, and handed it down to Mrs. Armour. Fighting back her overwhelming impulse to rush down the stairway, Miranda gave her siderolls a few unneeded adjustments. A groan of dismay made her turn startled eyes toward Mrs. Armour. "That unfortunate sister of mine! What an inconvenient time to pay me her monthly visit! I must think of some good excuse to send her away."

"Send your sister away?" Miranda was shocked. These cold-blooded English! Were they totally lacking in natural feeling?

"I really mustn't inflict her upon Lord Fortescue. She's a woman of no position—made an unfortunate marriage, and now she's widowed, she's forced to mingle with the most unsuitable people—that strident Montagu woman and that hideous Dr. Johnson."

"Dr. Johnson!" cried Miranda. "Oh, please let me meet your sister!" The plump little woman gave her an astonished look. Clearly, a well-brought-up heiress was not expected to admire Dr. Johnson. She had better pretend a less intellectual interest. "To be truthful, my dear Mrs. Armour, I'm a trifle nervous about finally meeting Lord Fortescue. Another visitor might help make conversation less awkward."

Mrs. Armour beamed at her maternally. "I understand you, my dear. What young lady wouldn't be nervous on such an occasion? We'll invite poor Amelia to stay, then. But I warn you, she'll bore you to tears."

Miranda was not bored at all. Mrs. Amelia Hester turned out to be a most amusing companion. At any other moment, Miranda would have thrown herself delightedly into a conversation so wholly concerned with the latest works of her favorite London authors. But keyed up as she was, she found herself responding to Mrs. Hester with only half her attention. The other half listened alertly for the knock that would herald Lord Fortescue's arrival.

At last it came, the long-awaited signal. Mrs. Hester kept chattering away, but Miranda had ceased to hear her. The whole of her being was focused on the drawing-room door. In a minute he would enter, the man in the blue frock coat and the dancing eyes and the voice that was like a caress....

The door opened. A man stepped through it. But it wasn't Lord Fortescue, not *her* Lord Fortescue. This was a much stouter man, with a drink-reddened face and thick blubbery lips. She rose to her feet to greet the stranger, aghast at this sudden blow to her expectations. The newcomer made her the barest excuse for a bow, then raised his quizzing glass and surveyed her through it, as though inspecting some prime example of horseflesh.

"Enchanted to meet you, Miss Fitton. My cousin

Charles's description did not do you justice. Or is it the impeccable English taste of our charming hostess that has worked a transformation? Whatever the reason, I must tell you the result is most satisfactory." He paused, smacking his lips as though savoring a sweetmeat. "Most satisfactory indeed. But enough of these pleasantries. Mrs. Armour, with your permission?" Before Mrs. Armour could answer, he sank heavily into a chair and motioned to Miranda to take the one beside it. "Now, my dear Miss Fitton, let us begin what I sincerely hope will be an extended acquaintance."

There ensued the most boring half hour Miranda had yet endured. Lord Fortescue seemed to have little conception of how to pay court to a woman. Indeed, he seemed to feel little need to make the effort. *I am here to be admired,* his manner proclaimed. Mrs. Armour's fawning response more than fulfilled his evident expectation. Mrs. Hester was more reserved, though she held her own with him in a spirited discussion of the merits of several racehorses. Miranda was tongue-tied, trying with all her might to find some way to tell him that the meeting was all a mistake. But, taken off guard as she was, she could scarcely summon up an intelligible sentence. The crowning horror came when she found herself, for lack of a ready excuse, accepting his invitation to a masquerade ball that night at the Ranelagh gardens.

Just as she was deciding that she'd have to feign illness or fainting to bring the call to an end, Mrs. Hester came to her rescue. "Dear Laetitia," she said to her sister, "will you do me a prodigious favor? Let me steal this charming young lady and carry her off to Mrs. Cholmondeley's house for an hour or so. Dr. Johnson is sure to be there, and Miss Fitton has told me how much she admires him."

"Oh, I couldn't force the poor girl," murmured Mrs. Armour, darting angry looks at her imperturbable sister.

"Oh, yes, Mrs. Hester, I'd love to go with you!" Miranda was fully aware of Lord Fortescue's raised eyebrows. But she didn't care. To get rid of this odious suitor, and meet the great man at last! For the first time since she'd set foot in London, Miranda Testa was thoroughly happy.

Chapter Three

"What a prodigious relief," sighed Mrs. Hester, settling back onto the seat of the post chaise. "How pleased I am to be able to snatch you away from that tedious discussion."

Miranda smiled at her warmly. What a nice little woman she was! Not nearly so dumpy as plump little Mrs. Armour, and she clearly had far more wit. She felt a pang of remorse at neglecting this new friend so shamefully. She'd been scarcely more than civil as she waited for Lord Fortescue's knock, and then had ignored her completely. It had been all she could do to respond to her suitor's lumbering efforts at conversation while her mind was whirling with all those unanswered questions: Who was the smiling young man who had rescued her book? Why was he using Lord Fortescue's carriage? Would she ever see him again? How could she rectify this appalling mistake of inviting Lord Fortescue's attentions?

Now she put all that out of her head, resolved to

cement this promising new friendship. "The pleasure is mine," she said. "It is very kind of you to invite me to Mrs. Cholmondeley's. I hope all these visits are not too fatiguing, after your sad bereavement?"

Mrs. Hester looked puzzled for a moment. Then she threw back her head in a ringing laugh. "Poor old Ned Hester, you mean? Good lord, he's been dead these eight years. But of course, it's my gown that deceived you. It's not meant for mourning, my girl. It's merely that I think black suits me. Don't you agree?"

"Indeed, Mrs. Hester, I was just admiring your gown. Mine seems ostentatious beside you, with all these flounces. I fear Dr. Johnson may think me a frivolous chit."

"Not a bit of it, child. He'll love you. He adores young girls fluttering round him. I assure you, your gown is quite perfect. This severe look of mine is a necessary evil; a lady novelist must exude the utmost decorum to keep any reputation at all."

"You write novels, madam? How enchanting!"

"Didn't my sister tell you? No, of course, she wouldn't. She finds my profession shocking. Thank God it's over, my courtesy call for the month. Ah, here we are in Hertford Street. Let's hope the good doctor's arrived. I can see you're dying to make his acquaintance."

Miranda's heart started pounding. So she really was going to meet Dr. Johnson. If only *Maestro* MacCrae could be here with her now! But what could she say to him? Her mind had gone blank. She curtsied and smiled as Mrs. Hester introduced her to Mrs. Cholmondeley, a bright-eyed bubbling woman who seemed to be everywhere at once. The room was full of people—more women than men—all seated in twosomes or threesomes on little chairs, talking a mile a minute.

Mrs. Hester led her to the corner where Dr. Johnson was holding court, his heavy bulk sunk deep in a velvet armchair, a circle of admirers seated and standing around him. "You've grown up in Florence, Miss Fitton? I congratulate you on your good fortune. My friend, Mr. Baretti, is never done singing the praises of that renowned city."

What a pleasant man he was! Not handsome, of course, with those massive scarred features, but rather noble looking. And not at all pretentious, for so distinguished a man. She felt a new surge of courage. "Indeed, sir, as Euripides tells us, *The first requisite of happiness is birth in a famous city.*" She said it in Greek, of course, and was pleased to see him look startled.

"A scholar as well." His eyes were warm with approval. "Are all the young ladies in Florence so well instructed?"

"I had a Scottish tutor, sir. He grounded us in the classics, and modern writers as well. It was he who first read us your sublime preface to the works of Mr. Shakespeare."

"Aha!" barked the big man sternly, as though he'd just found her out in some infamous crime. "I detect the mark of another sojourner in Florence!" What in the world had she said, to turn him so suddenly stern? "I mean Machiavelli," he said. "You've learned from him how to flatter."

"Oh, no, sir, I assure you—" she stammered. Then she saw the glint in his eye, and knew he was only teasing. The look of cold reproof gave way to a mischievous smile. "I hope you've not gorged on the sauce and neglected the meat? You've read the plays as well as the preface?"

"Over and over, sir." Miranda's eyes grew bright with remembered enjoyment. "We used to act them out, the three of us—"

Dr. Johnson nodded. "Ah, yes. You have brothers? Sisters?"

Miranda felt herself reddening. "A foster sister, sir; a peasant girl, really, but a special pet of my father's. She shared my tutor's instruction. Indeed, she spent all her days in our villa, returning only at night to her mother's cottage. She was my closest companion all through my childhood. It was she who played Hamlet to my Ophelia, Romeo to my Juliet. Mr. MacCrae filled in with the other parts."

"Ha!" said a voice behind her. "So you're fond of Shakespeare? You must come and meet our dear Theo." Miranda felt a firm hand on her elbow, tugging her out of the circle around Dr. Johnson. A quick wave of anger surged through her. Who was this woman who dared to intrude on her glorious moment? Then she saw it was Mrs. Cholmondeley, and managed a civil smile. Of course no accomplished hostess would stand idly by while an obscure young girl monopolized her chief attraction. All the same, it was disappointing. To be received so warmly, and then have the meeting cut short.

Mrs. Cholmondeley was leading her into the opposite corner, where a man and a woman sat chatting. At Mrs. Cholmondeley's approach, the woman looked up with a smile, and the man quickly rose from his seat. Miranda stifled a cry when she saw his face. The blue-coated man from this morning! Was it really he? Yes, there was no doubt about it. His astonished look showed he was as startled as she.

Miranda felt very strange. Everything around her seemed to melt into the distance. She couldn't have spoken if her life had depended upon it. Thank goodness Mrs. Cholmondeley was chattering on in her usual sprightly fashion! "Mrs. Bolt, I must tear you away. Lady Hawke's demanding to meet you. Miss Fitton, this is Theophilus Moreland, one of our finest new players. In a few months from now, he'll be the toast of the town."

The young man looked alarmed. "Please, my dear Mrs. Cholmondeley! That's not to be public knowledge."

"Oh, fie on this secrecy, Theo. You should copy my dear sister Peg and tell them all to go hang. There's nothing at all disgraceful in being a player. I'd be on the stage myself, if I had the talent. Now, entertain this young lady. She's as mad about Shakespeare as you are."

Mrs. Bolt was on her feet, smiling at her hostess's high spirits. Mrs. Cholmondeley seized her arm and marched her brusquely away. Miranda sat down on the chair she had left, grateful that her trembling knees had not given way completely. What was the matter with her? The man certainly wasn't a monster. Why was this unexpected meeting affecting her so strangely?

Theo Moreland seated himself cautiously beside her, as though she were some strange beast which might suddenly attack him. "Mrs. Cholmondeley tells me you have some interest in Shakespeare?" he asked stiffly.

Miranda found her voice. "You already know that, Mr. Moreland. Is it really necessary to pretend we have never met?"

She was surprised to see the cautious look change to complete abashment. "A thousand apologies, madam. I fear I was very awkward this morning. I was taken off guard, you see. It's difficult to explain—It involves a close friend of mine whom you haven't yet met."

"If you mean Lord Fortescue, I have indeed met him. Only an hour ago in Mrs. Armour's house."

The abject face turned suddenly radiant. "You've consented to see him at last? How glad I am! That changes the picture completely."

Yes, I consented to see him, and heartily wished I hadn't, thought Miranda. But she knew she mustn't say that. It would cut off the flow. "I'm afraid I don't understand," she said. "How does it change the picture?"

"Lord Fortescue confided in me some months ago how very zealous he was to win your hand in marriage." He stopped abruptly, clearly embarrassed. "I hope you won't think we bandied your name in gossip."

"Not at all," said Miranda. "You said he's a very close friend."

"A very close friend indeed. We share all our secrets. Well, then; he had also told me of his lack of success in pursuing your acquaintance. When I realized who you were this morning—When you gave me your kind invitation—"

Miranda felt herself blushing. "I must have seemed like a forward hussy."

"Oh, no, not at all!" He leaned forward eagerly, as though to reassure her. "I found our encounter most elevating. I would have loved to pursue our discussion. But knowing Lord Fortescue's devotion, I hesitated to venture onto ground he had marked for his own."

Miranda's heart leapt with delight. So it wasn't her own bad manners that had turned him so icy! She started to say, *I assure you the ground's still unclaimed,* then checked herself. She'd better tread carefully here. "I'm still in the dark, Mr. Moreland. Is Lord Fortescue so jealous a man he'd begrudge us the innocent pleasure of conversation?"

That lively face of his! How fast his expression changed. Now he was looking concerned for his friend's reputation. "I assure you, Miss Fitton, Lord Fortescue's a most genial man—in the general way. But in this particular matter, with his feelings so much engaged— I feared some misunderstanding might ruffle his temper."

Just as I guessed, thought Miranda, *the man's a brute.* "A daunting prospect," she said aloud. "A suitor so quick to misunderstanding—"

"Truly, Miss Fitton, I've given the wrong impression. He's really the best-tempered man in London. I assure you he has all the virtues that make a good husband." His eyes had gone soft with a pleading look. These strange English men! Her would-be husband behaved like an unfeeling log, while his friend did all the courting! But perhaps this was the English custom; to woo, as it were, at third hand—like Lord Fortescue sending Charles to woo Amanda, or Duke Orsino sending Viola to woo Olivia.

"All the virtues!" she protested. "How can you say that? When he lacks all appreciation of art and music?

32

When he tells me how lucky I am to *shake free from that barbarous Florence?"*

"He is uninformed in some spheres, I'll grant you. It's the fault of his education. But you will remedy that. You can open his soul to new beauties, widen his vision—"

Miranda caught her breath in dismay. "You've married me off already? To a man who proclaims his intentions of marriage to half of London before he's even made my acquaintance? Come now, Mr. Moreland. You must admit, it's my fortune, not my own poor self, that's aroused this ferocious devotion."

Theo Moreland's face creased in a stubborn frown. "Isn't that how most good matches are made? With an eye to advantage? It merely proves Fortescue's good sense."

Miranda could endure no more. "When was *good sense* a phrase to be used by lovers!" she exclaimed, her eyes hot with outrage. "Did Romeo prate of *good sense?* Did Juliet hymn the virtues of *advantage?"*

The earnest face relaxed in a rueful smile. "A truce, a truce, dear Miss Fitton. I'll abandon that field for the moment, and leave it to you to choose a less controversial topic."

"You already know my choice." Amanda smiled at him warmly. "The works of Mr. Shakespeare. You're a player, Mrs. Cholmondeley says?"

Theo cast a quck glance around them, then leaned confidentially toward her. "It's my highest ambition, has been since I was a boy. I've done some rehearsing, but haven't yet made my debut. It's my uncle, you see— he's threatened to cut me out of his will if I take to the stage. He claims I would be disgracing the family name."

"How awful for you!" said Miranda. "What a prejudiced man he must be!"

"It's a general prejudice. Mr. Garrick has managed to rise above it, but he's an exceptional man."

Miranda gazed at him with glowing eyes. "I'm sure

you're exceptional too. There's such fire in you, such spirit. You'd make a marvelous Romeo. Have you ever played it?"

Theo's face lit up with pleasure. "That's the part I'm rehearsing now at Drury Lane. Mr. Garrick seems to be pleased. He wants me to make my debut in January—an anonymous gentleman, you know, the way he himself first appeared."

"That's wonderful! Why all this hesitation? Mrs. Cholmondeley is right; you should tell you uncle go hang."

"It's not quite as simple as that," said Theo, smiling at her rush of high spirits. "But your words give me courage, Miss Fitton. Perhaps I *will* take the plunge. But tell me now, what do you think of our current Drury Lane players? I think Mr. Barry is fine. Or do you prefer Mr. Aickin?"

Mirada made a *moue* of disgust. "Would you believe I haven't yet been to the playhouse? The Armours complain that it's boring, and I've no one else to escort me."

"But of course you have, now you've met Lord Fortescue. He always takes a box for each new production."

I don't want to go to Drury Lane with Lord Fortescue. I want to go with you. But of course, she couldn't say that. "Perhaps I shall see you there, in Lord Fortescue's box?" She felt her heart sink as she said it. Did she really intend to encourage that insufferable *milord*'s advances, for the sake of a few scattered meetings with Theo Moreland? She was astonished to find that was *exactly* what she intended.

Struck dumb by this realization, she listened to him declaring what an enchanting prospect another encounter would be. *That's all very well,* thought Miranda, *but what am I doing? Condemning myself to an eon of boredom, for the barest chance of seeing this man again!*

Just then Mrs. Cholmondeley came bustling up to them. "You've spent enough time with this scapegrace," she said to Miranda. "Now you must come and meet Dr. Burney. Theo, make your adieux. Can't you say something Shakespearean? Oh, yes, I have it, of course: *Parting is such sweet sorrow—*"

I know a line to cap that, thought Miranda, aghast at the way the world clouded over the moment she left the presence of Theo Moreland. *That line of Olivia's, when Viola captured her heart.* Even so quickly may one catch the plague....

Chapter Four

"Indeed, Lord Fortescue, the place is a fairyland.
It quite outshines *Maestro* MacCrae's glowing description." Miranda gazed in amazement around the great
circular hall. It seemed to pulse with light, like an
enormous diamond, the flames of a thousand candles
in the sconces and chandeliers extending the glow of
the huge pillared fireplace at its central core. A host
of brightly garbed revellers promenaded around the
room, or bunched into little clusters, laughing and talking. There must be five or six hundred. She'd never
seen so many people inside one building before, not
even inside the *Duomo* on Easter Sunday.

She was finding the evening more pleasant than she
had expected. Lord Fortescue had settled her into a box
in one of the dozens of alcoves that ringed the Rotunda,
and plied her with tea and all sorts of sweetmeats.
Really, the self-centered bore had become most obliging. What more could the man possibly do to please
her?

The answer leapt to her mind: *He might have brought his friend Theo.* Then she railed at herself for being a silly goose. She was making too much of an ordinary acquaintance. She'd been bemused by Romeo's loverlike tones. But those words had meant nothing to him. He was a player. Those lover's speeches were part of his stock in trade. Would she fall in love with every greengrocer who offered her a fine lettuce?

Lord Fortescue's voice broke into her reverie. "Shall we promenade for a bit and inspect the costumes? I think I detect a few friends who'd be charmed to make your acquaintance."

She assented quickly, glad to escape her oppressive thoughts. They joined the chattering throng circling the fireplace. Lord Fortescue kept up a running comment on the various costumes. "Look at that Turk over there—I swear those jewels on his turban are real, not paste—and look, here comes Don Quixote—what a clever costume—that Harlequin over there seems very sprightly. Do you think it's a man or a woman? And look at Minerva and Zeus! A bit too much flesh and too little costume—don't you agree?"

Miranda had her own reservations. She thought Zeus was showing his daughter more than a father's affection. Nevertheless, she found the whole scene enthralling. It was like some gigantic play on a huge circular stage, with everyone blessed with a chance at a leading part. She *oohed* and *ahed* obediently as Lord Fortescue pointed out each striking costume. "A delightful array, indeed. I feel like a poor drab thing, wearing only this domino. If I'd had a bit more time for preparation—"

Lord Fortescue looked down at her indulgently. "Don't distress yourself, my dear Amanda. That scarlet robe becomes you most strikingly. Of course, once we're married the ton will expect the new Lady Fortescue to display some clever costume."

Miranda felt herself bristle. How sure he was of his conquest! Here he was, taking their marriage for granted, when she hadn't yet given him leave to use any other address than the formal *Miss Fitton*. She was summoning up the phrases to tell him he'd been too familiar, when a startling apparition threw her thoughts into sudden chaos.

A woman in an elegant, black satin gown shimmering with tiny jet beads came sailing through the turbulent crowd, elbowing out of her way everyone in her path. A towering jewelled headdress proclaimed her some kind of queen. *Lady Macbeth,* was Miranda's first guess. She wasn't sure why she thought so. The total black of the costume, perhaps—or was it the glint of pure malice that blazed from the fine dark eyes as she snatched off her mask and came face to face with Lord Fortescue? "Villain!" she cried. "You faithless Lothario! What a fool I was to believe your false, empty vows!"

Lord Fortescue stared back at her as though turned to stone. The buzzing crowd grew silent. Miranda gazed at the fuming lady in frank admiration. So that's what the grand costume meant. Not Lady Macbeth after all, but the tragic Calista, shamed and abandoned in Mr. Rowe's play. How well she fell into the part! You'd have thought her passion was real, she mimed it so well. But surely she'd picked the last man in the world to match her fine challenge. Lord Fortescue was a far less competent actor. He *was* doing quite well at miming the proper fury, contriving to turn his face an alarming purple, but no words emerged from his writhing lips. Small wonder, Miranda thought. Surely no poet's lines ever lodged in *that* unromantic mind!

She was trying hard to remember Lothario's lines, thinking that she might prompt him, when a strange arm encircled her shoulders, and she was pulled away from the scene by a black-masked man wearing a yellow domino. His insistent strength propelled her out of the glittering hall into the surrounding darkness.

"Who are you! How dare you touch me! Release me this minute!" Her indignant protests rose to a panicky shriek. Her abductor seemed to waver a moment, then pressed his lips close to her ear, still hurrying her along the path through a grove of small trees, lit by occasional lamps.

"Please, Miss Fitton. It is I, Theo Moreland. I'm only trying to spare you an unpleasant scene."

Theo Moreland! So her wish was granted! But why had he swept her away in such an alarming fashion? And what would Fortescue think, to see his intended bride carried off by a man who claimed to be his good friend? She cast a glance back toward the glowing hall. Silhouetted against the light in one arched doorway, she could see Lord Fortescue's broad shoulders, draped in his black domino, and hear a few shrill words in a feminine voice: "Monster! Liar! Betrayer!" Clearly, they were both still caught up in that dramatic scene. What a novel departure from the usual stiff English manners!

But hadn't she learned from her reading what to expect at a masquerade? Remember young Bevil in Mr. Steele's play, almost running his sword through the masquerader who annoyed his father—and Mr. Fielding's clever Miss Matthews in her shepherdess costume, trapping poor Captain Booth into intrigue before he knew who she was? That's why the *bon ton* adored these costume parties; disguise was a license for all sorts of strange encounters. And what encounter could be more delicious than this one?

"Mr. Moreland," she said, her voice grown soft as a whisper. "I'm delighted to see you again. But this headlong rush, I confess, makes for difficult conversation."

His arm dropped away. She was astonished to find how she missed its insistent warmth. But she welcomed the freedom to face him, to look once more into the lively blue eyes. They were in a little grove now, surrounded by neatly trimmed hawthorns. He had shed his black velvet mask, and stood looking down at her anxiously. She reached up and pulled off her own mask, the better to meet his gaze.

"I humbly apologize for this sudden assault. My only intent was to spare you a distressing experience—"

"I assure you, I don't mind at all." Miranda was shocked to hear how ardent she sounded. *Be a bit more of a lady,* she scolded herself. *You mustn't risk it again, being too forward.* "A most amusing occurrence," she drawled in a worldly voice. "Who was the charmer in black? Is she a professional actress?"

"No, no—nothing like that." Theo looked unaccountably awkward. "You mustn't give her a thought. She's a woman of no importance."

"But she played the scene beautifully," protested Miranda. "I really thought she was set on scratching his eyes out! Does this sort of thing happen often at masquerades? I vow, they're most stimulating, these impromptu dramatics."

She heard him sigh with relief. "You have great self-possession, Miss Fitton. I'm glad you can take things so lightly. I feared you might have been shocked."

"Good heavens, my dear Mr. Moreland! I'll admit I'm not yet adept at your London manners, but I'm learning quickly. I'm really quite delighted with your masquerade customs. They present a welcome contrast to the boring social round I've been engulfed in."

The dimness of the light obscured his features, but she thought he was looking crestfallen. "Ah, yes; it must have been boring for one of your youth and beauty, all that pedantic talk at Mrs. Cholmondeley's."

"Oh, no, I didn't mean that!" Miranda forgot to drawl in her haste to reassure him. "I adored this afternoon at Mrs. Cholmondeley's. To meet Dr. Johnson himself! He's always been one of my heroes. And then—" She tempered her tone, remembering the need for discretion. "And then, the pleasant surprise of meeting again the man who rescued my book." She looked up at him fetchingly from under her lashes, imitating a favorite trick of Amanda's. It all went for nothing, of course. He couldn't see her face, here in the darkness.

As if in answer to her unspoken wish, a passing cloud

changed position, and the little grove was suddenly bright with moonlight. She could see Theo clearly now, smiling at her with that open, lively expression. "A pleasant surprise for that fortunate man as well, whose humdrum life seldom offers such gifts from the gods."

Miranda's heart skipped a beat. Had that meeting at Mrs. Cholmondeley's meant as much to him as it had to her? It seemed too good to be true. Perhaps he was just being gallant. But the look in his eyes, so openly admiring, made her sudenly bold. "We've met twice by chance. Perhaps our third meeting need not be such a surprise? I've already asked you to call—"

The moment the words were out, she knew she'd gone wrong again. His sudden look of alarm quickly turned to the icy mask he'd presented in Russell Street. "A kind invitation, indeed. But I fear a visit from me would scarecely be proper in your situation."

"My situation?" Miranda felt smothered, as though dark walls were closing in around her. "Perhaps you're not wholly acquainted with my situation. I haven't accepted Lord Fortescue's offer of marriage. Indeed, I have serious doubts that I ever will."

"Don't be so hasty, I beg you." Theo's voice turned soft with entreaty. "You don't yet know him. It's true, his good qualities don't strike the stranger at first. He seems a rather bluff fellow, thick-skinned and perhaps a bit pompous. But beneath that blunt exterior lies a sensitive heart, a keen intellect, and a soul designed by nature to comfort and cherish a woman."

"Mercy!" Miranda purposefully made her tone light, hoping to repair her *faux pas*. "What a paragon of all virtues! Surely no mortal man could live up to such a description."

Theo's face relaxed in a smile. "Perhaps I've allowed myself a trace of hyperbole. But the man's a prince, all the same. I'm sure you'll very quickly grow to love him."

Miranda pounced on the word. "So now you admit

love might have something to do with marriage? This afternoon you thought *good sense* was enough."

Theo's smile turned rueful. "I'll not deny love makes a marriage go smoother. But not every couple is lucky enough to find it."

Miranda glared at him. "I'd never marry a man I didn't love. That would be a sin against God."

Theo raised an eyebrow, looking amused. "Of course, every woman has her head stuffed full of such notions. It's part of what makes the sex charming."

"You call it a notion?" Miranda was outraged. "That sweetest of all emotions? That transfiguring passion? That heavenly fire that blends two souls into one? And yet you profess dedication to the poet who portrayed love most truly—" She broke off her tirade, abruptly aware that she was showing too much of her own heart. "I fear I presume too much on our short acquaintance. You've told me you admire Mr. Shakespeare. But perhaps, as a player, you approach him more coldly than I do."

"Not at all," Theo answered quickly. "When I'm speaking Romeo's lines, I'm fully convinced of love's glory. That's Shakespeare's genius. His marvelous words can turn that vague dream into firm reality. I think that's the reason I've always been drawn to the stage. It presents such a noble image of life at its highest, an ideal to strive toward, though in our mundane life we seldom attain it."

"Thank God we don't," said Miranda. "I shudder to think of a life where jealous Othellos murder their innocent wives, where bloody Macbeths climb to power over a mound of corpses, where the love of a Romeo and Juliet is horribly thwarted."

"I'll dispute that last point, Miss Fitton. Isn't that thwarted love far more sublime than the pawky emotions your off-stage lovers boast of?"

Miranda didn't think so. But prudence, reasserting itself, forbade her to argue the point.

"It's true the Bard uses that thwarting to rouse all

42

our noblest feelings," she said evasively. "And now you're about to play that ideal lover? What a glorious prospect!"

Theo's face turned gloomy. "I wish I could fully decide to take that plunge. I'm not sure I have the courage. I've told you my uncle's against it, and I'm sadly dependent on him."

"And the rest of your family? Are they, too, opposed?"

Theo's gloom deepened. "I have no family. I was an only son. Both my parents died several years ago of a pestilent fever. My father, God rest his soul, was the kindest of men. He would never have balked my ambition. But alas, all his small resources were spent on my education. I live on my uncle's sufferance. He's forever urging me to take up some learned profession—law, or the church." He screwed up his face like a wizened old man, then matched his voice to his face. *"If you want to stand up in front of a crowd and spout off nonsense, do it with honor. Don't descend to the gutter."*

Miranda laughed at the clever imitation. "It's clear you've a gift for acting, Mr. Moreland. You're bound to be a success. Why not trust to the stage to earn you a living?"

A gleam of hope flickered in the troubled eyes. "If only I dared! But the actor's life is a hard one. Even the great Mr. Garrick had hungry days at the start. Dare I take the risk, a player of no experience?"

"But you must take the risk!" Miranda flashed back at him. "That's the whole point of living, the need to take risks. Is a hungry belly worse than a stifled ambition? A poor man can be far more happy than any Midas. Look at Mr. Fielding's Amelia, content with her little family despite her sad lack of wealth."

The rueful smile was back. Theo gazed at Miranda as he would at a charming infant. "How eloquently you hymn the virtues of poverty. But that's easy for you. You've never been poor."

Yes I have! I've been poor all my life! Miranda bit

the words back, aghast at how close she'd come to revealing her secret. Not her secret only—Amanda's secret as well. If she didn't curb her unruly tongue, she'd bring both their lives down in ruin.

She drew a deep, calming breath, then said cautiously, "Do not scorn the experience that comes from imagination. It's true that my knowledge of what it's like to be poor comes only from books. That does not make it less true. I'm sure I could learn to pinch pennies as well as Amelia."

Theo's eyes widened. She could see her grave tone had impressed him. He was looking at her with a keen, appraising look, clearly seeing a woman now, not a child. "And those eloquent paeans to love? Do they stem from book knowledge too? They seemed far too fervent to spring from the printed page."

Miranda felt her heart pounding. *I know what love is all too well. I knew it the moment I met you.* Of course, she couldn't say that. But she wouldn't permit him to force her back to the schoolgirl role. "I know a great deal about love, sir. Like Miranda on her island, my heart has been fully formed by the poet's lines, a warm waiting nest for the unknown man whom Fate will send to fill it. Remember that lovely scene with Ferdinand?"

Theo's face glowed with delight. "You know that scene too? You're truly a thorough student of the great man's works."

"More than a student, sir. I've often performed the part. How does it go? Ferdinand asks her name—but of course, you don't know *those* words. You haven't studied the role."

Theo picked up the challenge. "I know the scene very well." He struck a gallant pose. *"I do beseech you/ Chiefly that I might set it in my prayers/What is your name?"*

"Miranda!" breathed Miranda. She felt a tiny *frisson* dart through her as she said it. Delicious, delicious— to give away her secret and yet to keep it.

"Admired Miranda." He reached out and took her hand, raised it gracefully to his lips. *"Indeed, the top of admiration, worth/What's dearest to the world!"*

At the sound of her name on his lips, her hand, with a life of its own, had tightened round his. She felt him go tense with surprise, tried to pull her hand away, but his grip kept it tight. For a moment they stood there transfixed, as though some Prospero had cast his spell over the moonlit glade.

"Moreland! Miss Fitton! So here's were you're hiding!" The booming voice shattered the spell. Theo let her hand drop and moved abruptly away. Miranda looked up in alarm at Fortescue's heavy-jowled face. They must surely be in for a dose of that easily ruffled temper about which Theo had hinted. And who could deny he'd a perfect right to be angry, finding his hoped-for bride and his friend in so compromising a position?

He didn't look angry at all. He was smiling broadly, as though at some secret triumph. "Well done, my dear Moreland." He reached out a hand to Theo. "Thank you for taking Miss Fitton out of harm's way. Now the danger is past, I've come to reclaim her."

Miranda was amazed. No man in Florence would have welcomed so calmly the abduction of a lady he cherished. A cold-blooded lot, these English! And that cool phrase, *I've come to reclaim her.* As though she were a piece of luggage, and Theo a docile porter!

"I'm in Mr. Moreland's debt." She made her tone demure to hide a surge of rebellion. "Let's not go back quite yet to that stuffy Rotunda. It's so much pleasanter here among the trees; and we'd just begun such an interesting conversation. Perhaps you would give us your thoughts on the subject of Shakespeare's plays?"

Lord Fortescue blinked in surprise. Clearly he wasn't used to having his wishes disputed. But good manners barred him from contradicting a lady. "Just as you wish, Miss Fitton. Shakespeare, you say? Wasn't he the fellow who wrote that capital play about the three witches?"

Miranda barely suppressed a giggle, and glanced at Theo to see how he took this example of Fortescue's *keen intellect*. Theo's face was stony again. He refused to meet her eyes. He gazed fixedly at Lord Fortescue, as he said in a crisp, dry voice, "Much as I cherish the pleasures of conversation, the duties of friendship transcend all mere pleasure. I trust I've fulfilled those duties. With your leave, I'll retire to my previous occupation."

Miranda felt as though she'd just been slapped. What a consummate actor he was, shifting from lively interest to icy disdain in the space of a minute. Well, two could play at that game.

She laid a hand on Lord Fortescue's shoulder and smiled her most fetching smile. "Mr. Moreland has indeed been a good friend to you. But he's been a poor one to me. He's kept me too long away from the town's most pleasant companion."

Lord Fortescue's face broadened into a fatuous smile. Theo bowed coldly, replaced his mask over his eyes, then turned away. Miranda groped about to find her own scrap of velvet. She'd learned a fine lesson tonight about London manners. There was safety in masks. She must take good care not to let hers slip again.

Chapter Five

"It's settled, then. Almack's this Thursday evening." Mrs. Hester leaned back in her chair, beaming with satisfaction. The motion dislodged a pile of books from the untidy desk beside her, sending them crashing onto the floor. Miranda sprang to retrieve them, but Mrs. Hester waved her away. "Pray don't trouble yourself. The floor's the best place for them." She glanced around the sunlit corner room with a rueful smile. "This may look like chaos to you, but it's my own personal chaos. I can instantly put my finger on any volume I need."

"I'm honored to be allowed inside your sanctum," Miranda assured her. "What a pleasant life it must be, the writer's vocation. So much more exciting than the dull social round in which most women here spend their days."

Mrs. Hester cocked a wry eyebrow. "My sister would scarcely agree." Her forehead creased into a frown. "She'll probably be shocked at the thought of my being your sponsor at Almack's. After all, she's your hostess in London, and her husband's your guardian. Perhaps it might be discreet to invite her to join our party? I'd have no trouble in finding another ticket."

"No, please don't do that!" The words leapt out before Miranda could stop them. She made haste to repair the damage. "I beg your pardon, madam. I don't mean to insult your sister. She's been prodigiously kind. But I'm such a green girl that I find her high polish daunting."

Mrs. Hester flashed her a confidential smile. "You needn't mince words with me. Laetitia's a bore. Especially to an active mind like your own. Though you may find me equally boring when I take on the role of your attendant dragon."

"I'm sure you could never be dull." Miranda smiled at her gratefully. "Though I daresay the evening at Almack's will be far more sedate than the Ranelagh masquerade."

Mrs. Hester's lively eyes gleamed with a new alertness. "I was meaning to ask about that. All sorts of delicous rumors have been floating around the town. But perhaps you don't care to discuss it?" She left the question dangling, softening her voice discreetly.

"I'd love to discuss it with *you*." Miranda felt herself flush. "I'm still very confused by what happened there."

"As well you might be." Mrs. Hester nodded sagely. "What explanation did Fortescue offer to the sudden descent of his outraged mistress?"

"Mistress!" gasped Amanda. "That woman in black was really his mistress? I thought it was all a jest."

Mrs. Hester's lips firmed into a somber line. "It's hardly a jesting matter. The whole town knows why Lady Barwell lives apart from her husband. She and Fortescue have been lovers for several years. We all thought they meant to marry, once her elderly husband made his natural exit. But now that *you've* come on the scene—"

"Good Lord!" cried Miranda. "No wonder the woman

was frantic!" A flood of light seemed to pour into her mind, illumining a host of puzzling events. "So that's why Mr. Moreland carried me off! To keep me from learning his friend's hypocritical secret! I suppose there were other friends lurking about to quiet that poor jealous lady?"

Mrs. Hester's eyes sparkled with glee. "It took three of them to subdue her, or so I've been told."

"And then he came back to me as though nothing had happened! That double-faced rogue! That vile monster! Offering me his hand, when his heart is pledged to another."

Mrs. Hester gazed at her shrewdly. "Come, come, girl; you're not quite *that* innocent. Surely Italian men take mistresses too?"

"Of course they do," Miranda admitted. "Men's nature remains the same all over the world. But at home, we don't keep such things a secret. An Italian suitor would make a clean breast of his past, and very likely pledge to give up his mistress—at least for the first year of marriage. It's the hypocrisy I detest. He's truly the vilest of men. I hated him at first sight, and now I find I had good reason for that reaction."

Mrs. Hester looked alarmed. "A curse on my meddling tongue," she said remorsefully. "I hoped I've not spoiled things between you."

"There was nothing between us to spoil. I've never encouraged his lordship. The zeal is all on his side. Now it seems even more suspicous, his haste to wed me. I'm surer than ever it's my money he wants, not me."

Mrs. Hester's look turned intent, like that of a dog tracking game. "Do you really think so, my dear? It's true, no doubt, that no man would sneeze at your fortune. But Lord Fortescue's scarcely a pauper. His father left him quite an extensive estate."

"That may very well be." Miranda stubbornly clung to her theme. "But the man seems in desperate haste to lay hands on my money." She went on to tell Mrs.

Hester how Lord Fortescue's cousin had been sent to woo Amanda; how his lack of success had been followed by the summons to London. "I'm sure it was all a pretext, just to get me within his reach," she concluded. "How else is one to explain all these strange maneuvers? It can't be a matter of love. He'd never even seen me before last week. No, it must be a matter of money."

Mrs. Hester looked grave. "An interesting tale," she said. "You've certainly started me thinking. I sincerely hope you're mistaken in your suspicions. But I'll make some discreet inquiries. They might set your mind at rest."

"My mind is made up already. I wouldn't care if he turned out to be rich as Croesus. The man's a boor. I won't have him. Nothing can change my opinion."

"You certainly sound determined." Mrs. Hester seemed mildly amused. "Why keep him dangling, then? Why not refuse him outright, and make an end to the matter?"

Why not, indeed? Miranda sat biting her lip as though deep in thought. But the pose was mere playacting. She didn't need to consider. She'd been over this ground already, a thousand times. Still, how could she tell Mrs. Hester the shaming truth—that if she drove Fortescue off, she'd never see Theo again.

But why should she want to see him? The man didn't care for her. She was nothing more to him than his friend's appendage. How silly of her to think him a kindred spirit, on the strength of a few poet's lines. No doubt he knew a hundred girls in London who could prattle on about Shakespeare as knowledgeably as herself—

Aware of the growing silence, she raised her eyes to Mrs. Hester's and found there a grave, understanding look. "I can see there's more to this tale than you care to tell at the moment. Don't let me press you, my dear. Our acquaintance is still very new. I hope you'll soon trust me enough to confide in me fully. I've already formed a deep affection for you. Perhaps I see in you my younger self—" She broke off abruptly. Her grave look turned to a smile. "Enough of these vaporous musings! We've a vital decision to make? Which of those three new gowns will you wear to Almack's?"

"You dare to accuse *me* of duplicity, Mr. Moreland? What of yourself? Surely your *actions* were far more worthy of blame than any mere *words* of mine!" Miranda glared at the man in the plum satin coat who sat on the small gilt chair beside her. His cautious glances toward their neighbors on either side shocked her into compunction. Good Lord, she'd been almost shouting! What a shrew he must think her, lashing out at him so. She halted her tirade abruptly, turning away from him to regain her composure.

How in the world had they blundered into this quarrel? The one man in London she'd desperately wanted to see—and here she was, scolding him like a fishwife. It had all been so pleasant at first. She'd looked cautiously around as she and Mrs. Hester entered the ballroom, hoping Lord Fortescue wouldn't be there. She'd been overjoyed to see Theo's lively smile as he caught her eyes, and absolutely ecstatic as he made his way toward her to ask her to dance. During their first minuet, she'd felt she was floating on air. Their talk had concerned mere trifles—the weather, the music, the latest coffeehouse gossip. Then he'd suggested a rest, and conducted her here to this quiet corner. The talk had grown even more pleasant, ranging over the work of their favorite poets. She found he liked Mr. Pope, abhorred Mr. Thomson, just as she did. Forgetting discretion, she'd made an incautious remark on how agreeable his company was. That's when it all had gone sour. He'd drawn back into himself, and said with an icy politeness, "Your words do me too much kindness. But at least, I may serve to fill in the gap until the *town's most pleasant companion* arrives to relieve your boredom."

She'd winced in shock at the bitter twist in his voice.

Fighting to keep her composure, she'd barely managed to murmur, "I don't understand your meaning. Do you really think I deserve that sarcastic tone?"

He'd seemed a bit taken aback. Perhaps she hadn't succeeded in hiding her misery. "I apologize for my tone, if it offends you. But I can't resist expressing my deep disappointment that a lady I thought so refreshingly candid should descend to duplicity."

"Duplicity? Surely you can't accuse me—"

Theo kept his voice low, but his eyes bored into hers like gimlets. "What else would you call it, madam, your conduct at Ranelagh? You declare for a good half hour how much you dislike a man, and then change to fawning delight the moment he comes in view."

Stung by the germ of truth in his accusation, she'd launched her own counterattack. And now here they were, glaring at each other across this immense abyss. "I'm sorry I raised my voice." She tried for a smile, but couldn't keep her lips from trembling. "Perhaps you've some right to accuse me. But look at your own behavior. You whisk me out of the path of an outraged mistress— and then praise her fickle betrayer for his faithful heart!"

Theo looked startled. *"Mistress!* Then you know—"

Miranda's chin lifted proudly. "I'm not quite the simple chit that you take me for. Yes, I know about Lady Barwell, small thanks to you. Is that not far worse duplicity, to pretend concern for me brought you to my side, when your only motive was to hide the crimes of your friend?"

Now Theo looked thoroughly cowed. He kept his eyes on the floor. His voice was so low she could barely catch the words. "You wrong me there, Miss Fitton. That was not my only motive."

Miranda's heart started beating wildly. "Not your only motive?" she echoed softly, scarcely daring to hope for the words she wanted to hear.

Theo twisted in his chair, locked the fingers of both hands together and stared down at them glumly. "I find myself in a difficult situation. There are things I might like to say—but the laws of friendship—"

Damn your pestilent laws of friendship! What of the laws of love? Miranda bit back the words. She watched him struggle with his conflicting emotions. Finally he raised his head. His face had grown firm with virtuous resolution. With a sinking heart, Miranda realized that friendship had triumphed.

"Perhaps I was less than honest in concealing from you the truth about Lord Fortescue's attachment to Lady Barwell," he said earnestly. "I feared the truth might shock your innocent heart. But I meant every word I said in praise of my friend's husbandly virtues. Every man of the world sows a few wild oats in his youth. He will put all such folly behind him, once you are married. You need have no qualms on that score. I beg you, Miss Fitton, banish all thought of this unpleasant incident. Do not let such a trifle rob you of so splendid a husband."

Miranda felt a chill in the space where her heart had been beating. A woman's life ruined for love, and he called it a trifle! How could so callous a heart accompany such a keen intelligence? And this was the man with whom she'd fallen in love! If he thought Lady Barwell's love was only a trifle, how would he value hers?

"I suggest we abandon this fruitless conversation." She didn't bother to hide her impatience. "Your friend's attachments have nothing to do with my choice. Even if his life had been pure as an angel's, I still wouldn't have him. I assure you, my mind's made up."

"How can you say that so soon? You've scarcely begun to know him." Miranda thought she detected a note of hope behind the surface dismay. She remembered his silent struggle of a few minutes past. Perhaps he was really longing to be convinced that there was no hope for Fortescue.

"I assure you, my dear Mr. Moreland, I know my own heart. There is no room there for your friend. It is already filled by—another." She lowered her eyes demurely, breathing a languishing sigh. A small pang of guilt assailed her. Playacting again! Perhaps she really *was* a hypocrite? But she'd merely spoken the truth. Her heart was indeed full to bursting—with love for Theo Moreland.

He gave her a searching look, surprised and concerned. "You're secretly pledged to another? Someone back in Florence?"

"Not pledged! I didn't say that." She let her eyes fill with sadness. "I have the misfortune to love a man who cares nothing for me."

"But how can that be?" Theo was clearly astonished. "Surely no man in the world could refuse the gift of so ardent and tender a heart? Especially when clothed in so lovely and graceful a form?"

A small glow of warmth flared under Miranda's breastbone. How pleasant to hear those words from these particular lips! "I wish I were free to speak, but prudence restrains me. Suffice it to say that I've never dared even to hint at how much I love him." She sighed again, and let her voice throb with emotion. "Like Viola, I have *let concealment, like a worm i' the bud, feed on my damask cheek—*"

His lips showed the tiniest quirk of amusement. She realized she'd overdone the dramatics, but tried to carry it off, nevertheless. "You may smile, good sir, if you wish, at a maiden's distress—"

"My dear Miss Fitton, I swear I'm not mocking you." How warm and caressing his voice was. Would it were always like that! "But you must admit, you're not really cut out for the role of *Patience on the monument.* Come now, ain't I right? You're much too lively for that."

Damn it, how keen the man was. He'd seen straight through her playacting. Miranda tried one more time to picture herself as a drooping Niobe, but bubbles of mirth kept gathering inside her chest. She finally abandoned the pose in a torrent of laughter. Then he started laughing too, as though he were joining her in some marvelous jest. The last hint of strangeness vanished; she felt closer to Theo Moreland than to anyone else in the world.

Finally their laughter subsided into mutual smiling. He shook his head at her in bewildered amazement. "Indeed, Miss Fitton, you're an extraordinarily congenial companion. No wonder my mind has been full of you these last few days—" He broke off abruptly. A wave of scarlet swept up from his chin to his forehead as he leapt to his feet in evident agitation. "What a crass fool I am! I've completely neglected to bring you any refreshment. Excuse me one moment, please, while I fetch you some lemonade."

The kernel of warmth under her breatbone blossomed out to fill her whole bosom. *My mind has been full of you.* Had he been cherishing visions as tender as hers? Had he too been picturing moonlight encounters, exchanges of love words, adoring kisses sealing heartfelt pledges? She checked her tumbling thoughts. *Not so fast, not so fast!* She was making entirely too much of that casual admission of interest, an admission he had clearly regretted the moment it crossed his lips. Still, wasn't it lovely to know that he saw her as something more than Fortescue's prize quarry in the hunt for an heiress?

She saw him threading his way back to her through the crowded room. How noble he looked, with that clear, blue gaze of his! He seemed to stand out from the chattering crowd as though some bright cloud of light was enveloping him.

Enough of this nonsense, Miranda, she scolded herself. *You must keep all your wits about you. Haven't you learned by now how your eagerness leads you astray?* By the time he reached her side, she had managed to mask her ardent feelings with a cool social smile. "So kind of you, Mr. Moreland." As she took the glass from his hand, her own hand started to tremble. Before she could steady it, a sugary pool was soaking into the canary silk of her skirt.

"A thousand pardons!" Theo instantly pulled a handkerchief out of his coat sleeve and started mopping up the sticky liquid. Even through three layers of heavy cloth, the touch of his hand on her knee was more than Miranda could bear.

"Let me do it, please!" Setting her glass on the little table beside her chair, she snatched the lace-edged square of cambric from him, and scrubbed away as fiercely as though she were back at the Villa Bertolini pounding clothes on the rocks of the little stream.

"Do you think it will stain?" His voice sounded terribly worried. "I should never forgive myself for ruining that lovely gown."

Miranda raised her eyes to his, eager to reassure him. "The fault was all mine, Mr. Moreland. It's a matter of no consequence. Won't you be seated again, and tell me about your rehearsals at Drury Lane? I've tried to imagine that playhouse, from Mr. MacCrae's description. It must be a beautiful place."

He sat down obediently, clearly relieved to be able to change the subject. "You still haven't been there? We must remedy that very soon." His face lit up as an idea seemed to strike him. "They're doing *The Tempest* next Friday. It's a fine production. Why don't we make up a party? I'll suggest it myself, the moment Lord Fortescue gets here. Do you think your friend, Mrs. Hester, would like to join us? Or would you prefer Mrs. Armour to chaperone you?"

He was rattling on about tickets and times and arrangements. Miranda was scarcely listening. Lord Fortescue's name had put a heavy damper on the pleasant sensations of just a moment before. *Forget about him!* she wanted to shout. *Let's form our own party without him!* But that was a hopeless dream. Theo was back in his role of Fortescue's faithful friend. Before that situation could change, she'd have to take the decisive step that would put her odious suitor out of the picture. If only she could be sure it wouldn't banish Theo as well—

She was startled out of her musing by a bulky, broad-shouldered figure, looming up between her and the chattering crowd. "Good evening, Miss Fitton," boomed an all-too-familiar voice. "I'm glad to see you've been suitably entertained. Will you do me the honor of joining me in the next minuet?"

She stared up at him dully, feeling the whole of her body clamp into a knot of revulsion. His hand was outstretched toward hers. She couldn't make herself take it. It seemed a profanation—that the hand that had rested in Theo's should touch that of this boorish oaf.

She gave a quick glance toward Theo, who had risen to greet his friend. He was smiling broadly, as though handing Miranda over to her rightful owner brought him pleasure and relief. *My mind has been full of you.* Could it be she had merely imagined those impetuous words?

"Please excuse me, Lord Fortescue. I've spent too long away from my friend, Mrs. Hester. I must go make amends before taking the floor again."

A dark look passed swiftly over Lord Fortescue's heavy face and was gone in an instant. "Perhaps the next dance, then. Meanwhile, let me escort you back to that estimable lady."

Suppressing a sigh, Miranda rose and accepted his proffered arm. The crowd around her seemed dim and far away, so absorbed was she in a cloud of confusing thoughts. *Stop being foolish, Miranda. You didn't come to London for romantic adventures. You came for the sake of Amanda. You must act like a well-brought-up lady, not a flighty rustic. Ladies aren't allowed to be foolish. Only poor peasant girls can afford the luxury of falling in love.*

A poor peasant girl—the thought was a piercing knife. She faltered and almost stumbled as the shock went through her. What part could Theo play in a peasant girl's life? Only a few more weeks and she'd be barefoot again. Amanda would marry her Charles; she'd come up to London and end this whole masquerade. Back they'd all go to Florence, saying good-bye forever to this enchanting, exasperating Theo Moreland.

Her hand tightened in protest. She realized with surprise that it was full of damp cambric. Theo's handkerchief! She really must give it back—but she couldn't bear to. At least she'd have something to prove he wasn't a dream. She pressed it into an even tighter ball, resolving to tuck it away in her bosom the moment she was alone.

How huge the ballroom seemed! It was taking an endless time, this walk back to Mrs. Hester. A sudden wave of fatigue made her shoulders droop. She squared them resolutely. Just a few more weeks to keep up this stupid pretense, and then it would be all over. She must do her best to get through the time that remained. She mustn't fail her darling Amanda. *But, dear God, I'm growing so weary. Let it end, let it end soon.* . . . The silent prayer faltered inside her, then abruptly changed course. *Soon, God, but not too soon. I must have one more chance to see Theo Moreland!*

Chapter Six

"Consider, my dear Mr. Moreland, what Mr. Shakespeare tells us of the pleasures of poverty. Rosalind in the forest of Arden is a happier woman than she was at the ducal court. Indeed, even Prospero in his island exile—"

Miranda broke off her argument abruptly. She'd just caught sight of herself in her mirror. What an absurd picture she made. This earnest maiden, gorgeously arrayed in a peach silk gown, deep in intellectual conversation with a square of cambric.

If anyone saw me now, they'd think I was mad and pack me off to Bedlam! Miranda picked up the carefully folded handkerchief. She couldn't resist giving it one final stroke before she tucked it away in the drawer of her bureau. How pleasantly smooth it felt! She had washed it out herself in her china handbasin and spread it out to dry across the face of this very same tattletale mirror. It had dried with scarcely a wrinkle. Even without the attentions of a laundress, it looked quite respectable enough to be restored with complete decorum to its rightful owner. Perhaps by tomorrow, the night of their Drury Lane outing, she'd be ready to give it back. And then again, she might not. She'd almost reconciled herself to losing Theo. But a souvenir of him—surely the jealous Fates would allow her that!

Just in time, she heard the footsteps approaching her bedroom door. Hastily, she dropped the handkerchief into a drawer. By the time the beaming Mrs. Armour bustled into the room, the evidence of her folly was safely concealed, and Miranda sat buffing her nails as though nothing concerned her but preserving the ladylike look of her fashionably pallid hands.

"My dear Miss Fitton! There's a very presentable gentleman below who claims acquaintance with you. A Mr. Theophilus Moreland. Do you care to receive him, or shall he be sent away?"

Did she want to receive him? *Dio mio,* does a Christian long for the sight of Heaven? Miranda could scarcely restrain herself from dashing straight down the stairs. But she knew she had better do something to answer the many questions that gleamed from the eyes of her inquisitive hostess. "Oh, yes; that amusing Mr. Moreland." She drawled out the name with a suitably languid air. "I *have* met him once or twice. He's a friend of Lord Fortescue's. I suppose I must receive him, if only out of courtesy to his lordship."

"Intelligent girl. You seem to be gaining a grasp of the social niceties. I'll have him shown into the drawing room directly." Mrs. Armour turned to leave, then paused on the threshold. "I'll be happy to chaperone you—"

"That won't be necessary." Confound the woman and her sly curiosity! "After all, a friend of his lordship— it . . . it may be he's bringing me some personal message—" She saw Mrs. Armour's raised eyebrows, and cursed herself for the telltale stammer. Her hostess nodded coldly and left the room, her back stiff with protest at her young guest's unseemly rashness.

Miranda drew a deep breath to compose herself, meanwhile anxiously consulting her mirror. A fine London lady stared back at her from the glass, her peach-colored silk gown sprigged with small yellow flowers, her well-powdered hair sweeping up from her forehead in a towering egg-shaped coiffure. What good luck she'd decided to complete her dressing early! But wasn't it strange, this unprecedented visit? Perhaps he wasn't here on his own account. Perhaps he was merely a messenger for his friend. Or perhaps—a horrid thought struck her—perhaps he was here to claim that handkerchief, filched so glibly by this sentimental fool of a girl. No, it couldn't be that. Even if he'd guessed the handkercheif's whereabouts, good manners would forbid him to demand its return.

The explanation was probably very simple. He was here on some mission concerning tomorrow's theatrical treat. *The plans have fallen through! I won't get to go after all!* A sick disappointment made Miranda go weak at the knees. *Don't be a silly goose,* she rallied herself. *Enough of these futile guesses. Go down and learn the truth from the man himself.*

Her reception, when she stepped through the drawing-room door, was all she could wish for. He'd evidently been pacing the carpet. He turned as he heard her enter, and his first look of trepidation dissolved into an admiring smile. "You're looking quite splendid this morning, my dear Miss Fitton. I hope you won't blame me for blundering in this way. I happened to be passing—I was on my way to a friend who lives nearby—I thought I might venture—"

Miranda was amazed. Theo Moreland at a loss for words? Whatever next? She hastened to reassure him. "You're very welcome here, Mr. Moreland. I'm glad you've finally accepted my invitation."

"Your invitation? Oh, yes; of course." A look of dismay wiped out the smile completely. "Good Lord! That book I promised! What a forgetful wretch I am! You shall have it this very day. I'll send my servant here with it—"

"Pray don't trouble yourself, my dear Mr. Moreland. Your presence is far more enlivening than any book. Won't you be seated, please? I'll call for some tea. Or would you prefer a glass of madeira?"

Theo was looking exceedingly awkward. "I really don't want to impose—I can't stay very long—oh, yes, hang it; a glass of wine would be most deucedly welcome."

A pang of alarm shot through Miranda's bosom. Something quite drastic must have happened, to stimulate such rashness of expression. She summoned the footman and asked him for wine and seedcake, then turned back to Theo, determined to face the worst. "Has something gone wrong with our plans for Friday night? Will we have to postpone our visit to Drury Lane? I assure you, I shan't mind at all if that's the case. You needn't feel the least bit unhappy—"

Theo blinked at her in confusion. She could see it wasn't the playhouse that troubled him. What else could it be? She seated herself in the chair across the graceful-legged little table from him, and assumed an attentive expression, hoping he'd feel emboldened to reveal the cause of his perturbation.

"Miss Fitton," said Theo suddenly, in a strangled voice, "I believe there are certain laws instituted by our Creator in the human soul which sometimes transcend the laws, reasonable and just though they be, that man has created himself . . ." He came to a sudden halt, obviously groping for words. Then he shot her a piteous glance, as though demanding succor. "Don't you agree?" he said in a kind of gasp, then sank back into his chair, his eyes earnestly searching Miranda's face.

Miranda was quite in the dark as to what that portentous statement might mean, but to this pleading gaze, there was only one possible answer. "Indeed, I agree completely, Mr. Moreland. Does not that theme run all through the Holy Scriptures? Even the pagan Greeks acknowledge the same. Socrates, for example—"

Theo's face lit up with delight. He leaned forward across the table. "I knew you would understand. It was my faith in your womanly sympathy that encouraged me to present myself here this morning. My dear Miss Fitton, if you knew what a struggle I've had these last few days! The claims of my own rebel heart pitted against those of friendship. I scarcely know how to tell you—"

Miranda's head started spinning. Could she really be hearing aright? Was Theo on the verge of making what Mrs. Sheridan's novels described as a declaration? *Dio mio, let it be true! He wants to say it, I know. He wants to tell me he loves me. But he can't get the words out. How can I help him? Perhaps I should reach out my hand? But no, that might be too forward. I can't risk that. If only Mrs. Hester were here to tell me how English young ladies behave in these situations!*

A discreet knock at the door disrupted her whirling thoughts. She sprang to her feet and was halfway across the room before she remembered that all she needed to do was to say, "Come in." She stopped abruptly, and uttered the ladylike phrase. A footman appeared at the door. "Beg pardon, madam," he said. "Lord Fortescue presents his compliments and asks if you are at home."

A wave of desolation swept over Miranda. What an evil trick of Fate! He *would* arrive at this crucial moment, just as her prayers seemed about to be answered! Could she send him away? She cast a quick glance at Theo. He had risen from his chair and was staring at the door in silent horror, like a condemned man preparing himself for the hangman's entrance.

No, there was no escape. Her suitor's arrival had given a whole new shape to the situation. Theo's guilty face told her how much he already regretted his rashness. With a sinking heart, she turned to the footman and told him to usher her visitor in.

A few moments passed, taut with silence. Lord Fortescue entered. He beamed complacently at Miranda, as though he was congratulating himself on acquiring some fine piece of horseflesh. Then his eyes shifted beyond her. His heavy frame went rigid with surprise. "Mr. Moreland! I was not aware that you were on such intimate terms with Miss Fitton."

"Please let me explain." Theo's face was stiff and pale. "Perhaps it was thoughtless of me to call on Miss Fitton—I thought as your mutual host tomorrow evening—I assure you, my presence here can be quite easily explained—"

"Indeed? Then pray, sir, explain it." The broad smile had disappeared in a dark flush of anger. "I find it exceedingly strange that you said not one word to me of your intention to call here. And even stranger that I find you thus *tête-à-tête*. Is not Mrs. Armour at home? Damn me, she might have taken a bit more care to protect my intended bride's reputation."

"That was my fault," cried Miranda. "I did not think such formalities necessary with Mr. Moreland. After all, a close friend of yours—"

"My friend? Is he really my friend? What sort of friend would interfere in so delicate a matter as a serious courtship? Unless—" He turned an accusing gaze toward Miranda. "Unless the lady herself encouraged such forward behavior."

Miranda opened her mouth to protest, but Theo was there before her. "Fortescue!" he exclaimed. "Banish that monstrous suspicion. The thought is unworthy of you. The fault is all mine, I assure you. I am ready to answer for it in whatever way you think best. But do not, I pray you, attribute the least jot of blame to this innocent lady."

Lord Fortescue's gaze shifted back to Theo. "Very well," he said in a milder tone. "I accept your assurance as to Miss Fitton's share in the matter. I suggest you leave us now, sir. I wish to speak privately with my future wife."

"At your service, my lord." Theo bowed stiffly and moved swiftly toward the door.

Your future wife! Never in a thousand years! Miranda compressed her lips to hold back the angry words. She was glad that Theo was leaving. His presence here would only complicate matters. Here was her chance to end this odious courtship once and for all.

The door swung shut behind Theo. Miranda whirled to face the broad-shouldered man, her eyes alive with fury. "Once and for all, Lord Fortescue, I am *not* your betrothed. You have no claim on me. I wouldn't marry you if hell was gaping before me and you were my only escape!" She saw him blink in surprise, and abruptly lowered her voice to a more ladylike pitch. "I hope I've made myself clear. Will you heed my wishes and abandon this hopeless suit?"

The heavy man gazed at her stolidly from under half-closed eyelids. "I feared as much. Mr. Moreland's extravagant notions have clouded your native good sense. I suppose I've myself to blame. I should have broken with him the minute he broached this nonsense of becoming a player. The man is clearly unbalanced. And now he's infected you—"

"Lord Fortescue!" Miranda's insistent voice broke into the rambling tirade. "How many times must I tell you? My decision has nothing to do with Theo Moreland." She took a deep breath, preparing to launch what he might deem a deadly insult. "I don't like you. I never have liked you. I never will like you, let alone love you enough to consider marriage."

Lord Fortescue blinked incredulously, as though one of his horses had suddenly burst out singing "*God Save the King.*" "Really!" he grumbled. "This is most disconcerting. Have you given this serious matter sufficient thought? Consider all you're refusing—a distinguished name, a social position beyond all your previous hopes—"

And an ass for a husband! thought Miranda. With an effort, she kept her voice prim and cool. "Yes, my lord, I have given it serious thought. What else do I need to say to discourage your suit. Must I put my refusal in writing?"

What was he thinking now? His bland surprise had changed to a look of indulgent pity. "My dear Miss Fitton, you're not yourself this morning. I know these little tempests. All women go through them at times. I suggest we forget the intemperate words that have passed between us. Let's wipe the slate completely, and start afresh. I'll leave you now; perhaps with some rest and recollection, you'll be restored by tomorrow to your usual sunny temper."

Miranda gaped at him, at a loss for words. What man could be so thick-skinned? She'd just told him in so many words that she couldn't stand him, and here he was, acting as though nothing had happened. A sudden panic swept through her. Perhaps she'd wind up marrying him after all. His relentless determination would swallow her up, slowly eroding her will, draining away all her courage....

As though he were reading her mind, Lord Fortescue seized on the moment to say in a level voice, "I'm a very determined man, my dear Miss Fitton. I always get what I want. And woe betide anyone, man *or* woman, who presumes to stand in my way."

The threat brought a vivid image swimming before her eyes—Theo's pale set face, confronting the blast of his erstwhile friend's anger. *Careful, Miranda. If you make him too angry, he may take it out on Theo. Better let things ride for the moment, till this morning's anger dies down.* She managed a tremulous smile, playacting the dutiful maiden. "Perhaps you were right, sir. I do require rest and quiet. May I bid you *au revoir?* We'll continue our conversation tomorrow morning—"

The complacent smile reappeared. "That's better, my dear. Give yourself time to judge where your true interests lie." A tiny frown puckered his forehead. "As for tomorrow morning, I recollect now that I have some pressing engagements. I fear I won't see you again till tomorrow evening. I'll call at five to take you and Mrs. Hester to Drury Lane."

"Drury Lane? You still intend to go? But it's Theo who made the arrangements. After your quarrel this morning, I scarcely supposed—"

"Quarrel?" Lord Fortescue beamed down at her like an indulgent uncle. "What quarrel are you speaking of? Haven't I already said we'll forget all the rash words we've spoken this morning?"

Miranda was torn between relief and incredulity. It was good to know that his anger at Theo had cooled. But what sort of monster could so blithely trot off to the playhouse arm in arm with a man whom he'd just accused of making ignoble advances to the lady he claimed for his own? *Dio mio,* these inscrutable English, with their mysterious codes of behavior. She'd never understand them if she lived a hundred years. Thank God, she'd be free of them all in a few more weeks.

"Very well, sir," she said demurely, "I'll leave you now, and see you tomorrow at five."

Chapter Seven

Theo Moreland, resplendent in a coat of pale blue French silk, rose politely to greet them as they entered the Drury Lane box. Miranda felt a pang of disappointment as she watched him fuss over Mrs. Hester, settling her chair so she'd have a good view of the stage. What else had she expected? An ecstatic smile when he saw her? An admiring gaze? Surely she should have known better. His impersonal manner toward her was a necessary precaution. He wouldn't risk reawakening his friend's suspicions.

She'd spent the whole day in a torment of jangled nerves, fearful he might send a message canceling the trip to the playhouse. She was cheered by the fact that he hadn't abandoned his plan, even after the ugly scene the previous morning. Surely that meant he was still longing to see her. Or did it mean that at all? Perhaps he was just being cautious. To cancel the playhouse engagement might be seen as an admission of guilt. Or had Fortescue's anger stirred up his original scruples about the duties of friendship? Was he now resolved never again to overstep those bounds?

Absorbed in her thoughts, she was only dimly aware of the scene around her. Theo had taken a very good box for them. They were perched just above the right side of the stage. If she leaned out over the railing, she'd be within whispering distance of the actors. A good thing, too; this noisy crowd chattering around them would make it hard to hear the Bard's precious lines. But perhaps they'd grow quieter when the big green curtain went up. She hadn't much faith they would. Those gorgeously decked-out ladies in the double-tiered row of boxes seemed far more intent on showing themselves to advantage than appreciating the play.

She was glad Mrs. Hester was with her. She'd invited Mrs. Armour, for the sake of politeness, and had been greatly relieved when that lady said she didn't much care for the playhouse. Now the resourceful Amelia was keeping the gentlemen entertained with her sprightly chatter, giving Miranda the chance to rehearse in her mind the crucial real-life scene she intended to stage tonight after the play was finished.

I regret to inform you, my lord, that the next time you call on me I won't receive you. Surely he'd understand that, no matter how thick his skin. Thank God she'd finally persuaded Mrs. Armour to back her up! She'd brought forward all sorts of objections, but Miranda's subborn insistence had finally carried the day. "Very well, Miss Fitton. I must bow to your wishes, regardless of the embarrassment to myself and Mr. Armour. But you're making a fearful mistake. Your callous behavior will surely become public knowledge. You'll find few eligible gentlemen who'll let themselves in for so rude a reception."

I appreciate your concern, dear Mrs. Armour. Perhaps I *am* being rash. But my mind is made up. I shall inform his lordship tonight of my irrevocable decision."

I regret to inform you, my lord . . . Miranda mur-

69

mured the sentence again under her breath. Lord Fortescue's anger wouldn't daunt her this time. She was sure he'd invite himself in when he drove her home tonight to Argyll Street. She'd deliver the verdict then. He'd probably protest and try to overrule her. But this time, she'd stand her ground. If it meant losing Theo too, she'd have to risk it. After all, God had already granted the *one more time* she'd prayed for. But perhaps she could find some way to assure him that the door so firmly barred against this oafish peer would swing open wide when Theo presented himself.

Could she give him some message tonight? If he'd been seated beside her, she might have risked a whisper. But Mrs. Hester was sitting between them, and Lord Fortescue hovered close at her left-hand side. Pass him a note, perhaps? No, that was dangerous too. If Fortescue happened to see it—a shiver of apprehension rippled down Miranda's spine. Better banish all thought of Theo until his irascible friend was safely out of the picture.

She realized with chagrin that she'd barely given a thought to the play that was about to unfold before her. Would this pestilent *milord* rob her of even *that* pleasure? Not if she could help it! As the big green curtain started its slow ascent, she thrust all thoughts of him out of her mind, and fixed her attention down on the jutting stage, where a group of sailors scurried around a ship's deck, surrounded by a daunting display of thunder and lightning.

She gazed entranced as the scene of panic at sea raced to its end, and the stage flats slid back in their grooves to disclose the rocks and palm trees of Prospero's fairy island. She found that she remembered every word of the dialogue between the old magician and his daughter, her namesake. She'd always known that *Signore* Fitton, God rest his soul, had chosen her name from the heroine of this play. She'd often wondered why he'd liked the name so well. Perhaps *mama* would know? Somehow she'd never quite found the right occasion to ask her.

Miss Rogers was playing Miranda tonight, with Mr. Packer as Prospero, and Mr. Vernon as Ferdinand. What a charming creature she made the girl out to be! She hadn't much to do in this scene. She merely acted as audience to her father, exclaiming prettily as he unfolded the tale of his exile from the throne of Milan and her birth on this desert island.

Miranda—the stage Miranda—fell asleep under Prospero's spell. Ariel appeared, wafted onto the scene by an almost invisible stage harness. Miranda, up in her box, gasped with pleasure, and ventured a glance at Theo to see if he too was impressed. To her utter confusion, she found he was looking at her. Both of them dropped their eyes abruptly. From that moment forth, Miranda kept her eyes fixed on the stage, determinedly concentrating on Caliban's grumbling, then waiting with beating heart for Ferdinand to appear—and fall in love at first sight with her charming namesake.

Songs. Music. A shadowy gauze curtain descending to separate the ethereal Ariel from the shipwrecked mortals. Here comes Ferdinand now. Only a few seconds more and he'll see Miranda . . . She held her breath to hear the familiar lines:

. . . Most sure, the goddess
On whom these airs attend!—Vouchsafe, my prayer
May know if you remain upon this island:
And that you will some good instruction give
How I may bear me here . . .

She felt Lord Fortescue shift uneasily beside her. She looked up at him questioningly. He was staring at her in surprise. She realized with dismay she'd been speaking Ferdinand's lines along with the actor. Her cheeks flamed scarlet. What schoolgirl behavior! "Your

71

pardon, sir," she whispered. "It's just that the play is so familiar to me."

He smiled indulgently and turned his eyes back toward the stage. Miranda clamped her lips tightly. She longed to glance past Mrs. Hester and see if Theo had noticed her gaffe, but she didn't dare to. *He* wouldn't consider it strange to see her mouthing the words. It wouldn't surprise *her* to see he was doing the same.

She kept her lips still and her eyes glued to the stage as the next scene sped by. Sebastian jested, Alonso mourned, Gonzalo planned his utopia. Then came Caliban, begging for drink from the servants. And then they were in the midst of her favorite scene of them all. Carried away by the tender flow of the words, her lips began moving again. *"Do you love me?"* she crooned with her namesake, then answered her question in tandem with Mr. Vernon: *"I, /Beyond all limit of what else i' the world,/ Do love, prize, honor you!"*

Her heart gave a startled leap as she heard a third voice join in. She saw with amazement that Theo was leaning toward her across Mrs. Hester, his eyes raptly fixed on hers, his lips alive with the Bard's fervent lines.

"I heard that, sir!" Lord Fortescue's voice shattered the playhouse hush. He leapt to his feet, sending his frail chair crashing onto its side. "You villain! I call you out!" He glared at the startled Theo, who looked at him with dazed eyes, still enmeshed in the Bard's enchantment. "Choose your weapon, and answer to me for your treacherous conduct."

Theo's eyes came alive with alarm. "Fortescue, you're mistaken. I was quoting the play, only quoting the play—"

"No more of your perjuries, sir. I heard what you said to this lady. You will meet me at dawn tomorrow in back of Marylebone Church, or acknowledge yourself a coward as well as a traitor."

Theo slowly rose to his feet, his face white and set.

"I accept your challenge. You know where I lodge. I will wait there to meet your seconds."

A surge of panic brought Miranda out of her chair, hands outstretched to pull Theo back. "Oh, no! You can't do it, Theo! You can't risk your life for such a nonsensical trifle!" Her anguished cry set heads turning in the other boxes. The actors on stage were almost forgotten as the playgoers gaped at the real-life drama unfolding before them.

"Try to be calm, my dear." Mrs. Hester's quiet voice and her peremptory tug at Miranda's sleeve brought the distracted girl back to her senses. She sank back onto her chair, leaving Theo free to make his way out of the box.

"The matter's out of your hands now." Mrs. Hester put a consoling arm about her. "It's become an affair of honor. The gentlemen must settle their quarrel between them."

Miranda was aghast. She couldn't believe disaster had struck so quickly. Would they really come out at dawn and thrust or shoot at each other till someone shed blood? The thought of blood brought a vivid image of Theo, a crimson pool jetting up through a rent in his waistcoat. *Dio mio,* she couldn't stand that. Couldn't she make them stop it?

"Lord Fortescue," she said in a quieter voice, "I've always considered you a man of good sense. Won't you try to understand what you just overheard? Mr. Moreland's an actor. He found himself caught up in the lines of the play. When he said the word *love,* it was Ferdinand's love he meant—"

"Don't try to excuse him, madam. It was more than mere words that incensed me. I saw the look in his eyes. I think you saw that look too. What else could explain your guilty flush at the moment?"

Miranda didn't think she'd been blushing. But when she raised her hand to her cheek, it felt hot to her touch. Her suitor's appraising eye seized on her unconscious gesture as a further proof of guilt. He glared at her sternly, as though she were on trial in the dock, and he judge and jury combined.

Miranda felt the pressure of tears behind her eyelids. How could she explain when he wouldn't listen? She shot an appealing look toward Mrs. Hester. That shrewd woman saw in an instant how perilously near she was to losing control. "May I suggest that it's time we left the playhouse?" Her mouth quirked in a fleeting smile. "The players would thank us, I'm sure. We seem to be robbing them of the crowd's attention."

Lord Fortescue looked surprised. Caught up in his anger, he'd scarcely noticed all the curious eyes. Now he cast a quick glance at their goggling neighbors, and quickly decided to take Mrs. Hester's advice.

In a matter of minutes, the black landau was rattling off through the shadowy streets, its three passengers sitting stiff and silent. Miranda thought ruefully of her earlier plans—the final refusal, the firm, ladylike dismissal. Those well-rehearsed words would be useless now. They'd only enrage him further. He'd be more convinced than ever that there was some intrigue between herself and Theo. She'd have to rewrite it completely, that next scene in tonight's strange drama. She must find some way to coax him into good humor, dangle some tempting reward that would quiet his thirst for vengeance. With a sinking heart, she realized what she would have to offer. It seemed a drastic step, full of half-foreseen dangers. Nevertheless, she'd have to risk it. There was no other way to save Theo Moreland.

Mrs. Hester pressed Miranda's hand meaningfully as she stepped down out of the carriage in front of her little house in Vere Street. Miranda knew she would have stayed at her side if she had asked her. She had toyed for a moment with the comforting notion of having a friendly witness to the approaching scene. Reluctantly, she had discarded the thought. Lord Fortescue's pride wouldn't let him discuss such a personal matter in front of a stranger.

As she watched her friend mount the front steps on

Lord Fortescue's arm, she struggled to find the right words to greet his return. They *must* have their talk tonight. She couldn't risk his leaving her on her doorstep. If she meant to keep Theo safe, it was tonight or never.

She tried out a series of phrases: *Alone at last?* No, that sounded too forward. *I believe, sir, there are private matters that merit our discussion?* Too stiff and lawyerlike. *I hope you'll step in for a moment at Mrs. Armour's. I've something to tell you in private.* Yes, that was the ticket! He'd surely snap at that bait.

Her heart seemed to turn to lead as she forced out the invitation. His angry face relaxed in a broad, knowing smile. He nodded smugly, and settled back on his seat with his old self-confident air. Damn this arrogant man! Was he reading her mind again? Did he already guess at the offer she planned to make?

But perhaps there would be no need for that drastic offer. She'd seen before how quickly his anger cooled. He was looking quite genial already. She'd try one more appeal to his compassion, before she was forced to the final, distasteful step.

Miranda stared down at the intricate figure in the drawing room's Turkish carpet. She should have known her appeal would be worse than useless. Now he was furious again, breathing fire and thunder. "Call the duel off? That's impossible, madam. Why are you so concerned to protect that villain? Perhaps he's succeeded too well in his base design to snare your innocent heart?"

"He's nothing to me, I tell you. It's you I'm concerned for. I fear you'll be wounded, perhaps even killed—"

He glowered at her skeptically. "If that's your only concern, there's no need to worry. I'm a far better swordsman than Moreland, as a number of men in London have learned to their cost. As for pistols, I know he won't choose 'em. He's never learned the use of that

75

excellent weapon. His pious uncle wouldn't allow him to own one."

Miranda tried to look reassured, though his calm appraisal had made her fears three times stronger. She nerved herself for the final distasteful offer. How could she raise the subject in a delicate way? "I'll confess, sir," she said demurely, "I have a selfish motive in wanting to stop this duel. It's bound to arouse some scandal. Surely you understand how reluctant I am to risk such a cloud marring our day of betrothal?"

"Betrothal!" The big man looked thunderstruck. Then the proprietary smile came back, and he beamed at her in delighted triumph. "My dear Miss Fitton! So you've finally realized where your true interest lies!"

Miranda gazed back at him silently, struggling to hide her revulsion. What a cold-blooded way to begin a marriage engagement! He might at least have *pretended* a lover's pleasure.

Her accusing look seemed to stir him into compunction. "Forgive me, my dear. That was scarcely a husbandly comment. But you took me quite by surprise. My feelings at this tender moment are so overwhelming that I cannot find the words to express my undying devotion. Still, they say one kiss is worth a thousand words. Let us seal this sacred contract in the time-honored way—"

He reached out to draw her to him. Miranda jerked out of his grasp, more by instinct than by design. "Excuse me, my lord; I've never had any illusions that this was a love match. I am sure you haven't either. We both agree what's at stake here—a simple contract, entered into for mutual advantage. In marrying you I acquire a rank and title, social standing, a proud ancestral name. You acquire a presentable wife and a handsome estate. The bargain's a fair one. It doesn't need to be gilded over with mawkish words like *love* or *devotion*."

Insensible to his own crudities, Fortescue gaped at her for a moment. "My word, you're a cold-blooded lady!

Your foreign upbringing, no doubt. You've had no instruction in the tender affairs of the heart."

"You're just as cold-blooded, sir. Why don't you admit it? Your sole interest from the first has been in my estates, not my person. Why else would you have courted me sight unseen? Very well, I've said I'll accept you. If you don't like my cold-blooded manner, you are free to withdraw your offer."

"Oh, no, I wouldn't do that!" Alarm flared in Fortescue's eyes. "Indeed, I am quite relieved at your sensible attitude. Since we're both being so candid, I'll admit my first offer of marriage was prompted by thoughts of your fortune. But the moment I met you in person, my zeal increased tenfold. To combine such personal charms with financial advantage—"

Miranda's commanding gesture silenced him in midsentence. "I have told you already I don't like these mawkish phrases. The contract is settled, except for the date of our marriage. Perhaps the first week in May? They tell me your flowers are lovely at that time of year—"

Miranda had little hope he'd accept so long a delay. She proved to be right. "Oh, no! I couldn't bear such a long engagement. To have such a prize within reach, yet not wholly mine? I protest, it's unreasonable. I'm sure Mrs. Armour would give you better advice."

Which prize do you mean, sir? Myself or my fortune. Still, what does it matter? You'll have neither of them in the end. "What date do you suggest?" she asked demurely.

"Tomorrow morning! Next week at the very latest!" Miranda felt a tremor of alarm at the intensity in his voice. He must be in dire straits indeed! She must try to satisfy him without too much risk to herself. She'd carefully worked out the date to be sure there'd be no mistake. Charles would be back in Portsmouth by the end of this month. Amanda would come of age the fifth of November. Allow a few days for some unforeseen delay— "These matters are not so simple, as I'm sure

Mrs. Armour will tell you." She gave him a pleading look, the submissive maiden imploring his understanding. "There are clothes to be ordered—arrangements to be made—all sorts of womanly matters a mere man may not be aware of. I suggest we compromise. Shall we say—November fifteenth?"

She could see he was disappointed. But in the face of her girlish pleading, he had no further grounds for protest. "The fifteenth it is," he said resignedly. "Though how I'll survive this interminable month, I can't imagine. I will try to sustain myself with thoughts of our future conjugal bliss."

Miranda grew tense with alarm. The way he said those words, caressing them with his lips like some kind of exotic sweetmeat! Still, why was she so concerned? There was really no risk that she'd ever be forced to encounter that *conjugal bliss*. Amanda and Charles would be here well before the fatal day.

Her burgeoning fears refused to be silenced completely. For the hundreth time, she wished she had persuaded Amanda to provide a Portsmouth address to which she could write. If only she knew how vital it was that she arrive promptly in London. Still, Amanda had given her word. She wouldn't break faith with her dear foster sister and friend.

"Indeed, my lord, the time will hang heavy for me, as well as for you. But I trust the end will be worth it." Some mischievous demon inside her impelled her to mimic Amanda's flirtatious smile. "When that great day finally arrives, you'll find Amanda Fitton a far different creature from the cold-blooded girl you now see before you."

There was no doubt about it now, the lascivious look in his eyes. "An enticing promise, my dear. And now, shall we seal the bargain?" His big hands clamped down on both sides of her shoulders. Miranda felt herself flinching as the blubbery lips came down toward her own. But she forced herself not to pull away. *Think of Theo,* she told herself. *Imagine those lips are Theo's. It's only for darling Theo that you're doing all this.*

The thick, eager lips met Miranda's. They rested lightly a moment, then became more demanding. She pushed him away with a girlish, reproving laugh. "Only a month, my lord. Until then, the proprieties! Shall I summon dear Mrs. Armour and tell her our news?"

"I suppose that's the proper thing." Lord Fortescue looked disgruntled. "Though perhaps we shouldn't disturb her so late at night."

"It *is* a bit late." Miranda's heart started pounding. Now was the moment to ask him. Had it really succeeded, this devil's bargain of hers? "Tomorrow will do just as well. You'll have to call early, though. She's going out at eleven." She gave a sudden start, as though a thought had just struck her. "But perhaps you'll still be engaged with Mr. Moreland?"

"Engaged? What engagement?" Lord Fortescue looked confused. Just as she'd hoped, the spurious betrothal had driven all else from his mind. "Oh, yes, I remember now. That stupid misunderstanding." He beamed at her fatuously. "That's all forgotten now. Just as you say, we mustn't stir up any scandal."

A surge of joy set Miranda's head spinning. She'd done it! Her plan had worked! A dangerous plan, to be sure. Lord Fortescue would be furious when he found out how he'd been tricked. But what did that matter? What did anything matter? Theo was safe. That was all she needed to know.

Chapter Eight

Mrs. Armour flew into raptures when Miranda told her the news. "My darling child! What a marvelous choice you've made! I'm sure your dear father is smiling at you from his place in Heaven. When the *ton* hear the news, there'll be a sensation. All the town's finest ladies will be gnashing their teeth with envy."

And one in particular: Lady Barwell. She almost said it aloud. Then she remembered that well-brought-up English young ladies never mentioned such items as mistresses. She was sure they knew all about them. How could they help but know? But, as she was quickly learning, in London hypocrisy was accounted a major virtue.

Mrs. Hester, on the other hand, was appalled by Miranda's news. She paced up and down her cluttered study, muttering angrily under her breath, then turning to hurl reproaches. "A girl of such unparalleled mind and spirit! To throw yourself away on this dimwitted oaf! I won't let you do it, Amanda! I'll go to my brother-in-law, beseech him to save his ward from this fatal mistake—"

"I'm sure he won't listen to you. He's been convinced from the first that I ought to marry his lordship. I believe that was part of his purpose in summoning me here to England."

"He'll change his mind when he hears what I've learned from my friends." Mrs. Hester's mouth grew firm with determination. "The man's gambling debts are enormous. He's on the verge of ruin. He's only marrying you to avoid disaster."

"I fancy Mr. Armour already knows all that." Miranda's voice was dull with resignation. "I ventured a question once as to whether Lord Fortescue gambled. Mr. Armour said every man of good breeding in London gambled. But I wasn't to worry. My fortune would be sufficient to sustain a few paltry losses."

"Unfortunate girl!" exclaimed Mrs. Hester. "To fall into the hands of such a negligent guardian! Imagine his pleading the cause of this venal fortune hunter!"

"I'm sure Mr. Armour thinks he's protecting my interests." Miranda was struggling hard to hide her true feelings. "It isn't so easy, he tells me, for a girl like myself to find a good English husband. With an exiled father, an Italian mother, no family connections in England—his lordship belongs to one of the realm's proudest families. Surely such credentials are not to be sneezed at, whatever his motives may be. Besides, once we are man and wife, his motives may change. That latest novel of yours describes most convincingly how a marriage of convenience becomes a love match."

"Stuff and nonsense!" snorted Mrs. Hester. "Such things only happen in novels. In real life, these matches grow worse instead of better. Love match indeed! What about Lady Barwell? It's true he's avoiding her now, so as not to risk spoiling this marriage. But after the wedding he'll be back in her cozy boudoir, while you sit at home and twiddle your foolish thumbs!"

"Surely every man must be allowed a few peccadillos. From all I hear people saying, there's no such animal as a faithful husband."

"Ye gods, this wicked city!" Mrs. Hester slapped her brow in desperation. "How quickly it's turned you into a jaded cynic! I assure you, there are hundreds of men with faithful hearts. My own dear Ned was one. And what of our poor Theo Moreland? Since he heard the news, he's been pining away with grief. There's a heart that would be yours forever, if you'd accept it. How can you spurn that pure gold for Fortescue's dross? If you'd seen the look of pain when I talked with him yesterday at Mrs. Delaney's!"

Miranda's heart started thumping. She drew a deep, careful breath to steady her voice. "Surely you're imagining things. If Mr. Moreland's in pain, it isn't on account of my coming marriage."

"My dear Amanda, I'm well past the age of imagining things. I know our dear Theo well. I've watched him glow with pleasure whenever he saw you. That night at Drury Lane, even a blind man could see that he was in love with you. And I'd have bet my last bonnet that you were in love with him." Her scornful glare faded abruptly. A look of dawning comprehension appeared in its place. "That night at Drury Lane! So that's what it's all about! You feared for your Theo's life. You threw yourself into the fire of Fortescue's wrath, a living sacrifice for the man you love! Such nobility! Such maidenly ardor!" Her glowing eyes dimmed to cold calculation. "But your daring ploy won't work, my dear romantic. I won't let it work. It's all very fine for the young fools I write about to immolate themselves on the altar of love. But it's not a suitable fate for my dear Amanda. You and Theo are obviously destined to love each other. *There's* the love match my darling deserves, and I won't let these stupid heroics cheat you of it. I'll send for Theo this instant, reveal what you've risked for his sake—"

"Oh, no, Mrs. Hester, I beg you. I'm sorely afraid

you're mistaken about Theo's feelings. You mustn't reveal my secret longing for him."

"Tush and piffle, my girl. I've seen the man's eyes when I happen to mention your name. He's fathoms deep in love, I can warrant you that."

In the midst of her perturbation, a warm glow of pleasure flared in Miranda's heart. So there was one sweet oasis in life's arid desert! Theo was as deeply in love as she was! But that gave her even more reason to dread Mrs. Hester's meddling.

"My dear Mrs. Hester," she said, "I'm deeply touched by the sympathy you express. But don't you see what's bound to happen if Theo learns my true motives? He'll raise some kind of a fuss, refuse to accept what you call my sacrifice, perhaps even avow himself a rival suitor. All the good I hoped to achieve will be undone. He'll be risking death at the hands of that brutal swordsman."

"Surely Theo deserves the chance to take that risk? To face the prospect of death for the woman he loves?" Mrs. Hester's eyes were bright with the light of battle. She reached for a bellpull with one hand, picked up a pen with the other. "I'll send a message this minute. You'll be in each other's arms within the hour. Let Lord Fortescue rant and threaten and flourish his sword. Surely Heaven will protect this pair of predestined lovers."

Miranda felt her head spinning. She'd never had much faith in divine intervention. In this day and age, mortals must look to their own protection. It was up to her to stop Mrs. Hester. She'd have to tell her the truth—that the marriage she feared so much would never take place.

She hesitated, assailed by a pang of guilt. She'd sworn to Amanda not to reveal the secret. *Tell no one,* Amanda had said, *no one at all, whatever the circumstances.* But surely she couldn't be blamed for trying to save a man's life?

"Mrs. Hester," she said abruptly, "I have something

to tell you. You'll respect my confidence? The facts I'm about to reveal must go no further. There's too much at stake—my dearest friend's whole future. You promise you won't breathe a word to a living soul?"

A servant appeared in the doorway with a questioning look. Mrs. Hester sent him away and pulled the door shut, then turned to Miranda, gazing fondly into her eyes. "My dear child, I give you my promise. You're like a daughter to me. I want nothing so much in this world as to see you happy. Whatever secrets you tell me, I'll keep as mum as the grave. I'd cut off my hand before I'd risk injury to Amanda Fitton."

Those shrewd, honest eyes. This woman meant what she said. Surely Amanda would forgive her for revealing their secret. "My name's not Amanda Fitton." Her voice sounded harsh in her ears. "Amanda Fitton's my friend and foster sister. We've been playing a trick on you all. I'm a poor Italian peasant. My name is Miranda Testa." She went on to explain the whole tangled situation—Amanda's engagement to Charles, her suspicions of Mr. Armour, her own reluctant decision to masquerade as Amanda. "So you see what a pickle our plot has landed me in," she concluded. "But I trust in Amanda to make things come right in the end. She'll surely be here in London well before the date of my loathsome nuptials."

Mrs. Hester was wide-eyed with amazement. "What a fascinating romance! I could never have plotted so ingenious a tale, not in my wildest flights. But aren't you putting yourself at tremendous risk? What if some trick of fate keeps your friend from arriving in time?"

"You don't know my dear Amanda. She's a very determined young lady. She's given her word that she'll see that I come to no harm. Nothing on earth can stop her from keeping that promise."

Mrs. Hester wasn't convinced. She pursed her lips doubtfully. "I'm sure she's the soul of honor, but it's still a tremendous risk. I advise you to go to Lord Fortescue and break this disastrous engagement before it's too late."

"Oh, no!" Miranda went pale. "I can't possibly do that now! Don't you see what he'd think? He'd be sure it was Theo's fault, and be furious with him again, more furious than ever!"

"Don't fret about Theo, my dear. We'll whisk him away from London. By the time your boorish suitor learns that he's lost you, young Mr. Moreland will be safely out of his reach."

A flicker of hope stirred deep in Miranda's breast. "If only that could be arranged! But I'm sure Theo wouldn't go. He's a gentleman, after all. He couldn't evade an honorable challenge."

"But it's not an honorable challenge. Surely you see that, my pet? When Theo learns of the underhanded scheme to lure Amanda to England, a plot that drove the young lady to substitute you—"

"*Dio mio!* You can't tell him that!" Miranda's knees went weak. Her head started whirling. "He's the one man in the world who must never learn that secret."

"He should be the first to learn it. I tell you, my dear, he loves you."

Miranda shook her head sadly. "He loves a highborn lady, Miss Amanda Fitton. A poor little nobody like Miranda Testa—he'd shake me off in disgust, like a clod of mud that threatened the shine on his boots."

Mrs. Hester gave a snort of exasperation. "This pestilent blight of rank! Thank God, we're beginning to break through those old rigid forms. It pierces me to the heart when I hear you demean yourself so. A clod of mud! You're no such thing, girl. You're a most extraordinary young lady. Yes, *lady,* I said, in the truest sense of the word. In intellect, education, and most of all in your pure and tender heart, you far surpass the poor creatures who pass for *ladies* among the *bon ton* of London."

Miranda felt her heart grow warm with pleasure. "What a marvelous compliment! How fortunate I am to encounter a friend of your wide-ranging sympathies. But Theo, I fear, has been bred to a narrower world. You see how he flinches at the thought of besmirching his name with the taint of the playhouse. And he couldn't bear to be poor; that's why he's afraid of his uncle. Surely he'd shrink in disgust from a girl who's known nothing but poverty all of her life."

"My dear, I'm sure you're quite wrong. It's you Theo loves, not your wealth and position. If only you'd let me tell him—"

"No, Mrs. Hester." Miranda's jaw was stiff with determination. "I forbid you expressly to tell him. You promised, remember, not to betray my secret."

"Couldn't I drop a hint?" Amelia's voice took on a wheedling tone. "Not the whole secret, of course. But surely he deserves to know that this sorry affair may soon have a happy outcome."

A wave of desolation swept over Miranda. "But there won't be a happy outcome. There can't be, for Theo and me. Once Amanda is safe, I'll go back to the villa in Florence, and never see Theo again for the rest of my life." The stark finality of the words pierced her heart like a knife. She burst into racking sobs, burying her head in her hands.

Mrs. Hester leaned over and gently patted her shoulder. "But surely you'll tell him the truth before you leave London. You'll see the joy dawn in his eyes; he'll declare his love."

"It wouldn't be joy I'd see!" Miranda's sobs grew louder. "God knows what I'd see in his eyes. Distaste, contempt, perhaps even hatred, once he knows how I've tricked him. I couldn't bear that. I just couldn't! I'd be left without even one happy memory. I must have my memories—memories of the few golden moments when Theo's eyes gazed into mine with pleasure and admiration. That's all I have, don't you see? That, and this flimsy trifle." She reached up her sleeve and pulled out the square of lace-edged cambric, now limp and bedraggled, pressed it against her eyes again and again, trying to stop the tears. It proved to be a vain effort. The precious reminder of Theo only sharpened her sense of irreparable loss.

Mrs. Hester sat quietly, her hand still pressing the weeping girl's shoulder. "I think you're foolish, of course, to doubt Theo's love. But all girls in love are inclined to be foolish. Never fear, I'll respect your secret—yours and Amanda's. There's nothing else I can do. I've given my promise. We'll just have to trust that fate will be kind for once. Once Amanda is here, and the secret's no longer a secret, perhaps the rest of the tangle can be unraveled."

Chapter Nine

Thus began the most trying few weeks Miranda had ever endured. The wedding preparations provided a constant tormenting reminder of her painful bargain, as seamstresses, glovemakers, shoemakers, jewelers, milliners, hairdressers and perfumers came and went in an endless procession. Even so, there were many times when she welcomed their presence. They provided a good excuse for refusing to join Lord Fortescue as he pranced and preened in the role of expectant bridegroom.

Once the news was out, invitations rained in on them both. It seemed Mrs. Armour was right; the whole town was agog to see his lordship's betrothed, this unknown heiress who'd snatched him from under their noses. Miranda hated it all—the routs, the balls, the dinners, the assemblies, the masquerades. She felt lost in a sea of hypocritical faces—smiling and murmuring felicitations, then turning aside to whisper in guarded voices, calculating the size of her fortune, wondering what Fortescue saw in so green and awkward a miss, commenting lewdly on Lady Barwell's reaction to her lover's betrothal.

Only once in those awful weeks did she have one happy moment. In the midst of a jabbering crowd at Lady Ossory's, she suddenly turned her head and saw Theo Moreland. He was standing alone on the edge of the gathering, staring gravely at her. When he saw her looking at him, he turned away abruptly. Miranda caught her breath. Surely he didn't intend to leave without saying a word! Surely he'd come and give her some sort of greeting, murmur some words of congratulation. The words would ring hollow, of course—but at least she'd see again those dancing blue eyes, hear again that melodious voice. . . .

A rakish looking man with a painted face distracted her, begging Lord Fortescue for an introduction. When she looked for Theo again, she found he was gone. With a pang of dismay, she saw herself through his eyes: a hardhearted minx, encouraging him, then blithely bestowing her hand on a man she professed to despise. She felt her strength ebbing away, and clutched at Fortescue's arm, afraid she was going to faint. *Oh, Theo, my darling Theo! It's all a mistake. I'd never marry this man in a million years. Come back, come back, oh, please, come back. I'll shout it out to the skies; I'll tell them all it's a fraud. . . .*

She came to her senses abruptly, and looked wildly around her, fearing she'd spoken aloud. But no one seemed to be shocked. Lord Fortescue was peering at her with concern, his arm around her waist, supporting her to a chair. "It's nothing," she managed to gasp. "A giddy spell, nothing more. The crowd, the excitement—"

She searched his eyes, wondering if he too had caught sight of Theo. A cold fear clutched at her heart: *If he saw his betrothed start to swoon at the sight of his friend*—No, the thick-lidded eyes showed no spark of suspicion. Theo was safe—but by what a narrow margin! She'd have to be more circumspect in the future, or her irksome bargain would lose all its point.

She struggled up onto her feet, forcing herself to smile, proclaimed herself fully recovered, propelled herself like a clockwork doll through the endless hours of tormenting chatter until, alone at last in her bedroom's merciful quiet, she sank to her knees and prayed, as she did every night, that Amanda would come in time to end this nightmare.

Day crept on after day at a leaden pace. Prayer followed prayer, becoming more fervent each night. Then it finally came, the day she'd been longing for, the fifth of November. That night London was brilliant with bonfires and fireworks—the traditional Guy Fawkes celebration. She stood at her bedroom window, her heart full of exultation, as she watched the showers of rockets. She knew they were celebrating the defeat of the Gunpowder Plot. But she had her own celebration: *Amanda's birthday*.

That sudden burst of joy kept her aloft for a few more days, then quickly fizzled away to a few feeble sparks. When the twelfth of November arrived, Miranda was desperate. Where in God's name was Amanda? She must be married by now. Why hadn't she come? She'd promised! She must have been caught in some terrible accident!

November thirteenth was a Friday. Mrs. Armour left the house early for a round of visits. Miranda, pleading a headache, stayed in her room all day, straining her ears for the sound of Amanda's carriage. The wintry sun struggled out of a cold gray fog, rose wearily to its zenith, and began to decline. Miranda could stand it no longer. She threw on some clothes in a higgledy-piggledy fashion, sent a servant to fetch her a hackney, and ten minutes later was trembling on the doorstep of her only friend in London—or perhaps in the whole wide world.

* * *

She was ushered into the cluttered corner room, where she found Mrs. Hester pacing up and down in a state of high indignation. "Miranda! You poor, poor child! To fall into this den of wolves! I've just come from a talk with my sainted brother-in-law. The dreadful man's greed far surpasses my worst expectations!"

"You went to see Mr. Armour? About this marriage?" Consternation gripped Miranda. "I hope you didn't tell him Amanda's secret!"

"No, no, my girl." Amelia sighed with frustration. "Though I can't help thinking I should have. But you've sealed my lips with that ridiculous promise. No, I went to plead the cause of Amanda Fitton, an innocent girl confided to his protection. I gave him my information on Fortescue's debts. I told him straight out how things stood with Lady Barwell. I pleaded with him to forbid this unfortunate marriage, to rescue his ward from this profligate scoundrel."

"What did he say?" Miranda asked eagerly. "Did he try to deny the charges?"

"Of course not. How could he? It was clear to me from the start that he already knew all I told him. He never batted an eye, but made some feeble jest about *sowing wild oats,* then launched into a flowery speech praising himself for finding so good a husband for this undistinguished young girl of dubious family connections. The smug, greedy hypocrite! I wanted to scratch his eyes out. If you'd heard the names I called him! *Whoremaster* and *pimp* were only the beginning."

Despite her distress, Miranda couldn't help smiling. "What a rare scene that must have been! Was he terribly shocked to hear those words from a lady?"

Mrs. Hester looked grim. "He pretended to be, of course. He swelled up like a turkey gobbler and ordered me from the room. But I knew my shot had gone home. His anger gave him away. He's made some infamous bargain with Fortescue."

Miranda gaped at her. "You're saying Lord Fortescue's promised to give him a share of Amanda's fortune? That my dear friend has been literally bought and sold?"

"I'm sure of it, child. There's no other explanation. Did you think I was joking in calling that monster a pimp?"

Miranda heaved a deep sigh of resignation. "I suspected that from the first, but I thought I might be mistaken. I know so little about English social customs."

"The selling of brides is one of our oldest customs," Mrs. Hester said drily. "Usually the poor girl in question hasn't the power to resist. But that's not your case, Miranda. One word from you, and this whole vile scheme would collapse. For God's sake, child, won't you let me reveal your secret? It can't hurt Amanda now. Her birthday has come and gone; she's acquired full rights to her fortune. She's probably already married to the man she loves—"

"No!" Miranda had to shout to make herself heard. "I made a solemn promise. I can't tell Amanda's secret until she herself gives me leave."

"Exasperating girl! Then at least, break off the engagement! Forget your precious Theo. What's a duel or two, more or less, compared with the mortal danger of being married?"

"No," said Miranda again, her chin beginning to jut at a stubborn angle. "I won't risk Theo's life. Amanda will come tomorrow; I'm sure she will. And if worst comes to worst, I'll have to go through with the farce. At least I'll have the comfort of knowing it isn't legal."

Amelia shook her head mournfully, as though at a loss for words. "Good Lord, girl, you call that comfort? *You'll* know it's all a farce, but Lord Fortescue won't. What will you say when he comes to demand his rights as a husband? Surely your sacred promise won't bind you then?"

Miranda felt her throat aching and knew she was going to cry. She fought back the tears and glared at Amelia fiercely. "I promised," she said. "Won't you stop goading me? I know my predicament. But I can't see any way out—any honorable way."

Amelia's face softened. "You poor, sweet child. You're like one of my high-minded heroines come to life. But my dear,"—she hesitated, tactfully searching for words—"are you sure you understand what we're speaking of? Has your mother given you any specific guidance as to the mutual duties of husbands and wives?"

Miranda didn't know whether to laugh or cry. What a high-flown way of describing so earthy a matter. "My dear Mrs. Hester, you needn't fear to offend me. Remember, I'm a peasant girl, not a lady. By the time my mother told me how babies are made, I had already learned it all from watching the farmyard."

"You do understand, then. And yet you would take that risk? You'd make a gift of yourself to that unprincipled boor?"

A hot tide of panic welled up from Miranda's stomach. "It won't come to that, it won't! Amanda will come in time." And, with words said more in supplication than true belief, "The good Lord will send her to save me."

Amelia's lips firmed into a line. "That's the sort of thing they always say in my novels, the poor silly geese, and they always *are* saved in the end. But when it comes to real life—" She stopped abruptly, slapping her forehead as though she'd just remembered some glaring oversight. Then she rushed to the bookshelves, scanning the long ranks of bindings. She pulled a book out and started flipping its pages. "The very thing! We'll take a leaf from this saccharine novel of mine! Do you know, my impossible child, that I once told a tale of this very situation—a pure young girl, forced into a fraudulent marriage. Now look; here's how she dealt with that plaguey wedding night question. Read it yourself, and see what you think of the scheme!"

* * *

"A preposterous demand! Who ever heard such impudent words from a bride!" Lord Fortescue, red-faced and sputtering, leapt to his feet and strode over to warm his hands at the handsome Adam fireplace, then turned to glower resentfully at Miranda.

She raised limpid eyes to his, pleased with the self-control that kept her hands lying loose and relaxed in her lap. "But surely you understand the weight of a sacred promise?"

"Sacred promise indeed! This confounded skittish notion! It's your foreign upbringing, I suppose. No girl reared in England would countenance such an idea."

Miranda tilted her chin at a haughty angle. "My father was brought up in England, Lord Fortescue. It was he who exacted my promise. He was terrified lest I meet the same fate as my mother, who died in childbirth before she was twenty-two."

"So you ask me to forego my rights for a whole blasted year? It's a bit late in the day for this kind of nonsense. Why wait till the morning before our wedding to make this absurd demand?"

Miranda lowered her eyes demurely. "Our acquaintance has been so brief, sir. Naturally, I hesitated to broach such a delicate subject. I assumed your magnanimous heart would yield to my pleas—"

"You assume too much, madam." The big man's voice rose to a roar. "Marriage is marriage. A husband's a husband. I won't tolerate any such foolish conditions."

"Will you not, sir?" Miranda raised her eyes and gave him a long, level look. "That's most unsporting of you, since *I'm* quite prepared to tolerate your mistress, Lady Barwell."

Fortescue seemed thunderstruck. He goggled at her in dismay. Finally he managed to gasp out a strangled question. "You know—about Lady Barwell?"

Miranda maintained her voice at the same even pitch. "All London knows about Lady Barwell. You could scarcely assume the gossip would not reach my ears."

"You knew about Lady Barwell, and still you accepted me?" His voice was low and subdued, no longer that of the lord and master. Miranda felt a small pang of pleasure in seeing how sheepish he looked.

"As I've told you before, my lord, I regard this marriage as a simple business contract—your name and rank in exchange for my fortune. The fact that you have a mistress—and one so demonstrably eager to maintain that position—doesn't at all affect the terms of our bargain."

Fortescue's blubbery lips curled into a sulky pout. "Surely you realize that contract implies the need for an heir."

"Naturally, sir." Miranda flashed him a brilliant smile. "I wouldn't dream of denying that wifely duty. But surely a brief postponement—"

"A whole blasted year! That's scarcely a brief postponement. Can you really expect any man to forego his natural rights?"

"We're not speaking of *any* husband. We're speaking of you. I'm sure Lady Barwell will be only too glad to supply any lack you find in our marital arrangements. And think of the advantage to you! You won't be obliged to lie and make excuses when you want to be with your mistress. You'll be risking no wifely tears or scenes of domestic outrage."

A smile of grudging admiration spread slowly over the heavy-jowled face. "You really mean it, don't you? By gad, you're a hardhearted wench."

"My heart is no harder than yours, sir. We've already established the fact that it's my fortune you love, not myself. If you choose to seek love elsewhere, what concern should that be of mine?"

He studied her face with a bemused expression, as if trying to fathom the thoughts beneath its surface. "You're a most uncommon woman, my dear Amanda. It's true I don't love you now. But I honestly feel I could learn to love you."

The heavy-lidded eyes were gazing at her with a new

expression that brought a blush to her cheeks. Miranda forced herself to keep her face blank, concealing her painful spasm of trepidation. "Back to our contract, sir. Do you accept my conditions? A year's postponement of my wifely duty? Please answer yes or no." She saw him hesitate, and pressed urgently on. "Of course if you like, we could simply postpone our marriage till I'm twenty-two."

"No! We won't do that." His voice was sharp with distress. "I accept your blasted conditions."

Miranda felt a brief spurt of triumph. She'd pulled it off! His creditors must surely be pressing him hard. She raised her eyes, and stared sternly into his. "You give me your sacred promise? You'll swear on your mother's grave?"

His face clouded over. "We don't hold with such heathen nonsense here in England. I give you my word of honor, the word of a gentleman. Surely that's enough to quiet your skittish fears?"

Miranda saw it was useless to press things further. "Of course," she said, smiling shyly. "And I, too, will keep to the terms of our contract. I won't detain you longer from that pressing engagement you mentioned. I assume it's with Lady Barwell?"

He turned red as a beet, and began to stammer denials. "Please don't pretend, my lord. You've agreed to the terms of our contract. One of the terms is your freedom to love where you will."

He smiled incredulously. "I can't believe it, by gad. A woman who isn't jealous! I'll take you at your word, and bid you farewell—till we meet tomorrow in church." With the briefest sketch of a bow, he hurried out of the room. Miranda watched him go, her heart full of questions. Mrs. Hester's scheme had worked. She'd extorted the vital promise. But would that promise hold? In the pages of novels, the English gentleman was a highly predictable creature. But when it came to real life—

Enough of these gloomy thoughts. You aren't married yet. You still have twenty-four hours till that fatal moment. Oh, Amanda, my dear Amanda, what in God's name is delaying your trip to London?

Chapter Ten

"*If any man can show any just cause why these two may not lawfully be joined together, let him now speak, or else hereafter forever hold his peace....*" Miranda stared fixedly at the ornate gold cross behind the unctuous clergyman's shoulder. Surely she'd hear it now, Amanda's high sweet voice, demanding a halt to the farce, setting her free from this nightmare.

The miracle didn't happen. The only voice she heard was that of the English cleric, inexorably droning on through the words of the ritual. As though in a dream, she gave the required responses, accepted the ring, forced her lips into a smile as she turned to receive the congratulations of the throng in the little chapel. She couldn't remember later how they reached Lord Fortescue's town house. Had they gone in the open landau or the gilded coach? All she remembered was leaving a sea of faces, indistinguishable faces mouthing indistinguishable words, on the chapel's steps, then meeting another sea of indistinguishable faces as she made her way through the grand saloon of the house in Portman Square in which she would henceforth preside as wife and mistress.

Somehow she got through the hours of festivity that followed the wedding. Somewhere she found the strength to accept the words of politeness and ignore the salacious sallies. She almost faltered once, when Theo came up to offer congratulations. She babbled some nonsense, refusing to meet his eyes, afraid she'd find them full of accusation. Lord Fortescue more than made up for her lack of warmth, grasping Theo's hand warmly, beaming at him with a smile in which Miranda detected a hint of malicious triumph. She breathed a sigh of relief when a new arrival attracted her husband's attention, allowing Theo to melt away into the crowd.

"So times are good in Jamaica?" All her numbed senses suddenly snapped to attention. She stared at the well-dressed young man to whom her supposed husband had just addressed that heartwarming phrase. The newcomer saw her looking at him and bowed politely. Lord Fortescue hastened to make the introductions. The young man, it turned out, was a naval lieutenant, whose squadron had just returned from a trip to Jamaica.

"Then you must know my cousin, Charles Halstead." Miranda went giddy with joy as Lord Fortescue asked the question she was aching to ask. He turned to her with a patronizing smile. "You remember Charles, Amanda? That earnest young man who began the negotiations that led to this happy day?"

"Of course I remember Lieutenant Halstead." Miranda was struggling to keep her voice cool. "He's a friend of yours, lieutenant?"

"I don't know him very well, but we're in the same squadron. I'm surprised not to see him here. Our squadron docked at Portsmouth more than a week ago."

"It doesn't surprise me at all," said Lord Fortescue sourly. "My cousin and I have never been very close." He gave the young lieutenant a broad, lascivious wink.

"I'm sure you young men have more interesting things to do once you're ashore than attend other people's weddings. Once he's had his fill of chasing after the fillies, perhaps he'll come by to give me the news from Jamaica. Meanwhile, I've my own correspondents. You've heard of Sir Lucas Trotter? He's an uncle of mine."

The lieutenant's eyes lit up with quick respect. "Indeed I have, sir. One of the colony's richest speculators. They say he's made a fortune several times over. I dined with him last month, along with your cousin Charles. The man sets an excellent table. He's a true connoisseur when it comes to food and drink."

"A connoisseur, d'ye say? Well, well; we must give some thought to his entertainment." He turned toward Miranda, smiling with smug satisfaction. "I've just had a letter from him, saying he plans to come for a lengthy visit. He expects to arrive in London the first week of December."

Miranda managed to murmur the proper responses—that his uncle's visit was a most agreeable prospect, that she'd be so pleased to meet Sir Lucas Trotter. But she scarcely knew what she was saying; her mind was awhirl with the startling news about Charles. If he'd landed in Portsmouth last week, where was he now? Why hadn't he and Amanda come to her rescue? Had something gone wrong? Some terrible accident? Or was it mere heedlessness? Had the newfound pleasures of marriage left no place in their thoughts for the lonely girl who waited for them in London?

The rest of the afternoon went by in a colorless blur. She smiled, she bowed, she murmured appropriate greetings; she went through the motions of being a happy bride. As the daylight dwindled, so did the number of guests. The multitude was reduced to a few boisterous clusters, who seemed determined to drink the punch bowls dry if it took them all night.

Miranda sank wearily into a chair in a quiet corner, gazing blankly at the noisy stragglers. Lord Fortescue came back with another glass of punch for her. She waved it away with an exhausted hand. He smiled down indulgently at her, and drank it himself. "You've been an admirable hostess, my dear Amanda. But I should have expected that. Good breeding always tells."

"Thank you, my lord." said Miranda. "I must admit, I'm growing very weary. Since most of the ladies have left, perhaps it would not be amiss for me to retire to my room?"

A pucker of annoyance creased Lord Fortescue's brow. Miranda looked up at him in trepidation. Surely he wouldn't forbid her a little rest! She couldn't stand one more minute of acting the happy bride.

"Of course, my dear." He didn't sound very pleased, despite his affable smile. "I'm sure our guests will excuse us if we retire to our nuptial chamber."

Miranda went rigid with horror. *You know I didn't mean that!* She gazed in shocked reproach at the bland, heavy face. Then, conscious of watching eyes, she rose without further protest, accepting his proffered arm, and let him conduct her up the curving stairway. A liveried servant opened the bedroom door. Moving as though in a dream, Miranda advanced on her new husband's arm toward an enormous bed, its sumptuous satin hangings glimmering in the light of a dozen candles.

At Fortescue's signal, the servants bowed and left them. The moment the door closed behind them, Miranda's fury exploded. "You promised! You gave your word! The word of a gentleman. Is this all it means? I kept my side of the bargain. My fortune is yours. You said you'd accept my conditions."

Lord Fortescue regarded her with distaste, as if she were a two-day-old herring. "There's no need for this unseemly display of temper. I gave you my word. I intend to keep it. But there's no need to tell the whole world of my wife's unnatural notions. If you'll take time to notice, my dear, you'll see there's more than one door to this bedroom." He walked stiffly across the room and threw open a smaller door that had been half hidden from them by an ornate dressing table. "My own chamber lies through this doorway. I'll retire there now, and welcome the chance to escape these female hysterics. Let me bid you goodnight; I trust by tomorrow you'll find yourself more composed."

With the curtest of nods, he walked huffily out through the second door. She could see he wanted to slam it, but caution restrained him; perhaps the servants would hear. He paused for a moment, then closed it gently behind him.

Miranda's knees went weak with relief. She flung herself down on the bed. How wonderful, to be alone at last! She shot a quick glance at the door through which the big man had vanished. If only she'd thought to ask him for the key! No, perhaps it was better this way. To ask for the key might have been too much of an insult. This peculiar thing called an English gentleman's honor had saved her thus far. She'd just have to trust in it a little longer.

And Charles *was* back in England. That part of the plan had succeeded. No doubt Miranda and he were already married. Perhaps at this very moment they were lying together in some magnificent bed as splendid as this one—or better yet, on some lumpy mattress in a shabby post inn on the London-Portsmouth road. Perhaps they'd be here tomorrow. . . .

She fumbled in the pocket of her gown and pulled out the lace-edged square of cambric embroidered with Theo's initials. She held it against her cheek, still thinking of Charles and Amanda.

Before she realized what was happening to her, the girl all London now knew as Lady Amanda Fortescue drifted away into sleep.

Amanda Fitton stared out of her sitting-room window, watching the chilly wind whip Portsmouth harbor into a bristling surface of white-capped points. A dismal country, this England. And Portsmouth must surely be the most miserable town in the whole cold, gray island.

The flag at the stern of H.M.S. *Worcester* was standing straight out from the mast in a stiff winter breeze. She hated the sight of it now. She'd been so happy to see it, the day of the ship's arrival. She'd thrown propriety to the winds, gone down to the dock herself, with only little Maria for company. She'd had some romantic notion of enfolding Charles in her arms the moment his foot touched the shore of his native island.

The humiliation of it! Watching face after face, as the ship's crew came down the gangplank. Twice she had thought she'd found him, and moved eagerly toward him, only to see the familiar face turn into that of a stranger. Then came that bitter moment, after the gangplank procession had dwindled to nothing. She'd clutched at the uniformed arm of a passing lieutenant, and begged him for news of Lieutenant Halstead. He'd pulled away from her with a haughty air, obviously taking her for some common tart. The look in his eyes when he told her Lieutenant Halstead had been delayed in Jamaica! As if to say, *Won't I do just as well?* She had wanted to turn and run. It had taken all her control to walk quietly and sedately back to her lodgings.

There was only one explanation. Charles hadn't received her letter. If he'd known she was here in Portsmouth, waiting to marry him, nothing on earth could have made him tarry in Kingston. Unless, perhaps, he was ill? Some tropical fever wasting his flesh away? A pang of horror assailed her. Perhaps he was dead by now! But surely, that officer would have said he was ill?

She shook off the black thoughts impatiently, like a dog shaking off a wetting. No doubt there was some very simple explanation. Charles would arrive any day now, perhaps this very morning. They could be married within twenty-four hours. The pleasant clergyman had been most obliging. *He'd* seen from the very first moment that she wasn't some sailor's trollop.

If only she could settle these jangled nerves! What in the world had become of that girl Maria? She should have been back by now with the London journals. Even though they were five days old, they brought with them the excitement of another world—a world far removed from this cold, gray, wave-lashed corner of England, where she waited in limbo for Charles to come make her his wife.

Just as she was about to scream with boredom, Maria came through the door of the sitting room, rattling off an unlikely story to explain her delay. Amanda was reasonably sure what the real reason was—the flirtatious stableman she'd seen making eyes at the girl. But what was the use of scolding? If the poor thing could find some pleasure in this gloomy exile, why should she interfere? Perhaps she should have sent her along with Miranda, and engaged a maid who was used to this dismal town. But they'd both been afraid Maria would drop some hint that would give away their whole scheme.

Lucky, lucky Miranda! No doubt the dear girl was having the time of her life, playing the sought-after heiress at ball after ball. *If I'd known how long I'd be stuck in this dismal hole—* Amanda backed off from the treacherous thought. Wasn't dear Charles worth it all? Of course he was. She tried to remember his face— adoring, tender. Her mind went blank. A sudden panic seized her. How little she knew, after all, of this man to whom she'd pledged the rest of her life. . . .

She snatched up the *Morning Chronicle* to distract herself from that dangerous train of thought. The first page was dull; more of the same old nonsense about *parliamentary reform* and *unrest in the colonies.* She turned to the inside page, with its advertisements for all the fine London shops. *Ann Jenkins in Lombard Street makes, cleans and alters all sorts of hats, viz. Leghorns, Bermudas, silk, straw, etc. John Exshaw, at*

*the Seven Stars in Maiden Lane, has a fine new as-
sortment of rich flowered silks, velvets, damasks, Man-
tua silks, silk serges.* She made a mental note to remember the names. Once she and Charles were in
London, she'd have the chance to assemble a proper
trousseau.

A name jumped out at her from the column of larger
print above the shopkeepers' notices: *Miss Amanda
Fitton.* Her heart gave a sudden lurch, then slowly con-
gealed into a leaden lump. She read the announcement
three times before she could bring herself to acknowledge its awful meaning. So it really *had* been a trap!
And now the trap had been sprung. *Oh, Miranda, my
dear, Miranda, what a horrible thing I've done!*

She sprang to her feet, filled with alarm and remorse. "Maria!" she cried. "Go tell the landlord to order
a chaise at once. Don't stand there gawking, girl! Go
talk to the landlord, then come help me finish our pack-
ing. We must be on the road to London within the
hour!"

Chapter Eleven

In the blue and silver bedroom of her Portman Square mansion, the new Lady Fortescue gazed bleakly at the woebegone face in her gilt-encrusted mirror. *Come, girl, put on your smile! It's time to go down to breakfast. Your bridegroom awaits below.* She saw the wan face in the mirror wince and grow even paler. Impatiently, she snatched up some Spanish wool and dabbed away at her cheeks. This hateful hour before her; it was surely the worst of the day. Pecking away at her breakfast, pretending to smile at his clumsy compliments, pretending to misinterpret the hints that grew broader and broader. *I hope you slept well, my dear? You're sure you weren't lonely? I was damnably restless last night. But new husbands, they say, are supposed to be restless. . . .* A ponderous wink at this point, and a look that was meant, she supposed, to convey a world of soulful desire.

She braced herself against the coming encounter, consoling herself with the thought that the awkward *tête-à-tête* would soon be over. It wasn't nearly so bad when the callers began arriving. It was still all a farce, to be sure; her face still ached with the strain of pretending pleasure. But at least it meant some diversion; some livelier conversation than that of her clod of a "husband."

Livelier conversation! She bit her lip in chagrin. What a sorry pass she'd come to, when the vapid drawing-room chatter she'd detested a month ago could loom on the day's horizon like a welcome oasis! Still, wasn't that just one more facet of the bitter bargain she'd made? She'd met Lord Fortescue's friends—the world of fashionable London—before she'd gone through the charade of becoming his wife. She'd already learned how different these popinjays were from the witty, exalted creatures of *Maestro* MacCrae's glowing imagination. Dear old *Maestro* MacCrae. She wondered where he was now. They'd had so few letters from him after he'd left the villa to go back to Scotland.

I wish he could see me now, in the midst of this witless mob, hear them chattering away about gowns and receptions at court and the latest scandal. No, not the latest scandal—they don't speak of that to my face. They wait till they're out the front door before they put into words what their sly smiles have told me—how Lord Fortescue frolics away the midnight hours with Lady Barwell, while his poor, naive gull of a bride is left to wait alone in an empty mansion.

What would you think of that for "elegant discourse," my idealistic old tutor? But of course, you weren't wholly wrong. There's another side to this city. I caught one glimpse of it at Mrs. Cholmondeley's. A sudden happy thought struck her. Perhaps she could send her a note, ask Mrs. Cholmondeley to call with some of her friends—Mr. Sheridan, Dr. Burney, perhaps the great Johnson himself! But no, they'd find it too boring. Even her friend, Mrs. Hester, had chosen to stay away, rather than be immersed in that empty chatter.

She fought back a moment of panic. She hadn't

thought Mrs. Hester would desert her so quickly. She'd caught one brief glimpse of her friend in the crowded chapel; in the three days since then, there'd been nothing further, not a word, not a sign. Perhaps she'd been gravely offended when Miranda ignored her advice? No, surely that couldn't be it. The woman had too much good sense. Perhaps she was busy writing, caught up in the throes of creation. Perhaps, even now, she was turning this grim charade into the magic pages of a gripping novel.

An image flashed into her mind—herself on the villa terrace, a book in her lap, the Tuscan sun warm above her, recalling this whole ordeal through the lady novelist's eyes. Her mind leapt ahead to the crowning scene when Amanda would finally appear, in the midst of the chattering crowd in her drawing room. The footman would bring in the card: *Mrs. Charles Halstead.* Miranda would leap from her chair and rush to greet her. They'd embrace on the drawing-room threshold; then Amanda would turn with a smile to the gaping mock-bridegroom. "You've been sadly deceived, Lord Fortescue," she would say. "You thought you had married a fortune, but you really aren't married at all. The girl who pretended to be Amanda Fitton is actually my foster sister, the child of Italian peasants. The real Amanda Fitton now stands before you—with her fortune secure in the bonds of a true legal marriage."

Then Charles would step out from behind her with a husbandly smile, Lord Fortescue would turn red and erupt into curses, the glittering callers would all make a rush for the door, eager to spread this new tidbit all over London—and from some unnoticed recess, Theo Moreland would step out to greet Miranda, his eyes alight with delight, his arms outstretched—

You fool! You prodigious fool! You know that can never be! Miranda sprang up abruptly, knocking the stool from beneath her in her haste to escape the coils of that hopeless dream. *Enough of this silly mooning! Down the stairs with you, now, and trudge through a few more hours while you wait for Amanda.*

She was pleasantly surprised to find the breakfast room empty. Lord Fortescue, it appeared, had already finished. He had left a message for her: he was in the library, conducting some business. He hoped Lady Fortescue would excuse his absence, and express his apologies to any friends who might call.

Cheered by this welcome reprieve, Miranda was able to eat a substantial breakfast. Then she seated herself in the drawing-room chair, ready to welcome the usual stream of morning guests.

Half an hour ticked by, an hour. The drawing room remained empty. What could be keeping them? For the past three days, the room had been full of people before eleven. Perhaps this was part of some strange English marriage custom—to honor the bride for three days and then ignore her. She picked up the book she'd been reading, Mr. MacKenzie's novel, *The Man of Feeling,* hoping it would help fill the time of waiting. But she found herself so tense with anticipation that she couldn't follow the story. The slightest sound had the power to distract her—the front door opening and closing, footsteps along the hallway—

As the minutes ticked on, she became more and more curious about all those openings and closings. The big front door in Portman Square seemed to be admitting a record number of callers. But none of them were for her. Whose could they be, those interminable footsteps? Why did they pass her by as though she didn't exist?

She crept to the drawing-room door and cautiously waited there, her ears intent on the sounds in the hallway outside. She gradually made out a pattern: a caller would be admitted, would pass by her door to the library down the hall, would be closeted there for five or ten minutes, and then would emerge and pass by her doorway again, obviously making his way back out of the house.

So that was the explanation! The callers were there

on business. But why so many of them? A terrible suspicion dawned in Miranda's mind. She waited for the next set of returning footsteps, then opened the door a crack, hoping to catch a glimpse of the visitor's back. She saw a man dressed in sober merchant's black cloth, a folded parchment firmly gripped in one hand. *His creditors! He must be paying them off. Good Lord, here's a new complication. I must learn more about it!*

Holding her breath, she tiptoed along the hall to the library door, applied one cautious ear to the gleaming oak panel. The very first words she heard confirmed her worst suspicions. "That bloodsucking thief!" The voice was Lord Fortescue's. "Damn him and his hundred percent. We agreed for fifty, I tell you. Why must you be so weak as to give him more?"

"He did have your signature. There's no way to get around that." The second voice sounded teasingly familiar. That ingratiating purr—where had she heard it before?

It came to her in a flash. It was Mr. Armour! Her greedy guardian was here for his share of the spoils. She pressed her ear closer, keeping a wary eye out for any new callers. The two men had lowered their voices. It was hard to catch what they were saying. The next words she managed to hear from Mr. Armour made her breath thicken with panic.

"... really no reason to worry. When the funds in the bank are gone, you can start selling off her land. In that part of Sussex, you'll always find plenty of buyers..."

A door hinge squeaked somewhere at the front of the house. She heard the advancing footsteps and sprang away from the door, hurrying back toward the drawing room, her mind in a whirl. *What havoc I've wreaked on Amanda! This scheme of ours was intended to save her fortune. But now it seems I've helped send it down the drain. Mrs. Hester was right. I should never have gone ahead with this pestilent marriage. If only I'd listened to her. Dio mio, what shall I do? Perhaps she can help me, even with things gone this far. I'll go to her instantly. I'll send for a footman at once and order my carriage.*

She caught her breath in dismay as she entered the drawing room and saw that she had a caller. A woman in a black velvet gown with jet bead embroidery was standing in front of the long narrow windows, gazing down at the traffic that swirled round Portman Square. Her towering coiffure was twisted and curled in the latest style, and trimmed with silk butterflies. How long must she linger there, murmuring empty phrases, before she could send this elegant caller away? "Good morning, madam," she said, trying to make her voice cordial. "Lord Fortescue has asked me to make his excuses—"

The figure in black turned at the sound of her voice. "My dearest Miranda, you needn't be formal with me."

Miranda's impatience gave way to delighted surprise. "Mrs. Hester! How wonderful! You're like an answer to prayer. How grand you look this morning. I was sure you were some sort of duchess—or a countess, at least."

Mrs. Hester smiled at her wryly. "Because my hair's not quite the usual bird's nest? I assumed all the *ton* would be out in force, so I felt obliged to wear my one fashionable wig. But perhaps I've come too early? Have you and Lord Fortescue had any callers this morning?"

"The only callers have been for Lord Fortescue. That's why I'm so upset. All his creditors must be descending at once. He's down in the library now, with that detestable Mr. Armour. They're using Amanda's money to pay off mountains of debts. We must do something to stop them, or my darling Amanda will soon be as poor as *mama* or myself."

"So he's seized his new fortune already! Here's a pretty pickle indeed! It seems your Amanda's plotting has brought down the very disaster she sought to avoid."

"It isn't Amanda's fault." Miranda felt duty-bound

to make the protest. "How could either of us have foreseen that she'd be delayed this long? Something terrible must have happened to keep her away, a far more stringent disaster than any mere loss of a fortune."

"So you see that at last, my dear?" Mrs. Hester's voice was warm with compassion. "I hesitated to urge my fears more strongly, but even before this unfortunate marriage of yours, I had a premonition."

"How right you were! Oh, why didn't I listen to you? But I had such faith, up to the very last moment, that Amanda would come just in the nick of time."

"Let's not cry over spilt milk," Mrs. Hester said briskly. "We've decided we can't afford to depend on Amanda. What's our next step to be?"

"Surely we've only one course? I must spill out the whole secret now, admit my imposture, and proclaim the marriage a fraud. At least, that will put a stop to this draining away of Amanda's estate."

"Your precious Amanda again! My dear, I implore you, it's time to forget Amanda and think of yourself. Don't you see what a dangerous trap may be closing around you? When Lord Fortescue finds how you've tricked him, his anger will know no bounds."

"I'm not afraid of his anger," Miranda said staunchly. "What can he do to harm me? The worst he could do is to fling me out on the street."

Mrs. Hester gazed at her for a moment, a look full of pity mingled with incredulity. "Do you really think he'll let you escape so lightly? When you threaten to snatch his new fortune away, and turn him into the laughingstock of London? Oh, no, my dear; you're in graver peril than that. Do you realize how many crimes you've committed? How severely you might be punished under the English law?"

"Crimes?" cried Miranda, aghast. "I've told a few paltry untruths, pretended to be someone I wasn't—"

"That's how you see things, perhaps. But how would all this look to an English court? *Grand fraud* and *sacrilege* would lead off the list of charges. No doubt

Lord Fortescue's lawyers would think of a few dozen more."

Miranda felt a chill of horror. "I didn't realize—" She stopped in mid-sentence, abruptly aware of how dire her predicament was. "It all seemed so innocent. Do you really think he'd insist on my going to court?"

Mrs. Hester pursed her lips grimly. "You'll be fortunate if he does. In a court, at least, you'll have a chance to explain. But the likelihood is you'll never come near a courtroom. There are hundreds of wretches now moldering away in Newgate to whom the chance of a trial would seem like life's greatest boon."

"But how can that be?" Miranda's head started to reel. The solid walls of the room seemed to waver around her. "The way *Maestro* MacCrae described it, the English system of justice is the best in the world."

"It may be the best in the world, but that still leaves it very imperfect." Mrs. Hester's mouth twisted wryly. She seemed to be forcing herself to speak words better left unspoken. "The English courts might give a very fair hearing to a rich English heiress like Miss Amanda Fitton. But a child of Italian peasants, an alien pauper—I fear she might find a quite different reception."

Miranda's heart started pounding. She felt as though she were choking, as though some tremendous hand had gripped her by the throat. "What shall I do?" she gasped. "I can't go on with this nightmare. I must take some kind of action."

"My dear, I agree with you. The longer you wait, the worse things will be for you. But don't move too hastily. Give me a chance to rally a few powerful friends to your defense."

"How long must I wait?" Miranda was desperate now. "I'm sick to death of deception. I'm afraid I'll blurt out the whole story the very next time I see that hateful face."

"Good Lord! You mustn't do that." Mrs. Hester looked gravely alarmed. "That would be suicide. You must give me your solemn promise that you'll say nothing to his lordship without one of your friends at your side to serve as your witness."

"Friends!" said Miranda harshly. "I have no friends in England, except for yourself."

"That's not quite true, my dear. You do have another friend, a man who loves you dearly. Won't you allow me to summon him to your side?"

"No!" cried Amanda fiercely. "I won't have Theo involved. I've spared him the threat of a duel. I won't risk reviving that threat."

Mrs. Hester sighed, shaking her head in frustration. "I wish you could see how that young man pines for you. To be *involved*, as you call it, in springing you from this trap would fill that adoring heart with the greatest pleasure. But I see from that stubborn look that I'm still forbidden to broach your secret to him. Very well, I'm already pledged to silence. But give you me your own pledge now: not a word to Lord Fortescue without some friend beside you to act as a witness."

"I promise, I promise. I won't breathe a word until I've consulted you."

"Good girl! I must leave you now, to reconnoiter my forces. Meanwhile, not a word, not a sign, not the barest hint to his lordship. You must play the new-married bride as if your whole heart was in it." She paused abruptly, as though a new thought had struck her. "That scene from my novel—your terms for the wedding night—I assume from the note you sent me he accepted your bargain?"

"Oh, yes, we've agreed on that. He's given his word to defer his husbandly duties until a year has gone by."

"Thank God for small favors," breathed Mrs. Hester devoutly. "You're safe on that score, at least. Let us hope in a few days you'll be out of this plight altogether. Good-bye for the moment, my dear. You'll hear from me very shortly. Until you do, you must hold steadfast to your promise."

"I will, Mrs. Hester, I will." The black-gowned figure bustled out of the room. Miranda watched her go with a sinking heart. She sank back into a chair and stared blankly at the ceiling. *Amanda!* a voice was wailing from deep inside her. *My darling Amanda, what can have happened to you?*

Chapter Twelve

"And what will my lady choose for her bedwear tonight?" asked La Sogghignatora. "The white lawn gown sprigged with pink rosebuds, or the lilac tiffany?" Miranda glanced up at her maid, surprised at the note of deference in her voice. She couldn't believe her eyes. The creature was actually smiling! The supercilious look had disappeared completely. She was no longer sitting in judgment on the ignorant miss from some barbarous foreign country, but offering her fawning service to the wife of an English peer.

"The lilac, I think." Miranda kept her face blank, suppressing her impulse to respond with a smile of her own. That wasn't the style of a lady. She remembered Amanda's tone with little Maria. Especially in one of her arrogant moods, she'd treat the girl like a stick of furniture. She'd never presumed to do that with Miranda. She had a special status at Villa Bertolini, based on those years of being Amanda's playmate—and that other, unspoken reason, always below the surface, never allowed into words. . . .

A knock at the door brought her sharply back to the present. Lord Fortescue! It could scarcely be anyone else. Her heart took a sudden plunge. She hadn't seen him all day, not even at dinner. He'd sent for a tray to be brought to the library. She'd dined alone, at one end of the ten-foot mahogany table, bathed in the light from the glittering chandeliers. She'd welcomed the solitude. The less she saw of his lordship, the less she'd be tempted to blurt out her dangerous secret. Now her brief reprieve had come to an end.

She made a sign to her maid to go open the door. Lord Fortescue entered the room and went straight to Miranda, obviously meaning to give her a husbandly kiss. She was already on her feet, instinctively warding him off with an outstretched hand. She saw his face darken briefly, then smooth into acquiescence as he took her hand into his own and bestowed on it a studiedly formal kiss. "So you're still full of maidenly vapors." His tone was that of a father teasing a sulky child. Miranda darted a glance toward La Sogghignatora, wondering what she'd make of these strange bedroom manners. But the woman was not to be seen; she'd already slipped discreetly out of the room, closing the door behind her.

Miranda forced a social smile to her lips. "I'm surprised to see you, my lord. You've been so busy all day."

"Come, come, my dear wife, you're not going to say you missed me? I thought we'd dispensed with such sentimental nonsense."

"Indeed, sir, I thought the same thing. But when you affect such an ardent style in entering my bedroom—"

His lordship seemed taken aback by her tone of reproof. "The servants," he muttered. "One must keep up an appearance. Though the thought did enter my mind that you might have grown settled enough in your new estate to view our relationship in a much more sensible manner."

"I don't think I know what you mean." She knew all too well, and hated the knowledge. "I'm not aware that I've showed any lack of good sense."

Lord Fortescue flicked at a comb on her dressing table, then picked it up to examine it minutely, as though he could read on its surface the proper words to convince this stubborn young lady. "You know what I'm speaking of." His voice was guarded and sullen. "That silly agreement I let you force upon me, denying me my natural rights as a husband."

Miranda fought back a sudden wave of panic. *Be cool, Miranda; be firm. The man is not wholly a monster. You've bargained with him before. You can do it again.* "You put things too strongly, my lord. I do not *deny* you those rights. You gave me your word of honor to accord with my dead father's wish, and *delay* your claims for a time. Are you telling me now you wish to rescind that promise?"

Lord Fortescue flushed. "I never go back on my word. But circumstances have changed since I made that unfortunate promise. If I'd known at the time that Sir Lucas was due to descend, I'd have never been such a fool as to let you constrain me."

Miranda gazed up at him in unfeigned surprise. "Sir Lucas Trotter? That uncle of yours from Jamaica? What interest has he in what occurs in our bedroom?"

"Surely you understand what I'm driving at." Lord Fortescue fumed with impatience. "What *doesn't* occur in our bedroom might very well cost me a fortune."

Miranda shook her head in bewilderment. What was he talking about? Some strange English family custom which made the bridegroom's uncle the judge of his wedding-night prowess?

Lord Fortescue saw her blank look and gave a contemptuous snort. "Must I really spell out all the facts in such obvious detail? Very well, then, if you insist. Sir Lucas has never married. My cousin Charles and

myself are his only heirs. I've always assumed he'd
divide his estate between us. But this sudden visit of
his raises ominous doubts. From what that lieutenant
told me, he and Charles have grown thick as thieves.
Perhaps Charles has tried to persuade him to leave the
whole fortune to him? Perhaps he's plied the old man
with all sorts of vicious gossip? Sir Lucas is said to be
very straitlaced; he takes a jaundiced view of any form
of amusement. Hang it, my dear, surely you see my
point?"

"You're saying your uncle is coming to put you on
trial? To judge for himself who really deserves his fortune?"

The heavy-jowled face relaxed in a smile of relief.
"At last, my dear, you're beginning to understand.
Charles has urged him to take this trip, counting on
my well-known love of amusement to provoke the
wrong opinion in Sir Lucas's mind. But two can play
at that game. Charles doesn't know what a striking
advantage I've gained since he saw me last. Charles
isn't married and probably won't be for years; he can't
afford it. But I have a wife—who may be carrying my
child, if all goes well."

If all goes ill, you mean. Miranda was shocked into
silence. She could see now, only too well, where this
conversation was tending. These cold-blooded English-
men! They bred their women for profit, as other people
bred cattle. She turned her face abruptly away from
him to hide her feeling of overwhelming revulsion.

His lordship misinterpreted the gesture. "These
maidenly fears again! My dear, it's not such a dreadful
ordeal. An experienced man of the world knows ways
of making it positively pleasant. Come, let me show
you."

He lunged clumsily toward her, seizing her in an
awkward embrace. The unexpected assault made her
lose her balance. She fell back onto the bed, with his
heavy weight almost smothering her. She struggled
against him, thrashing about on the bed, kneeing and

119

kicking. Her resistance seemed to surprise him; he stumbled back onto his feet and stood looking down at her with a hurt expression. "Really, madam, you're being very unkind." Then she saw his eyes grow full of puzzled chagrin, as he looked beyond her face toward the head of the bed. His hand shot out in a grasping motion. "What have we here!" His face contorted with fury. "A pretty memento indeed, to grace a shy virgin's bed!"

Too late, she realized what must have happened. Her thrashing around had dislodged the blue satin pillow, and exposed the hiding place of that fatal scrap of cambric. She made an impulsive move to snatch it out of his hand, but he deftly eluded her, holding the handkerchief well out of her reach. "Hell's cauldron, I know those initials. That traitorous dog, Theo Moreland! So that's how the scoundrel repays my efforts at friendship."

A new note of rage in his voice made Miranda's veins turn icy. "Oh, no! You don't understand. Please let me explain how that handkerchief came to be there."

"Silence, you devious bitch! I understand all too well. You and Moreland have been intriguing behind my back. I'll soon put a stop to that. If I can force that cowardly sneak to respond to my challenge, he'll be a dead man by sunrise tomorrow."

"*Dio mio!* You can't do that. All London knows you're the far better swordsman. If you challenge Theo and kill him, they'll call you a murderer! There are laws against dueling, you know. In this case, they'd surely enforce them."

"They'll do nothing of the kind." Lord Fortescue's glare was baleful. "No court in the world would condemn a husband from avenging a slur on his honor."

"You're not my husband! You never were, and you never will be!" The desperate words were out before Miranda could stop them. She hid her face in her hands, sick with dismay at betraying her promise to Mrs. Hester.

But Lord Fortescue was too caught up in his rage for any words of hers to make an impression. "I see it all now," he roared. "This is why you concocted that touching story, that pretense of a deathbed vow. It was all designed to preserve for your paramour the sole enjoyment of the marital right I should have long since exacted."

"You're wrong. You're completely wrong! I've had nothing to do with Mr. Moreland. I haven't spoken to him for weeks—except for a word or two after the wedding. That handkerchief means nothing, I tell you. I'd completely forgotten I had it. He happened to leave it with me by mistake in a public place. I wasn't even sure it belonged to him."

"God's wounds, I know better than that. Remember I caught him out once, when he dared to call on you at Mrs. Armour's. No doubt after that you both became more discreet. You met in more private places, with the full connivance of that unseemly jade, Mrs. Hester." He paused abruptly, seized in the obvious grip of a new obsession. "The hours you spent at her house during our engagement! I know he's a friend of hers, one of her disreputable troupe of mountebanks and scriveners. No doubt he's using her now, to carry his messages. I'll soon put a stop to all these sly tricks of yours. You'll drop that woman completely! She won't be admitted here. I'll give all the servants their orders tomorrow morning."

Miranda felt her panic rising again. She forced her voice to assume a pleading tone. "Surely you can't be so cruel—to cut me off from my only friend in England—"

"I am your husband, madam. I can give any orders I like here."

Miranda felt as though her heart was shriveling inside her. Their eyes locked together, his dark with contempt, hers blank with despair. Then he turned on his heel and strode out the door, letting it slam behind him.

Miranda stood frozen a moment, unable to summon up any coherent thought. She knew where he'd gone: to deliver his challenge to Theo. She'd tried so hard to avoid that fatal encounter. She'd offered herself as a sacrificial lamb. What good had it done? Theo again was in mortal danger—and the fault was hers, all hers. What a curse it was, this weak, sentimental heart. If she hadn't stupidly clung to that handkerchief—

No, it *wasn't* completely her fault. It all began with that fatal scheme of Amanda's....*Amanda!* Her circling thoughts came to a sudden stop. Of course! That was what she must do! She must go find Amanda herself, not stay tamely here waiting for her to arrive. Portsmouth, she knew, was not a very large town. Surely it wouldn't be hard to determine the whereabouts of the charming Miss Fitton....

A rattle of carriage wheels in the square below sent her flying to the window. She was just in time to see Lord Fortescue slam the door of his coach. At least, he was out of the way. But what of the servants? Pray God, his furious haste to arrange the duel had kept him from giving them those threatened orders.

She summoned La Sogghignatora and gave her own orders, in a voice now crisp with decision. "I want a post chaise. You must find one immediately. If anyone asks you why, you will say Lady Fortescue needs it."

The maid gaped at her in surprise. Her smile of fawning submission gave way to the familiar raised eyebrows. "At this time of night, my lady? That's certainly very strange—"

Miranda seethed with frustration. Was she to be thwarted now by this haughty servant? The thought brought a vivid memory of one of Amanda's tantrums—the blond girl furious over some trivial detail, little Maria venturing timid excuses, cowering under the wrath of her arrogant mistress....*How dare you contradict me. I am the mistress here....*

That disdainful wrath had never been turned on Miranda. But of course, she wasn't a servant, any more than she was a true lady. She was something in between, neither fish nor fowl. Perhaps that's why she found it so hard to handle La Sogghignatora. But she *must* handle her, she *must*—before the walls of this house closed around her completely.

"How dare you contradict me! I am the mistress here!" Her voice startled her with its likeness to that of Amanda. "Off with you now, and bring back a chaise in five minutes!"

She saw the scornful eyes grow bright with respect. With no further protest, La Sogghignatora turned and made for the door. "And when you've done that," Miranda called after her, pushing home her advantage, "hurry back here and pack up my things for the journey. We must be on the road to Portsmouth within the hour!"

Chapter Thirteen

"Gone to London! When did she leave? Is she safely married to Charles? Did he go there with her?"

"Gently, gently, my dear. Catch your breath first, and then we'll untangle the threads of this very strange story." The Reverend Mr. Entwhistle beamed at her fondly over his half-moon glasses. He picked up the cup of tea from the rectory table between them, took a brief sip, and rolled it around on his tongue, closing his eyes as though to savor the taste.

Miranda forced herself to curb her impatience. Life and death in the balance, and this maddening clergyman sat here sipping his tea! But she'd already gauged his temper in the first five minutes; she knew he couldn't be rushed. Resignedly, she picked up her own dish of tea, as she waited for the little round man to proceed at his chosen pace.

"Excellent tea," he said finally, replacing the cup in its saucer. "Well, now, let's get down to our story. You know, of course, that your friend Miss Fitton made me her confidant. They'll have told you that at her lodgings. She first approached me over two months ago, to arrange for her forthcoming marriage to Lieutenant Halstead, whose ship was expected back on the first of November. She said nothing to me at that time of this scheme of deception. I learned about that only a few days ago, when she sent me a letter explaining her trip to London."

"So you did marry them! Charles and Amanda are married! But why did they wait so long to travel to London?"

"Don't go so fast, my dear girl." The clergyman raised one pudgy hand in caution. "The marriage plans were delayed. Lieutenant Halstead's squadron came back from Jamaica on schedule, but unfortunately for Miss Fitton, he was not with them."

"*Dio mio!* Something's happened to Charles! Surely only some terrible fate could have kept him away, when he knew Amanda was waiting alone in Portsmouth!"

"Ah, there's the crux of the matter. *Did* Lieutenant Halstead know Miss Fitton was here?"

"But she wrote him way back in August, before we started for England—"

"I understand that. But did that letter arrive? That's what we asked ourselves, Miss Fitton and I, when his ship returned without even a message for her. We came to the sad conclusion that he'd never received her letter."

"Good Lord!" cried Miranda. "Then the poor man knew nothing at all of Lord Fortescue's scheme? How he plotted with Mr. Armour to summon Amanda to London? How she asked me to go in her place—"

Mr. Entwhistle's jaw jutted grimly. "Just so. He knew nothing at all. No more than I did myself, until three days ago. If I'd known of this rash deception, I'd have taken a hand myself, and exposed the whole scheme before it enveloped you both in this current disaster. I'm sure the strong-willed Miss Fitton was fully aware how I would have condemned her plan. But then, when she learned from the *Chronicle* that you'd actually gone ahead with this sacrilegious marriage, her conscience asserted itself and she wrote me the whole sordid story of her criminal actions."

"I'm not a criminal." Miranda's eyes stung with tears. "I was only trying to save my dear friend's fortune."

"Come, come, child, I don't blame *you*." The stern, moralistic tone was replaced by tender compassion. "You couldn't have realized what a viper's nest your friend was leading you into. Neither did she, I'm sure; the letter she sent me was full of the deepest remorse. That's why she dashed off to London so hastily, without pausing to consult with her friend and advisor. She was in such desperate hurry to make amends and rescue you from your terrible situation." He paused for a moment, as though he'd run short of words. An embarrassed flush rose from his neck to his forehead. He coughed discreetly. "It was most regrettable that you felt constrained to go through that fraudulent ritual. But of course, on your wedding night you must surely have explained to his lordship that you weren't really his bride?"

"No," said Miranda, keeping her eyes averted from his questioning gaze. "I see now I should have told him. But I kept expecting Amanda to come to my rescue."

Mr. Entwhistle looked very shocked. "You poor, dear defenseless child! This disaster is worse than I thought. What a loyal heart you must have, to sacrifice for your friend a possession far dearer to you than life itself—"

Miranda could feel her own blush rise to match his. "It's not quite as bad as all that," she said hurriedly. "But I don't want to speak of that now. It's Amanda I'm worried about. She has no idea of the storm that she's heading into." She quickly described Lord Fortescue's hair-trigger temper, his fury over her supposed intrigue with Theo, Mrs. Hester's warning that he might take legal action. "If Amanda confronts him now, in this bloodthirsty rage," she concluded breathlessly, "there's no telling what he may do. I must go back and join her at once, and bring Mrs. Hester with me. At least she'll have witnesses if he chooses to bring her to trial."

Mr. Entwhistle's eyes took fire as he realized the danger of the situation. "Bring witnesses, by all means. As many as possible! Have you no other friends than this one rather dubious lady? What of this Mr. Moreland? Surely he'd want to help you?"

Theo! He may be dead! She brushed the thought quickly away. Time enough to consider that awful catastrophe later. "No, I won't involve Mr. Moreland. Mrs. Hester said she might find some friends who can help us. I'll start back to London this minute, go straight to her house—"

Mr. Entwhistle looked concerned. "But my dear, that long tiring ride! You only arrived in Portsmouth a few hours ago. Won't you rest here, at least for tonight? My good wife and I entreat you to be our guest."

"A thousand thanks, my dear sir. You've been as kind to me as though I were your daughter. But I must hurry back to London. Amanda went there thinking she'd rescue me. Now I've had the good luck to escape, I must hurry as fast as I can to rescue her!"

Amanda Fitton paused at the marble mantelpiece in the Portman Square drawing room and adjusted her silver-gold curls with the aid of the gilt-framed mirror that hung above it. *I've won the first skirmish,* she told the face in the glass. *Now to regroup my forces for the main encounter.* Once her anger had cooled, she realized she'd been wrong to become so incensed with his lordship's servants. They'd only been doing their duty in trying to send her away. She'd have done the same thing herself, at the Villa Bertolini, if some strange miss had turned up on her doorstep demanding admission.

Even so, there'd been something strange in the look on the footman's face when she'd asked that he announce her to Lady Fortescue. She'd thought he was lying when he told her his mistress had already left the house. But then when she'd asked for his lordship, he'd become so disconcerted he actually stammered. *His l-l-lordship has gone out also.* A likely story! Both master and mistress abroad at nine in the morning!

She'd insisted, of course, on speaking to his superior. It was then she'd become quite certain there was something mysterious afoot. Those averted eyes, that air of apprehension—the head footman's whole demeanor smacked of some guilty secret.

She hadn't intended to show the letter so soon. But without that trump card, she'd have never entered the house. She saw what a shock it was to his already unsteady nerves when he read Mr. Faldini's letter introducing his client, Miss Fitton. His eyes had gone wide with surprise and disbelief. He'd ventured no further protest, had meekly invited her into the drawing room, and made her comfortable there, staring at her all the while in mystification. No doubt by now the whole household was in a ferment. They had just grown used to one Miss Amanda Fitton. Now here came another girl, claiming that same name.

Where could Miranda be at this hour of the morning? Perhaps the footman *was* lying. Perhaps she'd been here all the time, but under some kind of restraint from that horrible man. Who could tell what that grasping *milord* might have been up to. He must have used some kind of force to persuade poor Miranda into the fraudulent marriage. She'd been so sure things would never proceed to that pass. How blithely she'd brushed off the threat, back home at the villa. *All this nonsense about wedding nights....I tell you, it won't come to that.... Oh, Miranda, Miranda, what have I done to you?*

Her mind shied away from considering that thought too closely. After all, she was here was she not, prepared to rescue Miranda, bring the whole episode to a close? They'd go back down to Portsmouth and wait there for Charles....

Oh, Charles, where are you? What is keeping you from me? Those vows we made—you can't have forgotten so soon. I knew you only two days, but it seemed a lifetime. . . .

A sudden clatter outside brought her a welcome reprieve from unwanted thoughts. She walked to the long narrow window and peered down into the square. That must be Lord Fortescue! Ughh, what a brute he looked. Though one had to admit, he was dressed in the height of sporting fashion. But why was he wearing that sword? Surely no gentleman wore his sword in the street in these modern times? In Portsmouth, only the naval officers wore them. Of course, it might be a new fad. The *bon ton* might have grown bored with their walking sticks. Fashionable or not, the man was clearly a boor. That huge red face, sweating and streaked with dirt. No doubt he'd been out all night, carousing in some low haunt with his vicious companions.

She moved away from the window and settled herself in a chair, composing herself against the coming encounter. The minutes ticked by. His lordship didn't appear. Surely those worried servants must have told him about her? Had he already guessed her mission? Was he skulking balefully somewhere, reluctant to face the news of his true situation?

Just as she was ready to make another scene, the door opened and the tall, heavyset man entered the room. It didn't appear to her that he'd bothered to wash. His neckband was all awry, and his hair in dire need of powder.

"Who the devil are you?" he growled angrily. "What are you doing here, upsetting my household? I've trouble enough as it is, without some strange female descending on me with a ridiculous claim to be Amanda Fitton."

Amanda drew herself up in a regal posture, looking him straight in the eye. "I am Amanda Fitton, Lord Fortescue. I know you will find it strange—"

"I find it more than strange, madam." He was shouting now, his face red and strained, the veins standing out on his neck. "I find it incredible. I know Amanda Fitton. I married the bitch. She's as different a creature from you as night is from day."

Amanda felt her firm resolution wavering. The man seemed demented with fury. What if he lost his head and struck out at her? Then she chided herself for being a fearful ninny. He'd never dare to hurt her. She *was* Amanda Fitton. Her only problem was how to convince him of that. Naturally, the news had come as a shock. But once he became convinced, he would change his tone.

She drew a deep breath, looked into his outraged eyes, and said in a level voice, "The girl you married is named Miranda Testa. She does look quite different from me. Her hair is black, is it not? Her complexion tawny? She looks just like what she is: an Italian peasant girl, not an English heiress."

She saw the shadow of doubt dawn in his eyes. "What kind of lunatic lies are you telling now? Of course my wife has black hair. But she is Amanda Fitton, nevertheless. Her guardian, Mr. Armour, will attest to that."

Heartened by that uncertain look, Amanda's smile took on a triumphant glow. "Mr. Armour has been deceived as badly as you. When he sent me his urgent summons, I guessed that a scheme was afoot to annex my fortune. I knew no one in England would have any notion of the real Miss Fitton's appearance, so I asked my friend Miranda to come in my place. I really didn't intend for the masquerade to proceed as far as it has—"

"Masquerade!" Fortescue exploded. "It's you who are masquerading! I see your intention now. You're in league with that faithless bitch who had the temerity to desert her rightful husband. She's snatched herself away; now she thinks she can snatch her fortune away as well. Hell's fire to you both! You won't succeed with your plot; I'll see to that. I'll get her back under this roof, if I have to search the whole kingdom to find where she's hiding. I've already killed the man who tempted her from me, that treacherous scoundrel I once considered a friend."

Amanda's head was whirling. So the sword had *not* been for show! But what was all this about hunting down Miranda? "Am I to understand," she said cautiously, "that the girl you know as Miss Fitton is not in this house?"

"You know damn well she's not," roared Lord Fortescue, "since it's she who sent you here, thinking to unsettle me with this fanciful story. Did the little fool really expect me to swallow these lies, meekly give up my claim, and leave her free to join her shabby lover? She'll change her mind quickly, I fear, when she learns of the miserable death she's brought down upon him."

"Good Lord!" cried Amanda. "I don't understand all you're saying! Has our innocent scheme really led you to kill a man?" Her knees felt suddenly weak. She sank helplessly into a chair. "How could things come to such a horrible pass? My only goal was to marry my darling Charles—"

"Charles! What Charles is this?" The man was beside himself now, insane with rage. "Charles Halstead, no doubt, my treacherous cousin? So he had a hand in this scheme as well as Amanda! You're all in the plot together, trying to pull me down to total ruin. Well, you won't succeed, I tell you. No lying imposter will cheat me out of that fortune."

"I'm not an imposter, sir. I have a letter to prove it." Amanda tried vainly to keep her hand from trembling as she held the letter out to the furious man. He snatched it out of her hand and perused its contents. She saw his expression change. As his doubts overwhelmed him, his anger faded completely. When he looked at her again, his eyes had gone dull with defeat.

"A most curious document," he said in a leaden voice. "No doubt you were given it by my bitch of a wife. It does nothing to prove that you're the real Miss Fitton. No court of law would accept it as evidence."

"If you wish further proof," said Amanda coldly, "I

have witnesses in abundance. I'll summon my whole Florence household, my banker, Mr. Faldini, even the English consul, Sir Horace Mann. They'll swear before any court that I am the girl they know as Amanda Fitton."

Amanda saw the desperate look in his eyes, like that of a cornered fox facing the hounds. Her heart swelled with triumph. "I see I've convinced you that I'm the real Amanda. I'm sorry you were deceived, but you brought it on your own head by being so greedy. It's a great relief to know that my dear Miranda has already had the good sense to escape from her false position."

The look of defeat underwent a subtle change; he stared intently at her, the desperate look replaced by a glint of low cunning. "It's true I let your damned accomplice escape. It seems I am doomed to learn my lessons the hard way. Perhaps you've a few to learn too. You think you've ruined me, don't you? You think I'll throw in my hand, and tamely accept going down to total ruin. I warn you, madam, you much mistake your opponent. I still hold one trump card here. You've put yourself into my power. While you're in my hands, those treacherous friends of yours won't dare to move against me."

"Have you gone utterly mad? You're not seriously threatening to hold me for some kind of ransom?"

"Ransom? Of course not, Miss Fitton. That's far too dishonorable a word. I'm sure with a little time we could work out some suitable *gift* from your ample estates? Bestowed on me free and clear, with no legal quibbles, or boring talk about courtrooms?"

Amanda caught her breath in sudden alarm. Those ruthless eyes! The man meant every word. But couldn't he see how senseless a course he was taking? "You can't hold me prisoner here," she told him staunchly. "There are laws against that. The liberty of the subject—"

His face half-relaxed in a bold, sardonic grin. "There

132

are laws against dueling, too. They won't be enforced against me. I've told you I just killed a man who threatened my honor. Do you think I'll permit *anyone* to threaten my fortune?"

Amanda shrank back in her chair. She searched his face, hoping for reassurance. She found no comfort there; his eyes seemed glazed with the look of incipient madness. *I've got to escape. I've got to get out of this house.* She glanced longingly at the door. He intercepted the glance, and moved to block her way. "My servants are very well trained." His voice was harsh and grating. "If I tell them to keep you from leaving, they may find rather rough ways of fulfilling my orders. I hope you'll accept your fate, and go quietly to the room I shall have prepared."

"You can't get away with this!" Amanda was on her feet, her breath coming fast and shallow. "I have servants as well, don't forget. My maid is outside in the chaise. When I don't return to her, she'll raise the alarm"

The sardonic grin grew broader. "Thank you for mentioning her. I'll see that your maid is told some plausible story. She'll have no cause for alarm. Now, if you'll take my arm, I'll escort you quietly to your place of confinement."

Amanda cursed herself for mentioning little Maria. As Lord Fortescue had said, she was no threat to him. What could she do for Amanda, a little Italian servant, alone in this strange foreign city with barely ten words of English?

Her heart sank another few notches. Was there really no chance of escape from this arrogant scoundrel? *That clergyman, Mr. Entwhistle.* He knows the whole story. He could summon the law. They'd listen to him. And Miranda is out there somewhere. She's a clever girl, and she must have a few friends here. And Charles will be coming soon—

Her racing thoughts slowed to a stop. Would Charles *really* be coming soon? She knew nothing at all of his current situation. Perhaps he was already wooing some beautiful rival. . . . No! Not Charles! She staunchly refused to believe it. Charles *would* come, she was sure—but he'd find himself walking straight into terrible danger. *I've just killed a man. . . . do you think I'll permit anyone to threaten my fortune.*

There was no use protesting further. It would only enrage him. Better to humor him, while she waited for rescue. Perhaps, once the first shock was over, she would find some way of bringing him back to reason.

She raised her eyes, and saw he was watching her with that madman's smile. "Very well, your lordship," she said, "you've won this round." She forced herself to glide decorously toward him, as though she were crossing a crowded ballroom floor. "Please conduct me to that room you so graciously promised. We're both a little fatigued. Perhaps in the morning, we'll discuss the whole question more calmly."

Chapter Fourteen

Miranda traveled back to London alone. La Sogghignatora flatly refused to go with her. "I've had quite enough of this scandalous behavior," she protested hotly. "You'll give me my wages at once, and let me go back to Dover."

There was no time to find herself another maid and companion. It was unheard of, she knew, for a lady to travel alone—but thank God, she was no longer constrained to act like a lady. Nor to dress like one, either; she abandoned hair pads and powder and twisted her ebony curls into a simple knot on the top of her head. What did she care for the innkeepers' questioning eyebrows, so long as she'd money to pay for a fresh pair of horses?

Three hectic days later, she arrived on the Vere Street doorstep, afire with impatience to know what had happened in London. It was Mrs. Hester herself who opened the door, a flushed, breathless Mrs. Hester, far more excited than Miranda had ever seen her.

"Come in, my dear child. Good heavens, look at your hair! Where on earth have you been? I've been quite frantic about you. Didn't you promise to make no move without me?"

Miranda began to explain, but the novelist cut her off short. "Don't bother to tell me now. We've no time to spare. We must go straight to him this minute. Come child, don't hesitate. The man wants desperately to see you, and it's surely he, above all, who deserves to be told why you left so precipitously."

She took Miranda's arm, urging her out toward the waiting carriage. Miranda drew back from her touch, her whole body tense with alarm. She'd counted on Mrs. Hester to help her confront that angry man who waited in Portman Square. She'd depended on her as an ally. Now she seemed to be changing sides, taking Lord Fortescue's part.

"Please let me tell you first what led to my flight." She was playing for time, giving herself the chance to feel out Mrs. Hester's motives. "I had no time to consult you. I suddenly found myself in a desperate situation."

"A desperate situation indeed! Though I fear that poor man of yours finds it far more desperate than you did! But I'm sure the sight of you will relieve him greatly. The dear man's half out of his mind; he's been calling for you all day—"

Miranda went numb with shock. "*The dear man*, you call him? After all I've told you about him! What strange sea change have we here? I was counting on you to protect me against that rough bully, not force me back into his arms!"

Mrs. Hester gave her a look of incomprehension, staring at her as though she'd gone suddenly mad. Then realization dawned. "You think I meant his lordship? Heaven forbid! It's Theo Moreland I mean, girl, that poor wounded wretch—"

"Theo wounded!" Miranda could feel all the blood rush out of her head.

136

"Yes, surely you've heard! The news of that ill-fated duel is all over London."

Miranda gave her head a sharp shake, trying to ward off the threatening cloud of blackness. "Then he *did* challenge Theo! Good Lord! On so flimsy a pretext! That cursed handkerchief! How could he risk a man's life for so trivial a matter?"

"What handkerchief? I've heard nothing of handkerchiefs. Lord Fortescue has proclaimed to the whole curious town that his disloyal wife has run away to join Theo Moreland. Of course, I knew you could have done no such thing. But most of the *ton* think Fortescue had good cause."

"*Dio mio!* What have I done!" She stumbled against Mrs. Hester, clutching at her for support. "It's all my fault, wretch that I am. It's I who brought down on his head this terrible fate."

"There's no sense in standing here blaming yourself like this," Mrs. Hester said briskly. "We haven't a moment to lose. Into the carriage with you!"

"Not a moment to lose! Dear heaven!" A knife-blade of fear lanced through her. "He's mortally wounded, then? He's on his deathbed? How can I bear to see him! How can I ever face those accusing eyes?"

"He's not *that* sorely wounded, though he has been hurt badly enough to bring on a touch of fever. He's in a delirium, babbling out all kinds of nonsense. Every second words is 'my dearest Amanda.'"

A spasm of remorse wrenched at Miranda's heart. "That fatal deception of mine! That's what brought down this ruin upon us." She was letting herself be half-dragged, half-pushed toward the carriage.

"A few words from you will wipe out that deception forever. Here's your chance at last, my dear girl. Tell Theo the whole twisted story. The poor man keeps raving that he can't bear to live without you. To know that you're not really married—it will give him a new lease on life."

Miranda slumped back in her seat. Her head dropped

137

hopelessly on her breast. "If he knew who I really am, he'd spit in my face. To risk his life for such a miserable pauper—and a lying schemer as well."

Mrs. Hester leaned over toward her and clasped both her limp hands in her own. "My dear, you don't do yourself justice. Whatever you've done, it's been from the noblest of motives. I'm sure he'll understand that. If there's any fault in this case, it lies with your friend Amanda."

"*Amanda!*" Miranda jerked suddenly upright, staring blankly at Mrs. Hester. "Good God, how could I forget her? This dreadful news about Theo must have driven all thoughts of *her* danger out of my mind."

"What's all this about Amanda? You have news of your friend? Well, at least there's some comfort in that."

"No comfort at all," moaned Miranda. In short quick phrases, she described her trip to Portsmouth, her dismay at learning Amanda had left there to come to London, her fear of what Fortescue's wrath might lead him to do to her friend.

Mrs. Hester's face became graver and graver. "You're right, my dear. Amanda may have walked into a den of lions. She mustn't be left to face that ruffian alone. I'll leave you at Dr. Johnson's, and try to find some of the friends I've spoken about."

"Dr. Johnson?" Miranda was startled. "How does the great Dr. Johnson come into this sordid affair?"

Mrs. Hester blinked in surprise. "Oh, dear, didn't I tell you? Theo is there at his house in Johnson's Court. We thought he'd be safer there than at his own lodgings. If that erstwhile husband of yours should learn that he's still alive—"

"Lord Fortescue left him for dead?" Miranda's head started spinning.

"Now, now, my girl. I told you he's not hurt that badly. But it's in his best interests to let it be thought that he's been killed. It's his strongest defense against Lord Fortescue's anger. Once that angry gentleman's rage has had time to cool, he may even feel some remorse—or at least some regard for the legal consequences."

"Small chance of that," Miranda said bitterly. "He boasted to me that no court would dare to judge him."

Mrs. Hester sighed deeply. "I'm sure that's no idle boast. But don't worry, child. I have friends as powerful as he." The carriage jolted sharply as it turned off the wide main street into a narrow alley. "Good, we've reached Johnson's Court. Dr. Johnson will be inside. Please make my excuses to him; tell him I had to go off on some urgent business. I should be back with you within the hour. If I'm longer than that, promise you'll wait for me. Don't go dashing off on your own—"

Before Mrs. Hester had come to the end of her sentence, Miranda was out of the coach and lifting the big brass knocker on the door of the little brick house. The door fell open abruptly. She almost tripped over the threshold into the arms of the portly figure who stood there, his scratch wig askew, his garterless stockings drooping. He thrust his massive head toward her and peered at her nearsightedly.

"Miss Fitton!" he exclaimed, making a hasty effort to straighten his wig. He stepped back from the doorsill and motioned her into the small dingy room. "My apologies, madam. I fear I've been somewhat distracted. It's no longer Miss Fitton, is it? I should have called you *my lady*. May I offer congratulations on your recent change of estate? Your coming here is really most apposite. I was just writing the news of your marriage to a friend of mine. He was also, I believe, a friend of your father."

Miranda seethed with frustration. Why must he waste all this time with social triva, when Theo might be dying. "Please, sir," she said, trying to keep her voice calm, "I've come to see Mr. Moreland. Mrs. Hester tells me that he's been asking for me."

The massive forehead was furrowed with disapproval. "She told you that, did she? I advised her against that sentimental mistake. You're already gravely compromised in this town's idle gossip. To come here now, alone and unchaperoned—"

Miranda flushed with shame. How must she look in the eyes of this firm moralist? A married woman, rushing to comfort her husband's wounded opponent! He couldn't help but believe there was some guilty secret between herself and Theo. "Oh, please, Dr. Johnson," she cried, "I know that my coming here must shock you deeply. But whatever I may have done, Mr. Moreland is innocent. He's suffered a terrible wound because of my folly. I must speak to him; I must! Take pity on me, dear sir. Can't you see my soul is in torment?"

She saw the craggy face grow soft with compassion. "Who am I to cast the first stone? You may have been rash, my child, but I can't believe you've been wicked. By all means, come in and see Theo. How can I turn you away, when I know what comfort the sight of you will bring my poor young friend?"

He beckoned her to follow as he made his shambling way into an inner room. Over his bulky shoulder, Miranda caught a quick glimpse of rumpled bed linens, a body turning and twisting, a woman leaning down to replace a compress. "Miss Williams," he said, "I've brought Lady Fortescue to see your patient. Lady *Amanda* Fortescue," he repeated meaningfully.

The woman straightened, and turned with a smile of welcome. "So this is the dear Amanda! I'm so glad you've come." Her gaze went straight past Dr. Johnson's shoulder. With a tiny shock, Miranda realized she must be totally blind. "Come over here, please, where Mr. Moreland can see you. Oh, wait, let me fetch you a chair."

But Miranda was already on her knees by the rumpled bed, oblivious of all eyes except those familiar blue ones, now glowing unhealthily bright and sunk deep in their sockets. A look of incredulous joy spread over Theo's face, easing the lines of pain. "Have my prayers been answered, then? Am I truly in paradise?" Miranda

140

had to bend close to hear the feeble murmur. "Oh, Amanda, Amanda, nothing shall part us now!"

"Hush, Theo, my dearest." She stroked his lips gently. How galling it was to hear him call her *Amanda*. Who would ever have thought the name of her dearest friend could pierce her heart like a dagger?

"Oh happy death, that leads to such glorious visions." Theo reached up a wondering hand and touched her cheek. The tenderness was more than she could bear. Impulsively, she pressed her lips to his, feeling his quick response, his arms closing around her, the sudden access of strength as he pulled her against him. For what seemed a timeless instant, they clung to each other. Then she struggled free from his grasp, pulling away from the bed and staring down at him with eyes full of remorse. "This will never do, darling Theo. We haven't reached paradise yet. We're still on this troubled earth with disaster looming all round us."

A look of alertness pierced through the glaze of fever. His hand closed on her wrist in a hard, unbreakable grip. "This is no bodiless spirit! Do we both live and breathe, my dearest Amanda?" A shadow of pain flickered across his face. "And Fortescue lives and breathes too? Oh cruel fate!" He struggled up and propped himself on one elbow. "Let me go call him out again, and let him finish the sad piece of work he began."

"Oh, no! You mustn't do that!" With a formidable effort, Miranda pulled further away, instead of embracing him as she longed to do. "You can't toss your life away so contemptuously. You have so much to live for, a golden future stretching out before you."

"Future!" The word came out like a bark. Theo's lean frame was racked with a fit of coughing. He flung himself back on the bed, his face turned away toward the wall. "What do I care for the future, when the woman I love is married to another?"

"But I'm not really married!" The words leapt out by themselves. She saw Theo pull himself upright, gazing at her with a heartbreaking look of hope. She gazed back at him for a moment, her breast a whirlpool of churning emotions. How often she'd longed to see that look in his eyes, that adoring look, the look that laid bare his soul. But that look was meant for Amanda, not for herself. If she told him the truth, that look would change to one of scorn and contempt. She couldn't bear to see that. She mustn't tell him. She must keep up the weary charade a little while longer.

"I didn't mean what you think," she said hastily. "In the forms of the law, we are married. You heard us yourself, repeating those solemn vows. But I'm his wife in name only, not in the flesh or the spirit."

His first glowing look faded quickly to a look of diffident comprehension. She could see he'd instantly grasped the one part of her secret she could safely afford to tell him. "Thank heavens for that," he said softly. "If you knew the torture I've felt, imagining you in his arms! I've cursed myself over and over for not being braver, defying his hair-trigger anger, urging my own poor suit for your lovely hand. That night at the playhouse—oh, how I welcomed his challenge. I longed for the dawn to come so I could make good my right to sue honorably for your hand—or die in that happy attempt. If his seconds had come to my door, I'd have welcomed them in with the greatest pleasure. But the weary hours dragged on, and they never came. And then, when I left my rooms and found White's abuzz with the news of your coming marriage—Oh, Amanda, Amanda, how could you have been so cruel? You knew I loved you; surely you knew I loved you." He struggled up toward her with a strange, wild look in his eyes.

"But I didn't know." Miranda was shaken by the passionate force of his words. "I hoped—but I didn't know. And I couldn't let you risk your life—"

"What's risk to a man in love? I defy all risk." Theo swung his legs out of the bed and onto the floor, struggling to push himself to a standing position. Miranda drew back in alarm, while Miss Williams, sensing a disturbance, rushed forward in an attempt to still her

142

atient. In the confusion that followed Dr. Johnson was irst to act. He grasped Theo's arm. "You're too weak, Moreland," he shouted. "Lie back in bed, before you do ourself worse harm."

Dr. Johnson then turned to Miranda. "You must eave now, my lady. His wits are sadly astray."

"My sword! Give me my sword!" cried Theo hoarsely, rying to shake himself free from Miss Williams's suportive arm. "I'll go call out the bully again. This time e'll taste cold steel. Now I know my Amanda loves ne, there's no man on earth can withstand my sword."

"No, darling Theo, you mustn't!" By the time she ad gasped out the words, Miranda found herself in the uter room, propelled there by Dr. Johnson. She sank veakly into a chair, sick at heart at the damage she'd aused. She'd come here to comfort Theo, not rouse him o frenzy. She looked up hopelessly at the burly figure owering above her, expecting to see a scowl of anger. She was startled at the depth of compassion in the half-blind eyes.

"You see how it is, my poor child? The man's quite ut of his mind. He's ready for any rashness. If you value his life, you must leave here immediately and go make your peace with that outraged husband of yours."

"Go back to that monster? Now that I know Theo loves me? Oh, no! You're asking too much!"

"I'm asking you to honor your obligations. The sacrament of marriage—"

It wasn't a sacrament. Amanda has come to prove that. She choked the words back in her throat, shocked at the sudden reminder of Amanda's existence. She must have gone mad herself, to thus so completely forget her friend's predicament.

"You're right, dear Dr. Johnson." She was overwhelmed with guilt for her callous behavior. "I'll go back to his house this minute. I'll go face Lord Fortescue's rage, and make my explanations. Find me a coach; please do. I've deserted my duty too long. My first thought now must be for my dear friend's danger."

"An admirable resolution, though reached some what tardily. It does credit to that forthright youn lady I knew as Amanda Fitton. Be assured, all m prayers will go with you on that thorny path wher duty now beckons." Dr. Johnson shook his head sadl and shambled out of the room to summon a servant

Miranda felt a sudden stab of compunction. Where wa Mrs. Hester? She'd promised to wait for her. The grav words rang in her mind: *Promise you'll wait for m Don't go dashing off again.* But other words followed words even graver, filling her soul with remorse *Amanda may have walked into a den of lions. Sh mustn't be left to face that ruffian alone.*

She felt a soft touch on her shoulder, and realize that Miss Williams had come silently into the room "The poor man is sleeping now," she said in a gentl voice. "The excitement of seeing you has quite wor him out."

"What have I done!" cried Miranda. "I should neve have come here. If I've made his wound worse, I shal never forgive myself."

"My dear, you mustn't think that. The joy yo brought him would heal a thousand such wounds. Wil you stay and watch till he wakes? I'll bring you a po of tea—"

"Lady Fortescue is just leaving." Dr. Johnson, reen tering the room, cast a meaningful glance at Miranda

"Oh, yes, I must leave, I must! But I'm so glad Theo is resting. God bless you, dear Miss Williams. You'll take good care of him till I come back."

"You intend to come back here, madam?" She didn't dare look at the big man's face, This time he would really be glowering. She could hear the horses stamp ing on the cobblestones outside the door. The promised coach must have arrived.

With a muffled sob, she gathered her cloak around her and blindly plunged through the door. "Yes, Dr.

Johnson," she called back over her shoulder. "I hope from the depths of my heart to be back in less than an hour. Meanwhile, remember your promise; Amanda Fitton is sorely in need of your prayers!"

Chapter Fifteen

Miranda paused outside the library door, straining her ears for the sound of voices inside. For an instant she thought she heard it, that clear imperious tone in which Amanda was wont to denounce some unfortunate servant's blunder. Then she realized that her keyed-up nerves were playing tricks. If he was really in there, as the servants had told her he was, he was there alone, biding his time, waiting for her in ominous silence.

Where *was* Amanda, then? She must have arrived in London three days ago. Perhaps she'd already confronted his lordship, and come away victorious. Perhaps Mrs. Hester's dire predictions had all been baseless.

A moment of sober thought banished that giddy hope. If Amanda had already triumphed, she would have sought out her friend. A few inquiries would have brought her to Mrs. Hester. Mr. Armour, his scheme defeated, would have had no reason to withhold that information.

So she hadn't confronted him yet. No doubt she was biding her time. That canny miss had none of Miranda's rashness. She wouldn't go barging into his lordship's presence until she'd taken good care to spy out the lay of the land. She was probably settled in some discreet hostelry sending out cautious feelers. Perhaps she'd already found a reliable lawyer, a man she could trust to take her case to the courts.

Then what am I doing here, waiting to beard the lion? She felt an overwhelming impulse to turn and run. It was quickly canceled out by an even stronger impulse to stay and face him. Now Amanda had come, she was free to reveal their secret. Why not blurt it out now, at once, and be free at last of this tangle of fraud and lies?

She touched the doorhandle lightly, then snatched her hand away as if the contact had burned it. She forced herself to take a steadying breath, scolding herself for her hesitation. *In, girl, and get the farce over. What can he do to you now that would be half so bad as what you've gone through? At least, now you know that Amanda's somewhere in London, ready and willing to come to your aid.*

She pushed the door open and cautiously stepped into the room. It took a few seconds for her eyes to adjust to its dimness. The only light came from the glowing coals in the fireplace, beside which the dreaded enemy sat, staring into the darkness. He turned as he saw her enter, but made no move to rise.

"So you're back," he said, in a cold, dispassionate voice. "I thought you'd come crawling back, sooner or later."

She'd been braced for his rage. This coldness threw her off balance. But she managed to match his tone with a voice just as cold. "Yes, Lord Fortescue, I've come back. But I haven't come back to stay. I'm merely

147

here to inform you that I'm not really your wife. You have no legal claim, either on me or the Fitton estates."

Fortescue raised a quizzical eyebrow. "Now that's a surprising statement." His tone remained as expressionless as though they were discussing the weather. "I spend four days of anguish, wondering what has become of my runaway wife, and then she walks in with her hair all in disarray like a common slut, and tells me she's not my wife. A ridiculous faradiddle! Half of London will swear they witnessed our marriage, and I have the signed marriage contract."

Here was the longed-for moment. She'd tell him the whole truth now. And then she'd go back to Theo, and perhaps she would finally risk the ultimate telling—A warm surge of courage welled in her breast. "I signed that contract, sir, with the name of Amanda Fitton." Her voice rang out, clear and defiant, through the shadowy room. "But I'm not Amanda Fitton. My name is Miranda Testa. I'm an Italian peasant, not a gentleman's daughter. The real Amanda Fitton is now in London. If you need any further proof of what I've just told you, I'm sure she will quickly oblige you."

She'd expected surprise, rage, shock. She saw none of these. The expressionless look never wavered. He stared at her through a long, tense minute; then finally broke the silence with a harsh, dry laugh. "You're wasting your breath, my dear. This farrago of nonsense will do you no further good. The imposter who calls herself the true Amanda Fitton has already approached me."

Miranda felt as though a huge fist had just knocked her breathless. "Amanda was here?" she gasped. "But when? What did she say? Where is she now?"

"That doesn't concern us, madam. It's all in the past. You'll find I'm a lenient husband, ready to grant you forgiveness. You'll settle back down to your wifely duties, and we'll forget all this silly nonsense your crackwitted young friend has been trying to foist upon me."

"But it's true!" Miranda shouted. "I'm not Amanda

148

Fitton. I have witnesses who can prove it! What have you done with Amanda? Let me see her this minute."

"I'm afraid, dear wife, that will not be possible. I've sent her where she belongs, to live among those unfortunate wretches at Bedlam."

"You've sent her to Bedlam? Oh, no, I don't believe you! Even a monster like you couldn't do that!"

"Could I not, my dear?" The quizzical eyebrow arched higher. "You really have no idea of what I can do when someone attempts to threaten my very existence. This golden-haired friend of yours presumed to do that. I hope she will very quickly learn her lesson."

A terrible conviction was beginning to form in Miranda's mind. "I believe you really mean it," she said in a horrified voice. "But you know she's not mad! You know what she says is true. I'll go get her out of that hellhole, and then we'll face you together! I'm not quite friendless, you know. Mrs. Hester is on my side. I've already told her that I'm not the real Amanda. She has powerful friends who will help us."

She turned to run out of the door, but he rose from his seat abruptly, clamped a hand on her shoulder, and swung her round to face him. "I wouldn't advise you to make any rash moves."

"It's you who've made the rash move." Miranda stared back at him like a cornered wildcat. "You'll rue the day you did this. Amanda's not mad, and you know it. When she tells her story in court, how you willfully sent her to rot in that horrible place—"

"That horrible place is a better place than the gallows."

The word clanged in her ear. "The gallows!" she gasped. "What on earth do you mean?"

"I mean that your fair-haired friend attempted to kill me." He released her shoulder abruptly, turned back toward the library table, and picked up a jewelled dagger. "When I refused to yield to her insane demands, she snatched this blade from the wall where I had it displayed and went for my heart. I wrested it from her before she could do any damage."

Miranda stood there aghast. Had it really come to this? Had Amanda's sharp temper led to that ultimate folly? Then she saw the cruel, secret smile, and knew he was lying. "You devil! You fiend!" she cried. "No court would ever believe you. They'd have only to look at Amanda to know that tender young girl never touched that dagger."

"The court will believe whatever I choose to tell them. After all, it's my word against that of a nameless stranger. If you know what's best for you both, you'll let things rest. It's only because I thought she was out of her mind that I didn't have her arrested. If you keep insisting she's sane, then the law must demand the appropriate punishment. Felonious assault on a peer of the realm."

"You wouldn't dare. We'll bring witnesses against you. Her banker, Mr. Faldini, servants who've known her from birth."

"Our courts move swiftly, madam. By the time your mistress's servants made the long trip from Florence, the verdict would already be in and the punishment given."

That's not true, she wanted to shout. *I know that it can't be true. No judge in the world would believe your lying story.* But a cold tide of fear swept the length of her bones. What did she know of the ways of English justice? Hadn't Mrs. Hester warned her about its dangers?

A slow smile of satisfaction spread over Fortescue's face. She knew he'd seen her hesitation. Now he pressed home his advantage. "Believe me, my dear, if you value your mistress's life, you'll do as I say—settle down as a dutiful wife, and let what you call 'this farce' continue unchanged."

"You called her my mistress!" Miranda snatched at the telltale word. "Then you know her story is true! That's why you've sent her away!"

How cruel that smile was, like a boy watching a fly struggling in honey. "I know it's true," he said, still in that toneless voice. "*You* know it's true. That golden-haired miss now in Bedlam knows it's true. But outside we three, no one in London knows. And no one in London *will* know. You're a competent actress, Miss Testa. You've already hoaxed all of London. They think you a highborn lady. You'll go on playing that part for as long as I tell you."

And how long is that? Forever? Miranda stared up at him, bereft of speech. He answered her unspoken question. "After the Fitton estates are bestowed on me as an irrevocable gift, I may see fit to let my charming young wife return to her native land for a lengthy stay, accompanied by her golden-haired servant, whose untrained, primitive mind so quickly succumbed to the pressures of civilized life."

Miranda's head was whirling. Could he do it? Make good his threat? Surely he couldn't! But how did she know? A sudden vision appeared in the spinning blackness—Amanda, white-faced and pleading, the hangman approaching—No! She couldn't risk that. The only safe thing to do was to accept this hideous bargain, play for a little more time, perhaps even face the loss of Amanda's fortune. What did a fortune matter, compared to a human life?

"Very well, Lord Fortescue." She stepped from his loosened grasp, bowing her head in defeat. "You have won this round of the game. It's up to you to set the rules of the next round."

Lord Fortescue heaved a sigh of mock relief. "I'm glad you see reason, madam. The rules? No real change, you'll find. We continue to play the game just as before. There *will* be one new player. Sir Lucas Trotter has just arrived from Jamaica. My uncle is resting now, fatigued by the journey. You'll meet him at dinner. He's professed himself utterly charmed to hear of my recent marriage. I trust that you, in your practiced role, will charm him still further."

A wave of nausea wrenched at Miranda's stomach. That hateful role still, just when she thought she'd shaken it off forever. She kept her head bowed in helpless acquiescence. She was at his mercy now. But perhaps she'd find some way out. There was still Mrs. Hester, perhaps her powerful friends . . .

Lord Fortescue's voice broke harshly into her thoughts. "Oh, and one thing more. I'd like you to write a letter. To your erstwhile friend, Mrs. Hester, breaking off your acquaintance. You must tell her you've lied to her ever since you met her. You may ask for her pardon, to make the thing sound convincing. But whatever you say, you must make it clear to her that she's not to take part in any quixotic scheme for your so-called rescue. You don't need to be rescued. You're a happy and satisfied wife."

Miranda stared up at him dully. "You'd take Mrs. Hester from me? My best friend in London?"

"You have two good friends in London," said Lord Fortescue coldly. "If you value the one friend's life, you must cut off all chance that the other continue her meddling. You understand me, I hope? You'll find pen and ink on that table. I shall wish to read the letter when you've composed it."

"Yes, my lord," said Miranda. "I'll write your letter." She walked to the writing table, picked up the quill, and prepared herself to sign away her last hope.

"Oh, madam, see how they shine! 'Tis like seeing a thousand trapped rainbows." The little maid fastened the clasp on the diamond necklace and stood back to admire the effect of candlelight on the jewels. Miranda forced herself to give her a smile. She owed that much to the girl's determined efforts to make her look splendid. What a comfortable thing she was to have around her, with her wholehearted admiration and quick elfin smiles. A welcome change from the haughty La Sogghignatora.

"You have a lyrical tongue, Ruth. Has someone taught you to read the works of the poets?"

"Oh, no, madam. I have no letters. But I often go to the playhouse, and hear the fine words that they do be speaking there."

The playhouse. A giant hand seemed to clench round Miranda's heart. *That night at Drury Lane. Theo and I entranced. And the awful sequel that launched me into this false marriage, and brought my darling Theo to the edge of the grave.* For the hundredth time that evening, she saw Theo's pale face and fever-bright eyes. How was he faring now? Was he sleeping soundly, soothed by Miss Williams's nursing? Or was he awake and delirious, calling her name in vain, railing against her broken promise that she'd return?

She should never have left him. She should have stayed by his side and let the whole world go hang. What a silly fool she had been, to think she could rescue Amanda single-handed. But she'd felt so powerful then, strong in her newfound knowledge that Theo loved her. And now she sat shivering here, as devoid of spirit as some cold porcelain doll, decked out in this panoply of satin and lace and towering powdered coiffure. The diamonds—Amanda's diamonds—seemed to burn through her skin. *That sweet, haughty pampered darling! What horrors she must be enduring! Surrounded by shrieking madmen, huddling from the cold under fetid straw, dining on bread and water—while I, in my borrowed feathers, strut and preen to charm Sir Lucas Trotter.*

"Are you ready, madam? The gentlemen are waiting." Little Ruth sounded anxious. No doubt her lord and master had sent her an angry command. She'd better not risk his wrath further by seeming to slight this all-important uncle.

She hurried down the curving stairway, steadying herself on the cool, polished wood of the bannister. Which one of his nephews would Sir Lucas Trotter resemble? His beefy arrogant lordship, or that slender young lieutenant who had stolen Amanda's heart? *Oh, Charles, Charles, Charles! What kept you on in Jamaica when we had such need of you?*

The answer leapt into her mind with a force that made her stumble. She clutched at the polished railing, retrieved her precarious balance, paused to consider the import of this new revelation. Sir Lucas, of course. Charles had met his uncle out there. He had lingered on with him, thinking to forward his chances at that tempting fortune. And when that uncle had boarded a ship for England, where had Charles been then? Perhaps at his side, accompanying him on the journey? Of course! He must have come with him. Charles must be here in England. He'd have learned by now of Amanda's dangerous plot and the fraudulent marriage. He was somewhere out there in London, ready to come to their rescue. Sir Lucas Trotter could take a message to him!

Her feet had a life of their own now, carrying her down the stairs in a dazzling cloud of hope. She arrived in the drawing room breathless, then abruptly slowed her pace to a proper decorum. She couldn't come out with the question she longed to ask. Fortescue mustn't guess at her newfound ally. She must be very circumspect in greeting Sir Lucas, then wait for a moment alone to ask about Charles, find out if Sir Lucas was also in on the secret.

The two men were warming themselves by the roaring fire—one broad-shouldered and burly, the other stoop-backed and slight. They turned toward her as she entered. Fortescue's face looked strained as he greeted her. The smaller man peered at her over his wire-framed spectacles, his black beady eyes appraising, his pinched little mouth not showing a trace of a smile. Miranda's joy faded abruptly. This dour little person in rusty black, his sparse hair twisted into an unkempt, unpowdered queue—could he really be that ebullient lieutenant's uncle? It hardly seemed possible. He had probably met his penniless nephew's advances with the same suspicious eyes he now turned on Miranda.

Fortescue had seen that look too, and was looking worried. "Dear uncle," he said, his tone unusually subdued, "may I present to you my bride?"

What a strange transformation then! One moment, all prunes and prisms; the next, a radiant smile. The small man was striding toward her, his arms outstretched as though about to embrace her. "So this is the happy bride!" His hands clasped her shoulders warmly, as he held her out at arm's length, as though to inspect her. "You've done well, young Edward. A delightful surprise to greet your doddering old uncle."

Lord Fortescue's brow was furrowed. "I didn't expect to surprise you. I assumed you'd have heard from Charles I had plans for marriage. Did he not mention his recent trip to Florence to carry my offer to Miss Amanda Fitton?"

"Amanda Fitton?" The little man seemed startled, as if the name were completely new to him. Then he gave his body a jerk and snapped his fingers. "Oh, yes. Of course. The charming Amanda Fitton. How stupid of me to forget that auspicious name. I remember now— he told me he'd played the matchmaker."

Lord Fortescue's face eased into a complacent smile. "He couldn't have known, of course, how well he argued my case. It was only after he left on his tour to Jamaica that my charming Amanda consented to come to London. Once she was here in person, there could be little doubt of the outcome."

"An admirable conquest, indeed." The seamed old face broke into a beaming smile. "I congratulate you, nephew. Your lady completely fulfills Charles's glowing description." He took Miranda's hand and leaned confidentially toward her, murmuring into her ear, "Young Charles was quite dazzled himself by the raven-haired beauty he met in those Florentine gardens."

Miranda stiffened with shock. *That raven-haired beauty.* Charles would never have used that phrase in describing Amanda. The old man was sending a signal with those whispered words. He knew very well who she was, but wasn't yet ready to expose her perilous secret. This was his way of telling her he was her ally!

Her head went giddy with joy. It had happened just as she'd hoped! Charles and he had traveled together to Portsmouth. Charles had found Amanda's letter, had told his redoubtable uncle about Miranda.

"Don't you think so, my dear?"

She came to herself with a start, aroused from her circling thoughts by the steel in Fortescue's voice. Both men were staring at her with questioning looks.

"I—I'm sorry," she said. "What were you asking just now?"

Sir Lucas smiled at her fondly. "I was merely remarking how eager I am to meet with you in our own private talk. You must tell me what means of persuasion this young scalawag used to secure your consent. Nothing reveals a man's character so fully as the strategies he uses in his wooing."

Miranda's heart started beating wildly. She was sure of it now! The old man was her ally. She could hardly keep from flicking a glance of triumph toward her so-called husband. That private talk would begin that hateful man's downfall. Once he knew where Amanda was, Sir Lucas would come to her aid. With this rich and powerful new friend, they'd have nothing to fear from any strange whim of an English judge.

"Sir Lucas," she said, "my time is at your command. I should like nothing better than the chance to enlighten you. Brief as our marriage has been, I believe that no one on earth could paint you a more candid portrait of my dear husband's motives and character."

In her new mood of confidence, Miranda found herself thoroughly enjoying the lavish dinner with which Fortescue welcomed Sir Lucas. He'd really done himself proud—salmon with fennel sauce, roast loin of veal, a pigeon pie made with egg yolks. Her body's eager response to the well-cooked food reminded her how hurried and scanty her meals had been during the past few days. Once her stomach was satisfied, Lord Fortescue himself provided amusing fare for her troubled mind. She could scarcely keep from laughing as she heard him presenting himself as a model of all the virtues.

"It's a terrible vice, this gambling. London is riddled with it. I myself, of course, would never go near the tables."

Sir Lucas nodded at him as though in approval, but Miranda noted a skeptical gleam in his eyes. "I'm at one with you there. I've never gambled myself. I've found much easier ways of earning my money. But I like the high spirits one tends to find in the cardroom, the zestful air of men who are risking big stakes. Haven't you felt that yourself? Oh, no; you've just said you never go near the tables."

Lord Fortescue looked confused and a bit crestfallen, but soon resumed his transparent efforts to secure his supposedly straitlaced uncle's favor. "I put things too strongly, perhaps. I'm not above an occasional game of hazard. But the one thing I will not do is bet on the races. *There's* the place where fortunes really go down the drain. The only greater folly than betting on horses is owning the beasts one's self."

Sir Lucas cocked a quizzical eyebrow at him. "You condemn the racecourse so strongly? I'm sorry to hear that, nephew. I had hoped for the pleasure of going with you to Newmarket. I have a fine stable myself, back in Jamaica. Arabian stock, most of them."

Lord Fortescue almost choked on a piece of the veal. Clearly he'd had a far different picture of his rich uncle's predilections. Miranda grew more and more pleased to find Sir Lucas so different from his nephew's description. How pleasant it was, to find so congenial an ally! And how amusing to see his lordship hoist with his own petard. Sir Lucas, it now appeared, had very little use for a puritan nephew.

"And what of the playhouse, uncle?" she asked mischievously. "My husband, of course, cannot abide the playhouse. But perhaps you and I will go there? We have some very fine actors at Drury Lane."

The little man's genial smile faded abruptly. His dark, merry eyes turned accusing; the mobile mouth twisted into a pinched-up grimace. "Actors!" he snorted. "Can't abide 'em. A parcel of indolent rogues, the worst class of ruffians."

Miranda was thunderstruck at the sudden shift in his mood. "Perhaps that was so in past years, before you left England," she ventured cautiously. "But conditions have changed since then. Quite a few gentlemen now take to the stage. And Mr. Garrick is received in the best of houses."

"Garrick! Garrick!" The little man was positively wheezing with anger. "Don't mention that odious man. He's the worst of all that scoundrelly crew!"

Miranda was tempted to hastily change the subject, but Theo Moreland's face suddenly swam before her, and a surge of loyal defiance made her bold again. "You surprise me, Sir Lucas. Most people believe Mr. Garrick a model of virtue. He's a careful businessman, a faithful husband—and even *you* must admit he's studied his craft."

"He's studied it too damn well!" Sir Lucas's emphatic fist came down on the table. "He's become an arch-devil. They say he can make you believe he's a different man every night. Now what is that, if you please, but sheer deception? Deception and fraud! The man's clearly a rascal. If a poor merchant like myself tried to pass himself off as a duke or an earl, he'd find himself plunked into Newgate before you could say Jack Harry. But here is this rascal Garrick, who nightly pretends that he is the king himself! And what does his impudence gain him? Instead of suffering his proper deserts, he's rewarded with fame and honors."

A crafty gleam crept into Lord Fortescue's eyes. "You think it a crime, sir, to be an imposter? You'd wish to see such a one punished? A flogging, perhaps?"

"Flogging's too good for such wretches. I'd have 'em transported. A good seven years in the canefields would teach them respect for their betters."

"That seems very harsh, dear uncle." Lord Fortescue pulled a long face, portraying himself as a man full of gentle feelings. "Seven years merely for pretending to rank above one's station?"

"It's the only way to cut out this cankerous evil!" The fist came down again, rattling the dishes. "An imposter, sir, is a threat to the whole social order. It's a mild punishment, I suggest, compared to his heinous crime. Transport 'em, I say again, or hang the rascals. It's all one to me. Let 'em dance at the end of a rope, and then we'll see how much they like the cheers from the galleries!"

What an odious transformation! Those eyes which had seemed so friendly now seemed to sparkle with glee at the thought of the gibbet.

"Perhaps you're right." His nephew smiled smugly, darting a glance at Miranda. "At least for the men. But surely you won't be so harsh when it comes to the women? A peasant girl, say, who pretends to be a lady?"

Miranda went stiff with horror. His air of triumphant malice seemed to transfix her. As though in a dream, she heard the old man sputtering on. "Why should I spare the women? Because they're supposed to be the gentler sex? They make just as good laborers, sir; my canefields are full of them. A few strokes of the lash make them work just as hard as the men."

Miranda swayed in her seat. The floor, it seemed, had given way beneath her. Where had he disappeared to, that powerful rescuer who would snatch Amanda to safety? This disgusting little man with the maniac gleam in his eyes at the thought of the whip coming down on her aching back—hers and Amanda's!

"What's the matter, my dear? You look as though you're not well." Fortescue's oily voice oozed with mock sympathy. All Miranda heard was the steely threat beneath it.

"I'm sorry," she said. "I *am* a bit indisposed. That dinner—too rich, perhaps. If you'll excuse me, I think I'll go to my room."

She had to hold fast to the table to push herself to her feet. Lord Fortescue made no move to help her. He was sitting back in his chair, a sly, catlike smile barely curving his lips. "Such a pity, my dear Amanda, to postpone your pleasant *tête-à-tête* with my uncle."

Miranda didn't attempt to answer. As she made her way out of the room, she could feel his gloating eyes burn into her back. Lord Fortescue, she was sure, knew how frightened she was. The last thing in the world Miranda Testa wanted was a quiet *tête-à-tête* with Sir Lucas Trotter.

Chapter Sixteen

"Miss Williams!" The name was called softly, almost in a whisper. The blind woman knew the voice at once.

Amelia Hester was standing just outside the doorway, obviously trying to catch any sounds from the sickroom. "My dear Miss Williams, how has your patient been faring these past three days? He's much improved, I hope, under your skillful nursing?"

"Indeed he is, Mrs. Hester. The fever has quite disappeared. He's still weak from loss of blood, but now that his appetite's back, he will soon become stronger."

"Heaven be praised!" Mrs. Hester's worried look gave way to a beaming smile. "Thank you, Miss Williams, for bringing me such good news."

"Good news in one way; not such good news in another." The blind woman's forehead, usually serene, was furrowed with lines of worry. "The fever's gone, but those feverish thoughts still remain. He insists he's determined to challenge Lord Fortescue. If only his dear Amanda were here to soothe him! Have you had any news of her?"

"Yes, she's sent me a letter. But I fear what she has to say would do nothing to soothe him. There's a gentleman waiting outside, however, who can give him important news about his beloved."

"Mrs. Hester!" came a voice from the inner room. "Surely that's you! I couldn't mistake that voice." Amelia was pleased to hear how strong and well Theo sounded. "Come in this minute, I pray you. Have you heard from my darling Amanda? Where is she? What does she say? Why hasn't she come as she promised?"

Mrs. Hester went into the sickroom. Theo was sitting in bed, propped up by a mound of pillows. Though he still looked a trifle pale, his eyes were no longer hollow and feverish. Mrs. Hester gave him a gentle, teasing smile. "So it wasn't only the fever that led to extravagant words like *my dearest Amanda*. When did your sentiments change? The last time we met, you swore you cared nothing for her—though your pale face and mournful eyes quite belied that claim of indifference."

Theo heaved a deep sigh. "Those terrible weeks just after Amanda's marriage. Of course I denied my love then. I thought she'd rejected me, for a reason I couldn't fathom. But now that I've heard that incomparable voice of hers call me her *darling Theo*—Oh, Mrs. Hester, please tell me where she is! I was out of my mind with fever that day she appeared at my side like an angel. There are so many questions I hadn't the wit to ask her. Why did she leave Lord Fortescue? Where did she disappear to? Why did he think she had taken refuge with me? Why, when she came here to see me, did she leave so quickly? Where is she now? Surely she hasn't gone back to Fortescue's house! She told me herself that she didn't consider that marriage a true one.'

"Help, Theo! A little mercy!" Mrs. Hester pretended to be overwhelmed by the string of questions. "Most of those fierce demands I'm not empowered to answer.

162

Not that I don't have the knowledge; my lips are sealed by a promise I now regret making. But I've brought a friend with me who's under no such constraint."

"Who is this friend?" Theo flung back the bedclothes and struggled to rise to his feet. "Take me to him at once."

"Theo! Enough of this nonsense!" Amelia could play the martinet when she chose. "If you're not back in bed in one minute, I shall leave this house at once and take my friend with me. Miss Williams!" She raised her voice loud enough to reach the outer room. "Come help me, please. Your patient will do himself harm."

Miss Williams hurried in promptly, clucking her own string of cautions. Theo gave up his attempt to get out of bed, and let the two women replace the bedclothes around him. When the bed was once more restored to its former order, Mrs. Hester, hands on hips, stood staring down at him, like a mother reprimanding a naughty boy.

"Now, Mr. Theophilus Moreland, you will give me your solemn promise that no matter what Lieutenant Halstead tells you, you'll not move a foot from that bed till we give you permission. Is that clearly understood?"

Theo looked sulky and avoided meeting her eyes. "You think I'm one of those characters from your novels, a marionette you can put through whatever paces you choose."

"Enough of this grumbling, Theo. Will you give me your promise? Until you do, you have no chance of learning your precious Amanda's secrets."

"Oh, very well," mumbled Theo. "I give you my solemn promise. Will you end all this mystery now? How long will you keep me in torment?"

Mrs. Hester disdained to answer. She left him sulking in silence and a few minutes later returned with a tall young man whose sun-bleached hair and darkened complexion proclaimed him just back from the tropics. "Mr. Moreland," she said in a formal tone, "may I present Lieutenant Charles Halstead, just returned from Jamaica. I'll leave you alone to make each other's acquaintance, while I go pay my respects to the excellent doctor."

Theo looked up into keen blue eyes, full of suppressed excitement. "You're welcome here, sir," he said. "I would rise to greet you, but my attendant dragons insist I remain in bed."

The lieutenant made a slight bow. "Stay where you are, sir, I pray you. Mrs. Hester has told me you have a serious wound. I am much in your debt for daring to fight with my cousin."

"Fortescue is your cousin? Why congratulate me, then, for trying to run him through?"

"Lord Fortescue is my mortal enemy. He's threatening the life of my future wife, Miss Amanda Fitton."

"*Your* future wife! What cruel jest is this? You're engaged to Amanda Fitton? When only four days ago she proclaimed her love for me, flung herself into these arms, ardently kissed these lips? Oh, no; I can't believe it." Theo fell back onto his pillows, overwhelmed with emotion.

Charles Halstead looked distressed. He sprang toward the bed and fell to his knees beside it. "Moreland, forgive me, I beg you. I'm an insensitive clod. That was indeed the cruelest sort of jest."

Theo turned a wan face toward him. "Why are you lying to me? You don't even know Amanda! Are you giving me some sort of test, to see my reaction?"

"My dear newfound ally, it's *you* who don't know Amanda. The girl you know is Amanda's foster sister. Her name is Miranda Testa. She's Amanda's dearest friend, and so when Amanda asked her to take her place—" He went on to explain the whole tangled turn of events—Mr. Armour's plot with Lord Fortescue to summon Amanda to London, Miranda's masquerade, Amanda's vigil at Portsmouth, believing her letter would soon bring Charles to her side.

"That's where the scheme went wrong. That fatal letter! It must have been lost at sea. If I'd had the slightest inkling of this dangerous scheme, I'd have surely returned with my squadron and helped my dear Amanda to rescue her friend. Instead, fool that I was, I dallied a month in Jamaica, improving my acquaintance with Sir Lucas Trotter, a very rich uncle of mine whom I met for the first time there. Imagine my horror, the morning I landed in Portsmouth, to be approached by a local clergyman who presented a letter Amanda had left for me. It said that my darling Amanda had gone to London to snatch her dear friend from the toils of a fraudulent marriage to my grasping cousin—"

Theo raised his hand abruptly, as though to brush away an enveloping mist. "It wasn't the real Amanda who married your cousin? But this girl I knew as Amanda—this lovely, spirited girl whose clear honest eyes seemed to draw me into their sea-green depths—"

Charles gave a little groan. "I know; oh, how well I know! Amanda has the same eyes. That girl is Miranda Testa. An Italian peasant girl, but a most remarkable one. She shared Amanda's whole life, was educated with her, became her sister in everything but name." He hesitated an instant. "I can make a few guesses about the situation—those sea-green eyes—you're a man of the world like myself; I'm sure you know what I mean. Of course, my darling Amanda hasn't the slightest suspicion—"

Theo gestured impatiently. "All this is beside the point, sir. What does her heritage matter? If she isn't the real Amanda, that means that the marriage I witnessed was really no marriage at all. Fortescue has no claim on her. She is free to give her love where she wills!"

"That seems to give you great joy, sir."

"The greatest of joys. It means I can marry the girl I love most dearly."

Charles looked a little surprised. "But the girl whom you fell in love with described herself as an heiress. It makes no difference to you that Miranda is penniless?"

"Miranda!" breathed Theo ecstatically. "How well

she suits that name. *Admired Miranda* indeed! What do I care for a fortune, when I know I have gained the love of this perfect creature?"

Charles threw him a dubious glance. "I take it, then, that you are a man of some means? If a fortune's not necessary—"

Theo cut him off with a wave of his hand. "I'm almost a pauper, but what does that signify? I did have some expectations of a legacy from my uncle. While I thought my love was an heiress, I took great care to remain in his good graces. I couldn't presume to ask her to marry a poor man. But now I am free—free to pursue the two great loves of my life—the stage and Aman—Miranda! Poverty will be bliss with her at my side!"

"A true lover's sentiment." Charles smiled at him wryly. "For myself, I confess myself glad to have fallen in love with an heiress. I'm sure I'd have loved Amanda, however low her estate—but you must admit, money makes love's path run smoother."

Theo had ceased to listen. He was now consumed with an urgent need for action. Forgetting his earlier promise, he was once more struggling out from under the bedclothes. "I must go to Miranda at once! Where is she? You must take me to her at once. I must hear from her own sweet lips the promise to be my wife."

"Moreland! Don't be a fool!" With a look of alarm, Charles Halstead clamped a restraining grasp on both Theo's shoulders. "She's back at my cousin's house. You mustn't go near the place. He thinks he left you dying. If you challenge him now in your weakened condition, this time you'll be dead for certain."

"She went back to Fortescue?" A dazed look crept over Theo's face. "I can't believe it! She was here, I swear it, professing her love for me! She told me herself he was not her true husband." His voice turned low and faltering. He shook his head in confusion. "But perhaps that was all an illusion, part of some feverish dream."

Charles Halstead's face was glowing with warm fel-

166

low feeling. "That was no dream, my dear Moreland. Mrs. Hester brought her to you four days ago. Miss Williams heard you declare your love to each other. Let me call Mrs. Hester in now; of the three of us, she's the one who knows the most about this tangled affair. Lie back now, there's a good fellow, and hear what she has to tell us."

Theo shook his head as though to clear his confusion. Charles stepped to the door and summoned Mrs. Hester. Theo tried to sit up when he saw her enter, but weakness compelled him to sink back onto his pillows. "My dear, dear friend." He smiled at her gratefully. "Have you heard this fantastic story that Lieutenant Halstead just told me?"

"Indeed I have," said Amelia. "I've know almost from the start who Miranda was. But she forced me into a promise that I'd not breathe a word to you. She feared if you knew who she was, you'd cease to love her. I take it that's not the case?"

"Cease to love my Miranda? Will birds cease to fly, winds cease to blow, the sun cease to shine?"

"Enough, my dear Theo; you've quite made your point. No more lover's rodomontade; what matters now is the plot of our little drama. What is our next step to be?"

"Surely that's evident. We must rescue her from that monster. I was ready to do just that, with my sword in my hand, when Lieutenant Halstead restrained me."

"Please, Theo, no more heroics." Mrs. Hester looked at him sternly. "Quite apart from the fact that you're still weak from loss of blood, you must realize that rescuing Miranda can't be our only consideration. Amanda is also in terrible danger."

Theo looked at her wide-eyed for a moment. Then his bewilderment cleared. "Oh, yes, the real Miss Fitton. Where is that young lady now?" He turned to Charles Halstead. "Her letter said she was on her way to London?"

"On her way to Lord Fortescue's house." Charles

nodded grimly. "Her intent, it seems, was to lay the facts before him. In her innocence of the world, she blithely assumed he'd calmly accept his fate. It seems that he didn't do that."

"Good Lord!" cried Theo. "She confronted that volatile man with the fact of his ruin? What was the outcome of that?"

"We don't know what the outcome was," Mrs. Hester broke in, "but we fear the worst. We know she went to his house. Her maid, Maria, waited outside in the chaise. After several hours had passed, a footman came out with a message to her from Amanda. He gave her a purse full of coins, said her mistress had chosen to visit in London alone, and instructed her to return to Portsmouth, there to await further orders."

"Surely the maid must have thought that was very strange?"

"Of course she did. But what was the poor girl to do? She speaks very little English, knows nothing of English customs. Amanda, I gather, is a somewhat impulsive young lady who becomes very angry when servants question her orders. Maria thought it best to go back to Portsmouth. There, at least, she could count on the help of some friends—including the Reverend Mr. Entwhistle, the same helpful parson who gave Charles Amanda's letter and then sent him on to me."

"So the last we know of Amanda, she was in Lord Fortescue's house!" Theo looked horrified. "He must have kept her by force. What of Miranda, then? You say she went back to the house. She must be his prisoner too. Surely she's in as much danger as your poor Amanda?"

"Potentially, yes. But I think she's safe for the moment. I saw her last night at Lady Harwood's assembly. Lord Fortescue, I believe, is forcing her to make a great show of being his loving wife."

"You saw her last night? What did she say? Surely you spoke to her?" Theo clutched at Amelia's arm. "You must have found some chance to see her alone."

"No chance at all," said Amelia. "Miranda cut me dead. I expected that, of course. I'd just had a letter from her breaking off our acquaintance. She claimed she'd been lying to me, that the story of Amanda's scheme was childish nonsense, made up to catch my novelistic attention."

Charles snorted contemptuously. "The brute made her write that, of course. You didn't believe it?"

"Not for a minute. I could never doubt Miranda's truthfulness. Her whole soul shines out through her eyes. That letter was written under some powerful duress."

"The monster has threatened her!" cried Theo wildly, struggling to get out of bed, then falling back in despair. "While I lie here in craven sloth, he may already have done her some harm."

"Calm yourself, Theo. Don't you see that he can't do that? He needs his supposed wife to parade around the ballrooms, silencing any question of his right to the Fitton fortune. But why should our poor Miranda choose to fall in with his wishes? If she decided to make a scene in some public place, she'd be free of him instantly. It's some threat to Amanda that's keeping her so quiescent."

"Surely he'd not be so mad as to harm Amanda!" Theo's eyes had come alive with imagined horrors. "The truth is bound to come out sooner or later. If he hurt Amanda—even had her murdered—"

"Murdered!" groaned Charles. "I pray you, spare me that word! It drives me half-mad with fear for my darling's life."

"Mr. Moreland! Lieutenant Halstead." Mrs. Hester's voice took on a schoolmistress tone. "Please subdue these unseemly hysterics. We need clear minds and firm hearts to conduct this adventure. However malicious he is, Lord Fortescue remains a peer of the realm. This means he depends on the power of his rank to subdue most enemies. He'll only descend to brute force as a last resort."

Theo stirred impatiently under the bedclothes. Mrs. Hester's voice softened. "Except, of course, when some foolish romantic young man decides that his honor compels him to risk suicide." She looked at Theo and sighed maternally.

"So Amanda is still in his house, perhaps being kept under guard as a prisoner?" Charles's voice was sharp with impatience. "What we need is some evidence then, to persuade a magistrate to order a search. Could we send a note to Miranda, ask her to go to Bow Street and swear out a complaint?"

"She'd never agree," Mrs. Hester said crisply. "The brute has her utterly cowed by his threats to Amanda."

Theo groaned in exasperation. "That pestilent villain! To think I once called him my friend! You're right, Mrs. Hester. My gallant Miranda would never desert her foster sister. If only we could persuade her that saving herself might help save Amanda as well."

"That's out of the question, I fear. She'd think it too great a risk. And so, my young friends, it seems we have only one option."

The light of understanding dawned in Charles Halstead's eyes. "If she won't join us willingly..." he mused.

"Then we must take her by force." Theo's voice was full of urgent resolution. "Oh, God, this pestilent wound! If only I weren't so weak."

"Have patience, my impetuous Theo. We have a full seven days to plot our attack. Lady Sudbrooke's giving a ball in her house in Chiswick a week from tonight. The *ton* will be out in force. Fortescue's sure to want to parade his wife there. Now, what do you think of this plan? When I tried it in one of my novels, some of my readers thought it a trifle unlikely...."

Chapter Seventeen

...Forgive me for not being more candid concerning my present difficult situation. Suffice it to say that the fate of my dearest friend hangs in the balance. For the moment, my darling Theo, our watchword must continue to be *silence and caution*. If your love for me is equal to that which I bear for you, you will abjure any thought of rash action and wait patiently until you hear from me further. I hope and pray that the day will soon arrive when I will once more hear your own sweet voice speaking those words of love which brought me to such heights of exaltation. Until then, dearest Theo, you must rest content with this assurance of the eternal love of your devoted...

Miranda eased herself back in her chair and stared thoughtfully at the letter on the table before her. Then she leaned forward again, and deliberately set down the signature: *Amanda.*

With a little sigh, she dusted the paper with sand to absorb the superfluous ink; then folded it into a compact square, sealing it shut with a blob of red wax. *There! That's done. Now where on earth it that girl?* She looked impatiently at the door, as though her very gaze could compel the little maid's entrance. She was still not completely sure she should trust her. A few days ago, it would have seemed out of the question. Surely all Fortescue's servants must be in league against her, forming a solid phalanx between herself and any attempt at help from the outside world.

But she'd gradually come to believe that Ruth might be an exception. From the very first moment they met, a strong current of sympathy seemed to flow between them. It hadn't been long till the shy, concerned comments began: *You seem unhappy, my lady. It must be lonely for you, with his lordship closing you off from all visitors.* Miranda, still cautious, had met these advances with some noncommittal answer. Then the girl had grown bolder, and come straight out with that surprising suggestion: *If you wanted a trustworthy person to carry a letter...I have a brother...Surely you have some friend who is longing to hear from you...*

Miranda was startled at first. Could the little maid read her mind? Then she realized that the servants' quarters were probably buzzing with gossip about her supposed affair with Theo Moreland.

Timeo Danaos et dona ferentes. She remembered the ominous way *Maestro* MacCrae used to give that warning. Full of suspicion, she confronted the girl directly. "A very kind offer, Ruth. But can I trust you? How do I know you won't go straight to his lordship? The friend to whom I'd be writing is a man he considers dead. If he learns that he's still alive, and finds out his whereabouts—"

The little maid had burst into a flood of tears. "Oh, madam, I can't bear this coldness. You've been so kind to me. No high and mighty airs, no scolding and shouting. You treat me more like a sister than like a servant.

172

Do you wonder I've grown to love you? His lordship's my master, it's true, but he rules by fear; you rule by love. I'd risk anything for you, even his anger. Only trust me, my lady. Give me the chance to prove how much I love you."

The girl had seemed so sincere, so hurt that her daring offer had been met with distrust. Miranda had decided to risk it. She thought of Theo lying in Dr. Johnson's bedroom, fretting for her return, wondering why she was delayed. At least she could let him know that her heart was still steadfast. And perhaps—who knows—he could rally some friends around him and—

No! Those were dangerous thoughts. She must put them out of her mind. One ill-advised move from outside, and Lord Fortescue might put his threat against Amanda into action.

She broke the seal and unfolded the letter, then picked up her quill again and carefully underlined the crucial phrase: *wait patiently until you hear from me further*. She folded and sealed it once more, then sat there tapping her foot, afire with impatience. What could be keeping Ruth? Surely she knew how badly she was needed!

Just as she thought she couldn't bear waiting a moment longer, she saw the bedroom door open and the little maid slip through it. Miranda sprang up from the writing table to greet her. Her face was flushed, and she seemed to be short of breath. *What now?* thought Miranda. *Have we some new complication?* "Where have you been, Ruth," she asked, trying to keep the note of annoyance out of her voice. "You said you'd be coming straight back after having your supper."

"Oh, madam, I'm dreadfully sorry. It was the tray that kept me. Cook had no one to carry it up, so she lighted on me. I tried to excuse myself, but she wouldn't have it. I hurried as fast as I could."

"Dear child, wait and catch your breath. Where did

173

you carry this tray, that it's winded you so? To whom were you taking it?"

A look of consternation spread over little Ruth's face. She clapped her hand over her mouth. Her eyes shifted around the room, looking everywhere but into Miranda's. Finally she gulped and said in a shaky voice, "It's Tom, the underfootman. He's been very ill, and can't leave his room in the garret. He must have his food brought to him."

She's lying. She can't be trusted! The instant conviction brought a bitter bilious taste to the back of Miranda's throat. She'd been counting so much on the chance Ruth seemed to offer. Now she saw how rash she'd been in accepting the girl's pretended allegiance. When she'd lied about so innocuous a matter as where she'd carried a tray, could one really expect her to safeguard this dangerous letter?

"Have you finished your letter, my lady?" The girl still found it hard to look her straight in the eye. At least she had the grace to feel guilty for her attempt at entrapment. "The letter?" Miranda feigned to be puzzled. "Oh, that whim I had this morning. No, Ruth, I've changed my mind. You needn't have hurried so fast. I won't need your services now for the next few hours."

She saw the girl flinch as though Miranda had slapped her. "You have no need of my help, madam? But surely—I thought you'd decided—"

Miranda deliberately pretended to misunderstand her. "Help with undressing? Not yet, Ruth. I'm far too restless yet to take to my bed. A few hours of solitude now, to prepare me for sleep..." She looked meaningfully at the girl. *Go now, and leave me alone,* she wanted to shout. *You're Fortescue's spy, like all the rest of them here.*

The maid seemed to read in her face the unspoken message. "I'm sorry, my lady," she said in a tremulous voice. "I hoped I could help you. I'll leave you now.

174

Please call me the moment you need me to help you undress."

She turned to go, but just as she reached the door, a few sharp raps made her halt in her tracks. She darted a glance at Miranda, then opened the door a crack and exchanged a few hurried words with a servant outside. Then she raised her voice—*for my benefit?* Miranda wondered—and repeated her answer more loudly. "No, she can't see him. She's already gone to bed. Please convey her regrets to Sir Lucas, and tell him she's much too tired to receive him tonight." A few more murmured words from the servant outside; then Ruth closed the door and turned again to Miranda.

"I hope I did right, dear madam. I can see how strongly you need to be left alone. And I know you don't like to tell lies. But that's what servants are for, to tell your lies for you." She gazed wistfully up at Miranda, obviously hoping that her intervention would put her back into favor. But Miranda had learned her lesson: *trust no one.* "You presume a little too much, Ruth," she said coldly. "In the future, permit me to make my own excuses."

Ruth's lower lip trembled. A stricken look filled her eyes. Without further words, she turned and went out of the room. As the door closed behind her, Miranda sank into a chair, breathing a sigh of relief for the privilege of being alone at last.

And who was it earned you that respite? The girl you spoke to so harshly. Miranda brushed away the accusing thought. Ruth had her own reasons, no doubt, for wanting to be accepted as Miranda's ally. Still, whatever her motives, she'd gained her one more postponement of that dreaded *tête-à-tête.* But how much longer could she manage to put him off? She was running out of excuses. Headaches, a dizzy spell, inordinate tiredness—Sir Lucas must think it strange that a lady who bloomed so brightly at the breakfast table should become such a wilting flower by the time he came home in the evening from his affairs in the city.

The curious thing was that, much as she dreaded his power, she preferred his company to that of anyone else in that household. He was such a congenial companion on most occasions. He had none of his nephew's haughty airs, but treated everyone as though they were his equals. He seemed to spend half his time below stairs; she'd even seen him gossiping with one of the coachmen.

Once in a while, when Fortescue happened to broach a tender subject, he'd explode into passionate fury, as he had the night they first met. It was impossible to predict what would trigger these outbursts. The anti-slavery movement, the fashion of quizzing glasses, the different varieties of tea—it took but a word or two on one of these disparate subjects to turn him into a choleric stranger, ranting and raving, the maniac gleam in his eyes. Fortescue, clearly bewildered, had given up his attempt to pose as the champion of virtue, having found that a mention of *sin in high places* would bring but a sly quip or two, while the words *sound economy* might set off a tirade.

To Miranda herself, he was never less than cordial, the epitome of the doting old uncle. But what did he really think of her? That confidential whisper about the *raven-haired beauty*—what had he meant by that? He wasn't in league with Charles Halstead; his tirade against imposters convinced her of that. Or was he playing some game, pretending to hate her falseness only for her protection, awaiting the proper moment to appear as an ally?

She quashed that thought instantly. Hadn't she learned her lesson: *trust no one here?* All this kindness of his was meant to soften her spirit, tempt her into the trap of confiding in him so that he could use her own confession against her. No, she'd have to hold fast to her first instinctive reaction: *don't give him the chance to question you in private.*

An insistent rat-a-tat-tat broke into her speculations. She sprang to her feet in dismay. She knew that knock. Why had Fortescue come to see her? That wasn't his habit, not since she'd come back from Portsmouth. He might play the husband in public, but in private, he made it clear, he wanted no bedroom encounters with the child of Italian peasants.

She'd thanked her stars for the gift of privacy. Was even that to be snatched from her now? The knock came again, more insistent. "Come in," she said, hating the way her voice quavered. She knew in her bones that whatever he'd come to say would bode her no good. But there was no use resisting. This was his house. She was his prisoner.

He opened the door, stepped in, and closed it behind him, then leaned back against it, regarding her with an insolent stare. "I've come to inspect your gown, madam. The one you've chosen for Lady Sudbrooke's ball."

"My gown, Lord Fortescue?" Miranda was startled. What did this new whim mean? "That's a rather strange request. Surely that's a matter between myself and my seamstress."

"It has been, in the past. I have come to remedy that unfortunate situation. The gown you wore to Lady Harwood's assembly was not at all up to the mark. So plain and severe, with scarcely a satin bow or a bit of ruching."

"It suited my taste, sir. I don't like all these fancy trimmings."

"I'm not concerned with your dubious sense of what suits you. I'm concerned with maintaining my credit before the world. If an Englishman's wife is not dressed in the latest fashion, the whisper goes round that his credit is open to question. There's been far too much such talk where I am concerned. I want to quash it completely. Now, if you'll show me your gown?"

"I haven't decided yet. You know that these balls give me no pleasure. Won't you make some excuse for me, and go by yourself?"

"I don't choose to go by myself. I choose to go with

177

my wife. Surely you understand why I need you besid
me? All London saw me marry a dark-haired Amanda
Fitton. They must continue to see that dark-haired lady
beside me. They must grow so used to that sight that
a fair-haired Amanda would be unthinkable. Then if
your golden-haired friend should ever be brought to
court, her protests would be dismissed as an obvious
falsehood."

Miranda felt a pang of fear shoot through her. "You
plan to bring her to court? But you said if I'd hold my
peace, you wouldn't press charges!"

"My temper is wearing thin. I had hoped she would
quickly see reason, but the girl remains obdurate. I
had not expected a gentleman's daughter to be such a
virago. No doubt it's the influence of all those barbarian
Italians."

"You've seen Amanda? You've gone to Bedlam to
talk with her?"

"Gone to Bedlam? Of course not. Why should I suffer
the noise and stench of Bedlam? I can see Miss Fitton
whenever it suits my fancy. I've told you before, the
power of an English peer is far beyond your peasant
understanding."

Miranda's heart plummeted. What could she do
against this powerful man, who could summon Amanda
back and forth from Bedlam at his slightest whim?
"How is Amanda faring?" she asked in a humbler tone.
"Do they feed her well? Does she have a cell of her own,
or is forced to mingle with all those mad people?"

An amused smile. "I assure you, Miss Fitton's privacy is thoroughly respected. Despite a few minor hard-
ships, she's in a more comfortable place than Sir Lucas's canefields."

The final jab broke through her shaky resistance.
"I can't bear these threats," she cried. "*I'm* the imposter. Let me go to Sir Lucas. Let *him* say how I'll be
punished. Amanda's committed no crime. She's never
claimed to be other than what she was born—an English gentleman's daughter."

"You forget that this gentleman's daughter attempted to stab me."

"That's a damned lie, and you know it!" Miranda was shouting now, regardless of consequences. "You don't dare to bring those trumped-up charges against her. No court will believe you!"

His lordship seemed taken aback by her furious onslaught. He reached out to pat her shoulder, obviously trying to soothe her. "Calm yourself, please, Miss Testa," he said in a quiet voice. "There's no need for all these hysterics. Neither you nor your friend need ever go near the canefields. She'll come to her senses soon. I've no doubt of that. Before the year is out, the two of you will depart for Italy. The *ton* is already aware of your inexplicable love for that heathen country. I'll pretend at first you are there on a lengthy visit. After a suitable interval, a divorce can be arranged. Meanwhile, however, I need the visible presence of a rich and wellborn wife to shore up my shaky credit. You will provide that presence for as long as I tell you. I think I've made myself clear? Now, show me the gown you intend for Lady Sudbrooke's."

Chapter Eighteen

Miranda sat stiff and straight as the traveling chariot jolted through the woods on its way to Chiswick. Lord Fortescue's choice for the evening was a gown of pale green damask, lavishly beaded with seed pearls, its overskirt looped with wine-colored velvet bows to reveal a quilted petticoat of pink figured silk. Her voluminous black velvet cloak was trimmed with ermine. She felt uncomfortable, as ostentatious as a barnyard hen that had sprouted peacock feathers.

She dreaded the evening ahead. That empty chatter, those supercilious smiles, the pitying looks when they thought she wasn't watching. Lavish compliments to her face; behind her back the same old malicious gossip. *Oh, yes; Lady B.'s still very much in the picture. If the little bride only knew. Fortescue's managed to get the best of both worlds.* And she was expected to go smiling through this jungle, as if her heart was full of joy instead of despair.

The only good thing one could say about this unpleasant excursion was that it meant another evening away from Sir Lucas. On the question of balls, he'd come down on the puritan side. *These frivolous pastimes. I've little taste for 'em, nephew.* So they'd left him behind in the mansion, much to Miranda's relief. The canny old man had been growing very impatient with her excuses. She'd seen him looking at her with a shrewd expression, as if he'd finally come to some conclusion about her. Any moment now, he'd confront her, demand the truth—and then the fat would really be in the fire!

She shot a quick glance at the burly man to her right. Warmed by an excellent dinner, he'd fallen into a doze, his chin sunk into his chest, his mouth gaping open. He seemed better tempered today than he'd been for weeks. Had he seen Amanda again? Had she given him the impression that she was about to yield to his greedy demands?

A week ago, the thought would have filled her with panic. Now her feelings were painfully mixed. Of course she still hoped for Amanda's continued defiance; it proved she had not succumbed to her fearful ordeal. But more and more often these days, she found herself thinking that surrender would not be the end of the world. The estates were important, yes; but scarcely worth a life of perpetual torment. If Amanda gave in, at least they could go back to Florence. She might have to sell some land, but surely there'd be enough left to keep her in modest comfort. A fleeting memory rippled toward her through the dusk—Theo's worried look; her own confident voice: *A poor man can be happier than Midas.* It might take Amanda some time to agree with that sentiment. But she'd learn to be happy with less, especially if her dear Charles were there to console her. . . .

The chariot jerked to a halt, almost flinging her out of her seat. Surely they hadn't reached Chiswick already? She peered out the windows, but could make out nothing but tree trunks. Why were they stopping here in the midst of this wood, obviously miles from nowhere?

Throw down your arms! No tricks, now! The words rang out sharp and clear through the murmuring dusk. She saw them then, the two masked men with pistols, one confronting the coachman, the other already grasping the handle on Lord Fortescue's side of the chariot.

"What in damnation!" Fortescue was awake now, groping in vain for a sword that wasn't there. The masked man's pistol was pointing straight at his head. As he became fully aware of his danger, Fortescue shrank back into the seat and grew very still, as though by avoiding all motion he could make the intruders disappear. "If you want my purse—" he muttered between clenched teeth.

"Out of the coach, sir." The words had a guttural sound, as though the highwayman was disguising his voice. Fortescue didn't move.

"Out, if you value your life." The pistol came closer, held in a steady hand that showed no signs of wavering.

"Damn you to hell!" Fortescue slowly shifted his heavy bulk through the open door. He stood with his back to the chariot. There were two men facing him now, both holding pistols. Miranda caught a glimpse of the coachman, stretched out on the road a few feet ahead of the carriage. His arms and legs were bound; his mouth was gagged. No doubt they'd tied up the footman just as securely.

She gazed at the scene in horror as the man with the guttural voice proceeded to gag and bind Lord Fortescue. He went through the ordeal in silence, not deigning to protest further. The second man's pistol hovered ominously close to his head.

She squeezed back into her corner, as though she hoped to become invisible. What in the world were they after? Why didn't they search his pockets, take what they could find, and then let them proceed on their way? Why truss the victims up like Christmas geese?

Her heart leapt into her mouth as she heard the

doorlatch rattle beside her. A rough hand reached in and seized her by the shoulder. "Come along, miss. Out of the carriage." She felt as though she'd suddenly turned to ice. What did they want with her? "I have no money," she gasped. "Only these rings and earrings. You're welcome to those." The highwayman ignored her frightened offer. He clambered up into the chariot, snatched her up in his arms, then leapt to the ground and hurried to a spot where two whinnying horses stood tethered, a little way off the road in a grove of saplings.

"Help!" shrieked Miranda. "Help!" In the quiet woods, the shout sounded as loud as the peal of a hunting horn. "Hush, my darling," whispered a voice close to her ear. "My darling Miranda, it's Theo. Be still now. We've come to your rescue."

The warm tide of joy flooding her veins turned her limp as a baby. She threw her arms round his neck, and clung to his muscular frame like a drowning swimmer. How strong and agile he was! He must have recovered completely from that awful wound. And he'd called her *Miranda!* He'd found out her secret! Mrs. Hester must have told him, despite her promise. But it hadn't turned him against her; he still called her his darling; he'd come to her rescue. "Oh, Theo!" she cried. "Why did I ever doubt you?"

A hurrying figure flashed past them. The second masked man reached his horse and leapt into the saddle. "Hand her up to me, Moreland," he said in a low, urgent voice. "Here, Miranda, give me your hand." It wasn't the guttural voice she had heard before. He spoke like a gentleman. There was something about him that brought back a teasing memory. The Bertolini gardens—a golden-haired girl walking beside a handsome, uniformed man—"Lieutenant Charles!" she exclaimed! "So you've come at last—"

Her words were cut short by an urgent shout from Theo. At the very same moment, she heard the sound of hooves, and saw the slight, crouching man galloping down the road toward them. *Halt or I shoot!* The words came out in a roar, much too loud a sound for so small a man. Charles's horse shied away abruptly. She felt herself falling back into Theo's arms. He lowered her to the ground, then quickly let go of her and awkwardly tried to pull the pistol out of his belt.

Hands in the air! The horseman had reached them now. He was pointing a pistol at Theo. She saw a flickering gleam from his wire-rimmed spectacles and knew at once who it was.

Numb with disappointment, Miranda watched Theo raise his hands into the air. She glanced up at Charles. His hands were in the air, too. *Dio mio,* thought Miranda, *you're not going to let him subdue you? He's just a feeble old man; he can't do you any harm.*

"Throw down your arms," commanded Sir Lucas firmly. Miranda could see the fanatic gleam in his eyes. His maniac fit was upon him. Perhaps it was just as well that Charles and Theo seemed ready to do his bidding. Behind her, she heard Charles's pistol hit the ground with a thud. Theo was staring up at the mounted man as though under a spell. His pistol was still in his belt. Miranda held her breath. Would he reach for it after all? Or would these two strong men meekly surrender themselves to the little merchant?

She felt it before she saw it; Theo's sudden lunge toward Sir Lucas's stirrup. Then all hell seemed to break loose—a flurry of shouts and blows, the quiet night split apart by a deafening blast. Instinctively, Miranda threw up one arm to protect her eyes from the powder flash. When she opened them again, Theo was on the ground, Sir Lucas's pistol grasped tightly in his hand. Charles was urging his horse straight toward Sir Lucas. His sword was out, the point toward Sir Lucas's throat. "He's got another pistol," he was shouting to Theo. "Mount, man! Mount and away! I can't hold him off more than a minute."

Sure enough, the small man's hand was resting on the butt of another pistol. But with Charles's sword at

184

his throat, he was evidently content to let it stay in its holster.

Theo was stumbling up from the ground, still holding the now useless pistol. She could see his anguished eyes, looking at her through the slit in his mask. He was trying to give her some kind of instructions, but he couldn't force his voice above a whisper. At last he gave up in frustration, ran for his horse, leapt into his saddle, and rode off into the night. Charles wheeled his own mount and immediately followed his fleeing comrade. An obviously shaky Sir Lucas slid down from his horse and helped Miranda to pull herself up off the ground, peering anxiously at her all the while.

"What did the ruffian want, girl? Has he injured you? What good luck I decided to come with you after all!"

"I'm quite unharmed, Sir Lucas. You need have no concern about me. But Lord Fortescue and the servants are bound and gagged." She gazed after the little man as he hurried around to the other side of the chariot. She swayed on her feet, feeling utterly spent and lifeless. *Collect your wits, Miranda! You must act as though you're glad to be rescued. You can't let them know how you welcomed those gallant abductors.*

She became abruptly aware that her teeth were chattering. She hadn't noticed the cold until this minute. She gathered her cloak around her and started back toward the carriage. She found Fortescue chafing his wrists and muttering curses. Sir Lucas was bending over the coachman, untying his hands and removing the gag from his mouth. "How much did they take from you, Edward?" he called to Fortescue.

"They didn't want my purse," his lordship shouted back. "The ruffians were after my wife. They meant to snatch her away and hold her for ransom."

Sir Lucas undid the last knot. The coachman slowly got to his feet, a sheepish look on his face. "I'm sorry, my lord," he said to Fortescue, "but I didn't see that pair till the rascals were right on us. With them pistols and all—"

Fortescue brushed him away with an angry gesture. Sir Lucas came back to join his nephew, obviously deep in thought. "Then it wasn't a random attack? They were here of set purpose? They knew you were passing this way? But how could they know?"

"Obviously, someone told them." The pale moonlight was throwing deep shadows across the burly man's face. She couldn't see his eyes, but to judge from the tone of his voice, they were full of pure murder.

"Dear, dear!" exclaimed the little merchant. "Here's a pretty kettle of fish. Who could have told them, I wonder? Who knew you were coming this way?"

"Only three people." The answer ground its way out through gritted teeth. "The coachman. The footman. And my estimable lady."

She could see the small man's face peering up at his nephew. He didn't look startled. He merely looked interested, as though an alleged abduction was a nightly occurrence. "'Pon my word, dear nephew, you lead an exciting life. I swear I can't fathom its tortuous intricacies."

He cast a quick glance at Fortescue. The man was staring grimly into the shadowy woods, obviously lost in thoughts of revenge on his attackers. "You've scarcely been candid with me," Sir Lucas continued. "I must turn to your excellent lady for information. Let's all go back to your house, now, and proceed at last to that long-promised *tête-à-tête*."

Chapter Nineteen

"We'll take it again, from the top." The prompter's caustic voice had an edge of weariness to it. "A little more fire, Mr. Moreland. You're supposed to be deeply in love. But perhaps, at your tender age, you haven't yet encountered that burning passion?"

Theo clamped his lips firmly together, suppressing an angry retort. He *hadn't* been putting much feeling into the part. If only his head didn't ache so abominably!

He focused his gaze on Miss Mansell's face, gazing down at him from the stage box-balcony. Instead of her cool blue eyes, he imagined Miranda's vibrant green ones, gazing worshipfully up at him as he carried her through the trees to the waiting horses. He felt a surge of warmth—half joy, half anguish—arising from some obscure source beneath his breastbone. He willed the warmth into his voice, heard it suffuse the familiar lines with an unaccustomed richness:

*"But soft! what light through yonder window breaks?
It is the east, and Juliet is the sun! ..."*

Once launched on the tide of words, he felt himself carried along as though by a rushing current. He no longer had to grope for a half-remembered line; the words were engraved on his mind, waiting and ready. They came soaring out through the dusty air of the playhouse, filling the space with a leaping sense of excitement. Miss Mansell, startled at first by his sudden aliveness, quickly rose to the challenge, and matched him lyrical note for lyrical note. The lovers fenced, parried, finally declared themselves in a burst of passionate verse. The immortal duet moved sweetly down to its close:

*"Sleep dwell upon thine eyes, peace in thy breast!
Would I were sleep and peace, so sweet to rest!"*

Theo came to himself with a start. It seemed as though someone else had been speaking the lines. He felt tired, wrung dry of all spirit. He couldn't have felt more fatigued if he'd been at hard physical labor all day and night. The previous evening's hard-riding excitement had not drained him half so severely.

"*Bravo*, Moreland! That scene was excellently played." A small, dark-eyed man rose from his seat in the pit and advanced toward the stage. The prompter turned toward him with a gesture of deference. "Good morning, Mr. Garrick. I didn't know you were there. We've had some rough spots this morning, but I believe our new Romeo is finally beginning to get the hang of his part."

Theo felt awkward and foolish, as though he'd arrived half-dressed in an elegant ballroom. He hadn't expected Garrick at this rehearsal. He was semiretired these days and left most of the playhouse business to his assistants. True, they'd spent many hours together, across at the Bedford, discussing the craft of the player over their coffee. But there they had met as equals, fellow idolaters of the world's greatest poet. This was a different encounter—a raw, untried player, presenting himself at the court of the king of the English stage.

"You—you think it will pass? My performance, I mean?" Theo hated himself for the high, reedy sound of his voice. Where had they gone, those round, resonant tones which had just been reverberating as far as the galleries?

"It will do; oh, yes, I'm sure it will do. You've a month yet before your debut. I do have some comments I'd like to give you in private. Will you step in my office a minute?"

Theo's heart took a dive toward his boots. The stern note in Garrick's voice boded no good. Even worse was the call to a private conversation. Praise could be given in public; if one wanted to cushion a man against humiliation, one detailed his faults where public ears couldn't hear them. Sick with apprehension, Theo followed the little man along the winding corridor behind the greenroom and into the little study where he conducted his business.

Garrick sank into a chair beside a rickety table loaded with higgledy-piggledy piles of playscripts. He waved Theo into a threadbare armchair beside it. He stared at him intently for what seemed an interminable period. What was he thinking now? Was he about to cancel Theo's performance? Was he searching for words to let him down lightly?

Finally the great man spoke, in a quiet, offhand voice. "That's a nasty bruise on your forehead. Were you practicing in some tavern for your new calling?"

Theo felt himself flush. He knew Garrick didn't approve of the common run of players, who roistered through life in the London underworld. He himself led a model existence, drinking only in moderation and going home early at night to his charming wife.

"You know me better than that," he said with a show of spirit. "I received that bruise honorably, defending a lady."

"Aha! So you *were* one of those amateur highwaymen! I was sure it was you under that mask. But what was your business with Lady Fortescue?"

Theo gaped at him incredulously for a long, tense moment. He finally managed to gasp an astonished question. "Someone told you about that affair? But how—what in the devil—it happened only last night—"

Garrick's mobile face, heretofore bland and impassive, relaxed in an impish grin. "No one told me, dear Moreland. I saw you myself. Your mask slipped a little when you made that grab for my pistol. It gratifies me to see your look of amazement. Didn't I play my part well?" He pursed up his mouth and puffed out his cheeks, miraculously changing every line of his face. Straightening up in his chair, he thrust out his chest in a martial attitude. *"Halt!"* he barked, the slight hoarseness of age in his voice, *"Halt or I'll shoot!"*

"You were the man who came galloping up on horseback? The man with the brace of pistols?"

Garrick made a little mock bow. "I admit it freely. It was I who gave you that bruise. Your lunge took me by surprise. I struck out at you with my pistol and accidentally discharged it. I'm glad to see I've done you no lasting harm. But I'm deucedly curious to know how you came to be there. I had hoped Lady Fortescue might consent to tell me, but before I could ask her, the poor woman swooned dead away."

Theo's mind was a whirl of quick calculation. Garrick had caught him out squarely. How much did he dare to tell him? Was he in league with his lordship against Miranda? Theo couldn't believe it. He seemed far too pleasant a man for that sort of scheming. All the same, he'd better be wary of telling him too many secrets.

"I had private reasons for what I attempted last

night," he said in a stiff, formal voice. "Before I share them with you, I believe I've the right to know how *you* came to be there."

"A fair request." Garrick thrust out his hand as though sealing a bargain. Theo's inherent caution kept him from reaching to grasp it. Garrick let his hand rest in midair an instant, then flicked his wrist upward as part of a graceful shrug.

"You'll hear my story first, eh? It's easily told. I've been playing a part off stage these past ten days. I've been staying at Fortescue's house, pretending to be his uncle, Sir Lucas Trotter. Surely your charming Amanda has mentioned me? Or am I wrong in believing you know each other?"

"Her name isn't Amanda. She's playing a part as much as yourself." The words had popped out before he had time to think. He caught his breath, awash with consternation. He shouldn't have given away Miranda's secret. Perhaps there was time to retreat, throw Garrick off the track with an alternate explanation. He looked into the merry shrewd eyes, trying desperately to concoct a believable lie. He found he was too confused to think at all clearly. He might as well tell the truth. The great actor's interest was obviously aroused to high pitch. He'd worm out the whole tangled story, sooner or later.

"It's a complicated affair, sir." He proceeded to give all the details he'd learned from Charles—how Miranda's foster sister had coaxed her to take her place; how she'd found herself forced into a fraudulent marriage; how she'd run away to Portsmouth to find Amanda; how she'd come back to spend one ecstatic hour by his bedside, and then disappeared again, drawn back to Fortescue's house by some unknown coercion. Garrick drank it all in, his eyes growing bright with delighted wonder.

"And I prided myself on my excellent masquerade! Your Miranda has beat me all hollow! What a marvelous romance! We must write it all down and play it on Drury Lane stage. So the elegant Lady Fortescue is really a peasant? No wonder she went so pale when I said that my nephew Charles had praised her raven-haired beauty. The true Amanda, I take it, must be fair-haired?"

Theo was suddenly overwhelmed by a flood of anguished suspicions. "Charles told you Miranda was dark? But where did you meet him? He's never mentioned your name. Is he playing a double part?"

"Calm yourself, Moreland; it's nothing so sinister. I've never met Sir Lucas's other nephew. I made up that compliment on the spur of the moment. When I first started playing my part, I didn't know Amanda Fitton existed. My old friend, Sir Lucas, neglected to mention her. But I perceive you're completely at sea; it's time I made clear what induced me to take on this part."

He settled back in his chair, a ruminative glow in his eyes. He was obviously set on making the most of his story. "I met Sir Lucas—plain Lucas Trotter then—some thirty years ago shortly after I made my debut in London. We quickly became firm friends, and we kept in touch with each other over the years since he went out to Jamaica. Early this fall I received a surprising letter. Sir Lucas, he said, was beginning to feel his age, and was ready to make a decision about how to dispose of his quite considerable fortune. He had always assumed that the fairest thing to do was to split it equally between his two nephews, Charles Halstead and Edward Rainey, Lord Fortescue. But Charles, who was visiting him, had brought some disturbing news. His report of Fortescue's habits had stirred my old friend's suspicions that his hard-earned wealth might quickly be gambled away, once Fortescue had it in his possession. But of course, Charles himself had a pressing interest in the matter. Sir Lucas felt he needed a candid opinion of Fortescue's character, and lighted on me as a trusted, detached observer. He asked me to give him my judgment as to what sort of use his fashionable London nephew was likely to make of a fortune bestowed upon him."

"That's what led you into this strange masquerade? A few questions in the back room of White's would have served as well, with far less trouble to you."

The impish gleam flared again in Garrick's eyes. "I considered that course. As you say, it meant far less trouble. But all these years of listening to London gossip have turned me into something of a cynic. I didn't want to do Fortescue an injustice. There was too much at stake for him. So I hit on the scheme of playing Sir Lucas on the intimate stage of his lordship's London mansion. I wrote Fortescue a letter, couched in a fair approximation of my old friend's hand, and made it appear to have come on a ship from Jamaica. Thus heralded, I duly made my grand entrance, and was welcomed with cordial affection—born, as I now believe, of an even greater affection for Sir Lucas's money."

"He let you see the grasping side of his nature? He's usually more careful to hide it from casual acquaintances."

"But I was no casual acquaintance. I was there in his house, observing him carefully from every angle. At first he put on an impressive display of virtue. But I saw straight through his pretense; he's not a very good actor. He doesn't compare on that score with your precious Miranda."

"Miranda!" Theo echoed the name in ecstatic delight. "So you do agree that she's a remarkable person? What a steadfast heart, to embrace this ordeal so bravely! What resourcefulness, what marvelous spirit and wit!"

"She's quite a pleasant young lady." Garrick nodded approvingly. "But it must have given you pause, to find that the girl you loved wasn't really an heiress."

"Not for an instant, sir!" Theo's eyes flashed with scorn. "I'm no fortune hunter. I intend to make my own way. I was happy to learn my Miranda was a poor man's daughter. I suddenly saw a blissful future before us—

Miranda and I together, sharing each meager crust, huddling together for warmth in some threadbare garret—"

"A touching picture." Garricks's smile turned indulgent. "I trust it won't come to that. If the scene I witnessed today is any example, you've the talent to make yourself quite a respectable living. But enough of this; we're digressing. Go on with your explanation. You haven't said what's become of Amanda Fitton."

"We don't know what's become of her. We think she's in Fortescue's house, being held as a prisoner. Poor Charles is half-mad with worry about her."

"That was Halstead last night? Your companion in crime? What a pity I didn't know him. I'd have loved to hear his opinion on how well I was playing his uncle."

"Apparently, too cunningly for comfort. He said he thought it was you—Sir Lucas that is—but he wasn't quite sure. You sounded like his uncle, but the physical resemblance was not really that great."

Garrick's face clouded over. "A disappointing verdict. But of course, it's many years since I've seen Sir Lucas." Then his face brightened again. "Charles Halstead, of course, has seen him quite recently. Lord Fortescue, luckily, never knew him at all. He'd left for Jamaica long before he was born."

"We're digressing again, I'm afraid," Theo said diffidently. "We were talking about Amanda."

"So we were." Garrick's tone turned brisk. "You say you don't know where she is. That explains the attempt I blundered into last night? You thought Miranda would know if she's in that house? Aha! I see. That makes a little more sense of your mad escapade. But suppose she's been hidden away too carefully? I myself have lived in that house, and haven't seen hide nor hair—" He paused abruptly, slapping himself on the forehead. "By all that's holy! Of course! So that's the explanation. Damn my romantic soul, I was concocting all sorts of stories—a demented relative, a secret mistress. It's all quite clear to me now. Amanda is there, locked up in that garret room."

"Garret? What garret?" Theo was looking more confused than ever.

"Fortescue's garret, where else? It made me curious at once when I noticed the servants carrying those well-loaded trays. They fobbed me off with their tale of an invalid footman. But the food came from Fortescue's table, much too delicate for a mere servant's palate."

"Good Lord! Then she really is there!" Theo's eyes were bright with excitement. "Can't you get in to see her? Surely they wouldn't refuse their master's uncle?"

"Yes, they would. I've already tried." Garrick shook his head gloomily. "They pretended to fear for my health, said the footman had got the pox, and it might be contagious."

"The room must have some kind of window. Which side of the house is it on? Perhaps we could come at night, bringing a ladder—"

"With that mob of servants about? You'd be caught for sure, with no convenient horses to carry you out of the reach of his majesty's judges. No, I'll get in and see her myself, but not as Sir Lucas. Despite my advancing years, I can still run the gamut of parts. What sort of servant do you think Amanda would fancy—the cheeky Scrub, or the obsequious Meggot?"

"What does it matter, sir, so long as you get in to see her? Once we're sure she's there, we can go find a magistrate, have him prepare a warrant, and have the bailiffs search the house. We'll swear he's abducted Miranda as well as her friend. When they're safely out of the house, we can bring the whole matter to court, and wrest Amanda's fortune out of the greedy paws of my erstwhile friend."

He broke off abruptly, his exuberance suddenly chilled by the older man's frown. "I don't like that script at all. It lacks precision," mused Garrick. "One never knows where one is with our bribable judges. Besides, I hate courtroom scenes; they're lacking in color. We need a grand finale for this drama of ours—a *deus ex machina,* young lovers pledging their troths, all the loose ends tied up with one master stroke. You look skeptical, young Mr. Moreland. I'll show you I'm serious. But I'll have to have some time to prepare my scene."

"You won't try to rescue Amanda?"

"I'll see her and speak to her. I'll let her know she has friends who are working to help her. But rescue? No, that must wait for a few more weeks."

"A few more weeks! How can you be so cruel? Those girls are in torment."

Garrick's usually genial face assumed a formidable scowl. "I have offered my help, Mr. Moreland. If you wish to proceed on your own—"

"Of course we need your help!" Theo's voice was abject. "After last night's fiasco, we'd be fools to think we ourselves could do what's needed."

Garrick looked mollified. "I'm glad you realize that. If you want my help, you must take it on my conditions. It may ease your mind to know that I've already started to set out the final scene. If Sir Lucas falls in with my wishes, we have all the material we need for a classical denouement."

He saw the dubious look in Theo's eyes. "You think I'm being too frivolous? Prating about aesthetics when lives are at stake? I think you'll learn that the slowest course is the surest. This Fortescue is a fairly dangerous beast. We can't afford merely to wound him; he might thrash about in his death throes and do incalculable damage. We must finish him once and for all— and be sure that *he* knows that he's finished. That's why I cling to the thought of my master stroke. No, no, young Moreland—no questions. *I'm* the impresario here. You must each play the parts I give you, and trust me to weave all the strands into one grand effect."

Theo breathed a sigh of acquiescence. "We're in your hands, Mr. Garrick. Can you give me any idea how soon your scene will be ready?"

Garrick gave him a quick, darting smile. "I've picked a date that is already etched in your mind. The sixth of January."

"The night of my debut! But that's still a month away. You don't mean to say we must leave those young ladies in limbo?"

"Now, now, sir; contain your impatience. The poor things aren't being mistreated; they're warm and well fed."

"But their mental anguish—"

"Trust me to take care of that. I'll go see Amanda today." He paused as a new thought struck him. "Perhaps she'd be glad of word from her young lieutenant. Judging from what you've told me, she probably doesn't know he's back in England. Where is your friend, Charles Halstead? Perhaps he'll write her a letter that I can deliver."

"I'm sure he'd jump at the chance. He'll be as happy as I am to know that you've come to our aid. I left him across at the Bedford; if you'd care to accompany me there?"

"The Bedford it is. Let's be on our way at once. I'll sketch out the parts for you both, the two principal players, and start you learning your lines for our final extravaganza."

Chapter Twenty

Amanda backed away from the small, square window, watching the panes as she went. There was one certain spot where the light came at just the right angle to cast a reflection. Ah, yes; there it was. She could see a dim shape outlined on the windowglass, a dispirited figure in a lemon satin gown with a green-and-white-striped silk waistcoat. She forced herself to straighten the drooping shoulders and lift the chin high. The reflected figure took on a little more life. Then, as Amanda sighed with frustration, it drooped again.

Sick of the sight of her image, Amanda turned her back on it, sank wearily onto the narrow iron cot that stood in the corner of the garret room, and stared gloomily up at the ceiling. The man was truly a monster! Keeping her here all this time, with only the gown she'd arrived in. True, he had offered others, but she'd taken one look at them, and known them for what they were, some house servant's castoffs. She'd spurned them indignantly. Now she wished she'd accepted them. Even a drab muslin gown would have been a change. The lemon satin gown had been one of her favorites. Now she didn't care if she never saw it again.

She felt a stray hair tickling her nose, and impatiently brushed it away, then explored her curls with her fingers, wondering what they looked like after two weeks of neglect. She must appear a proper Medusa. Perhaps it was just as well that the room was without a mirror.

She supposed she should thank her stars that he'd shown a little more sense when it came to her underlinen. That, at least, she could change every day; he'd sent up a lavish supply of delicate cambric garments, nicely embroidered, obviously made for a lady. Miranda's, no doubt, left behind when she fled this house.

At least, that was one consolation. Miranda was free from his powerful grasp, out there somewhere in London, safe in the loving care of devoted friends. Any day now, they'd burst in the door and release her. This alarming adventure would come to a happy ending. She mustn't let him frighten her with his threats. Herself in danger of hanging or transportation? The thought was ridiculous. Such things didn't happen to Nicholas Fitton's daughter.

The clash of angry voices outside her door disrupted her brooding. It sounded as though the guard was arguing with a servant. Were they here with her tray again? It seemed scarcely an hour since she'd had her breakfast. This close confinement had destroyed her appetite. She must try to eat, all the same, to keep up her strength.

She watched the door inch open. This was a different servant, a bent old man who seemed to have trouble walking. He shuffled toward her, bearing the loaded tray in quivering hands. She suppressed an impulse to leap up and take it from him before he dropped it. It wouldn't do to forget her position; she was a lady. However humiliating their master's treatment of her, at least the servants showed her proper respect.

The trembling old servant placed the tray on the three-legged stool that stood beside the cot. "There, me lady, fall to." His voice was unnaturally loud for so feeble a man. And wasn't his form of address a bit overfamiliar? She gave him a gracious smile, and waited for him to leave. He peered at her from under his straggly thatch of graying hair. "I can't leave yet, me lady. I have instructions to stay and see that you eat."

The impudence of the man! She was sure the guard could hear that loud voice of his even through the thick wooden door. What would he think, to hear this old dodderer giving her orders? But of course, it was Fortescue's fault, another demeaning trick to humiliate her. Her best course was to ignore the annoying intruder. Once she finished her meal, he would have no further excuse to inflict his presence on her.

She picked up her spoon and started to eat her soup. The old man smiled and nodded, then shuffled away toward the door. What on earth was he doing? He had his eye to the keyhole, obviously checking to see what was happening outside. What strange maneuver was this? She'd often suspected the guards were spying on her. But a servant spying on them? It didn't make sense.

He gave a low grunt of satisfaction, as though something outside had pleased him. Then he straightened up abruptly, shedding a score of years in one quick, stretching motion. He moved quickly across the room and crouched on the floor beside her, his face tensely alert, his penetrating dark eyes fixed firmly on hers. "Please keep your voice low, Miss Fitton. We don't want the guards to hear us. I've come to let you know that you have good friends outside these walls. We're planning to rescue you. But you mustn't let Fortescue know that you expect us. He must think he's in full control, till the final moment."

For a moment she couldn't believe she had heard him aright. Perhaps she'd fallen asleep, and all this was only a dream? She reached out a testing hand and touched his shoulder. The rough frieze of his shabby waistcoat prickled under her hand.

"Oh, yes; I'm real enough." The man must have been reading her mind. "And so are your friends outside."

"What friends?" she said, astonished. "I have no friends in London, except for Miranda Testa." A sudden tide of joy flowed into her veins. "Now I see! Miranda has sent you to me. How is my dear foster sister? Is she safe and well?"

The crouching man nodded gravely, his eyes still intent on her face. "She's safe enough for the moment. As safe as you are. Though no one's entirely safe under Fortescue's roof."

Amanda went pale with shock. "Are you saying she's still in this house? But I thought she'd escaped, days before I fell into this trap."

"She did run away to Portsmouth, attempting to find you. But unfortunately she returned, hoping to come to your rescue. Now Fortescue has her frightened out of her wits. He's obviously made some dire threat against your welfare, and thus convinced her to play the docile wife."

"Oh, my poor Miranda! Will my conscience ever forgive me? To have led you back into the arms of that loathsome monster! Your fate makes my own paltry suffering seem like the merest trifle."

"Please calm yourself, Miss Fitton. The girl hasn't been harmed; I'll vouch for that. Don't be alarmed for Miranda. Remember that rescue is coming for both of you."

"Does Miranda know that? But of course she must; you said you're a friend of hers."

"A secret friend at the moment. She thinks I'm her enemy. I intend to change that impression within the hour."

Amanda stared at him with a puzzled frown. "This is all so very mysterious. It wasn't Miranda who sent you? Then who told you I was here?"

"Someone you know very well." An impish gleam crept into the stranger's eyes. "He asked me to give you this letter. It may help while away the hours till our next encounter."

One glance at the folded parchment bearing her name was enough to send her spirits soaring. "My darling Charles! I could never mistake his writing. But where did you meet him? How long have you known him? Is he still in Jamaica, or has he come here to London? Where is he staying now? How soon will I see him?"

The man laid a warning finger against his lips, reminding her of the urgent need for caution. "That letter will answer your questions, all but the last one. I'll leave you alone to read it, while I go seek out Miranda."

"Oh, yes. Miranda. You said you would speak to her." Amanda tried vainly to wrench her thoughts away from the beckoning letter. She wanted to rip it open, gulp down its contents at once. But that wouldn't be good manners; she'd have to wait till the stranger took his departure. What was he saying now? She'd been so transported with joy, she'd been only half-listening.

"I shall be very cautious as to how much I tell Miranda. She's not good at keeping secrets. Her face is far too transparent. Don't you agree?"

"Transparent? Oh, yes; I know what you mean. She hasn't the knack of making a white lie convincing. No proper sense of a ladylike reserve. I suppose it has something to do with her peasant background. Of course, you can trust *me* completely. I shan't show the slightest sign that I know of our coming rescue. Do tell me when it will be! I won't mind another day or two here, now that I've heard from dear Charles."

"It won't be a matter of days. Our plan is far from completion. It may be as long as a month before our great scene is prepared."

"A month!" Amanda was livid with horror. "What a cruel trick you are playing! To raise my hopes, then dash them into oblivion."

"Oh, come now, Miss Fitton." What a condescending smile he turned on her! "There are thousands of people in London who would gladly trade places with you. You've plenty to eat and drink; you're warm and sheltered. And, unlike your friend Miranda, you aren't compelled to mask your unhappy heart with a pretense of marital bliss."

Amanda flushed, feeling a pang of remorse. What a self-centered creature she was! The stranger was right; she hadn't much cause to complain, compared to Miranda. "A thousand apologies, sir. You are right to chastise me. I'll endure my confinement bravely for as long as it lasts. I'll account it my punishment for the harm I've done to Miranda with my luckless scheming."

"That's the right spirit, Miss Fitton. The time will pass quickly enough. I trust when we meet again, we won't have to speak in whispers." The stranger rose to his feet, standing erect a moment. Then his shoulders curved inward, his legs turned feeble and crooked, he reached for the barely-touched tray with a trembling hand. She gazed in astonished awe at the transformation. "Wait!" she called after him, then lowered her voice to a whisper. "You haven't told me your name." But the door was already opening. The tottering old servant passed through it, and left her alone.

She reached hungrily for the letter. Its reassuring crispness made her sure she hadn't been dreaming. She quickly broke open the seal and scanned the familiar writing. *My dear, dear Charles. So he really does love me. Not that I really had any question that he remained faithful. How delightful it will be to see him again! And how clever he's been, finding just the right person to make his way into this house. Who could that old man have been? He's obviously an actor. I wouldn't have thought my dear Charles would know that low kind of person. Still, he's just what we need to get me out of this fix. I must remember to see that he's properly rewarded....*

"Good afternoon, my dear niece. How pleased I am to see you up and about! I trust you're fully recovered from last night's fainting spell? Perhaps we can now resume our interesting conversation."

Miranda, startled, laid down the book she'd been reading, and forced herself to meet Sir Lucas's eyes. How had he known where to find her? She'd been so careful not to let anyone know she intended to spend the day in the library. She had counted on Fortescue's absence—affairs of business, he said—to allow her to hide there unnoticed. "Good afternoon, Sir Lucas." She did her best to make her voice sound cordial. "I'm surprised to see you here at this hour of the day."

"My commercial concerns have been brought to a happy conclusion. But my private affairs, I fear, remain unresolved. I hope you'll be able to give me some useful pointers."

"I can't think what you mean, uncle," parried Miranda. "How could I presume to advise a man of your experience? Surely Lord Fortescue is the person you need."

"Please don't play the fool with me, madam." Sir Lucas fixed her with a stern and beady eye. "Your husband has surely informed you of what's at stake in my visit. You must have guessed, both of you, that I'm here to make up my mind how to leave my fortune. That's why I need your help. Will you give me your candid opinion of Edward's chief vices and virtues?"

Miranda regarded him warily. He seemed so sincere in his quest for information. If only she dared to tell him the true extent of his nephew's vices. But it wasn't Edward he wanted to know about. He wanted to know more about her. He already had his suspicions, and now was setting a trap, hoping she'd take the bait and make some damning confession.

"My candid opinion?" she echoed, searching for neutral words to fend off his questions. "But surely, Sir Lucas, you know that I, as a loyal wife, would not

204

breathe a word that would injure my husband's prospects."

"Aha! That's just the point. Is he really your husband? Or are the two of you playing at masquerade?"

Miranda went stiff with alarm, her mind a blank. "I—I can't think what you could mean, sir."

"You know perfectly well what I mean." Sir Lucas's eyes seemed to be boring into her brain. "I don't know who you are, or in what relation you stand to my profligate nephew. But I know you're not the lady you profess to be. I've learned from a trustworthy source that the true Amanda Fitton has silver-blond hair and a fair complexion. 'Pon my word, just look at her blush! So you *have* been lying. Out with it, girl. It's time you told me your secret."

Miranda's heart seemed to have turned to lead. There was no further use in pretending. She'd have to tell him the truth, and take her chances. At least there was one ray of hope; he had already reached the conclusion that his nephew was as guilty as she.

She heaved a deep sigh and turned her face up to him in remorseful appeal. "I crave your mercy, Sir Lucas. It's true I've deceived you. I've masqueraded as someone above my station. My only excuse is this: I didn't do it for gain. I did it for love of a friend, hoping that I could prevent a great injustice. I realize now what a wicked thing I have done. You'll be quite within your rights in having me punished."

"Punished?" Sir Lucas sounded amazed. "What business is it of mine to see you punished? Surely that's a matter between yourself and your conscience?"

Miranda felt a giddy sensation, as if she'd been pressing for hours against an immovable door, and then it had suddenly opened. "I though—that first night at dinner—the way you denounced imposters—you said that a flogging would be too good for them."

The old man blinked several times, as though trying to retrieve an errant memory. "Did I really say that? How very unreasonable! I must have had too much wine. Forgive me, my dear; I sometimes get carried away. Now, if you please, proceed with your explanation. I assure you, whatever you've done, I'm quite ready to make full allowance for your youth and lack of experience."

He beamed at her, a kind, paternal smile. Miranda's last reservation faded away. She poured out the whole tale to him, watching his eyes all the while to see his reaction. The effect was gratifying; as she reached the end of her story, he seemed as fully convinced as she was that Fortescue was the villain of the piece. "So this dastardly nephew of mine has sent Amanda Fitton to Bedlam? To think my sister's son could be so depraved."

"You must have her removed from that hellspot as soon as you can." Miranda was glowing with joy. To find that the man she feared so had proved himself to be her staunchest ally! "I'm sure a word from you would be all that's needed."

"You flatter me, miss. My power is not that extensive. I'll do what I can to remedy this injustice, but I warn you, it's likely to take a considerable time."

"But how can my darling Amanda bear that horrible place? She's led such a sheltered life. We must get her out at once, before her tender nerves are completely shattered. There are others who might help us, if only you'll seek them out. Your nephew Charles—did you know he was here in London? And another friend of mine named Theophilus Moreland. And Mrs. Amelia Hester, the novelist; she said she had friends who might help."

"You overwhelm me, my dear. I'm very glad to hear of these friends of yours. I shall make a point of seeking them out at once. I'm sure we can work it all out in the end—rescue you from your present distasteful position, retrieve Amanda's fortune, and see her safely married to Charles. But I don't expect to be able to do all this quickly. My nephew's rank gives him a great deal of power; we must be very careful not to arouse his suspicions before we're sure of our ground."

Miranda gazed at him with a stricken look. "Are you saying you're not going to help us? That you're leaving Amanda to rot in that dreadful place?"

"I'm not saying that at all. I fully intend to help, to the extent of my powers. But those powers are somewhat feeble, compared with those of my nephew. We must proceed in this matter slowly, step after careful step. The first step, I agree, concerns your friend Amanda." He drew himself up, obviously fired with new resolution. "I'll make you one promise, my dear, which I hope will remove that despair from your pretty eyes. Whatever desperate course I have to pursue, Amanda Fitton will not spend another night confined to Bedlam."

Chapter Twenty-One

"What can be keeping Sir Lucas?" Lord Fortescue stared irritably at the gaily-dressed ladies in the boxes around them. "I vow, I'll be glad to see the last of this pestilential uncle. It was he who proposed this dubious entertainment. Now it's about to start, he's disappeared."

Miranda forced her lips to curve in a smile. She remembered the old man's whisper, as they left Portman Square this evening: *"Play your part well, girl, and leave me alone to play mine."* And what scene are you playing, my wily old Lucas Trotter? Or is that your name at all? I very much doubt it. Like so many people in London, you're not what you seem.

And yet, despite such doubts, she longed to trust him completely. He'd been so unfailingly kind this last weary month. His sly little hints of the coming rescue had time and again restored her flagging spirits. And he'd certainly proved his good faith by saving Amanda from Bedlam.

She fingered the crumpled note in her skirt's deep pocket. *My dear Miranda; we share the same roof again.* She knew it by heart now. She'd read it a hundred times since Ruth had brought it to her, almost a month ago.

Watch and wait. That was what Sir Lucas kept saying. *Don't let him suspect a thing; keep playing the docile wife.* She was growing very tired of watching and waiting. If only he'd tell her a little bit more of his plans. He kept making vague remarks about his *climactic scene.* Surely that must tie in with this night at the playhouse? Especially since he'd called it his *last night in London?*

She smiled again, remembering how adroitly he'd roped Fortescue into his plans. "You'll humor an old man's whim, on his last night in London. The son of an old friend of mine, Theophilus Moreland, is making his debut at Drury Lane...."

Fortescue'd given a start when he heard that name. Miranda knew why; he was shocked to know Theo still lived. He couldn't explain that, of course, to his rich old uncle. He'd been forced to grit his teeth and fall in with his wishes.

A sudden hush swept through the chattering crowd. The music had come to an end; the curtain was rising. The false smile on Miranda's lips turned into a real one. *Theo, my darling Theo! Whatever happens tonight, at least I'll see you once more!* She scanned the crowded stage, waiting for Romeo's entrance, scarcely daring to breathe. *There he is at last! That blue silk coat—he wore it that fatal night. Pray God it's not a bad omen!*

Her whirling thoughts were cut short by surprise and wonder as Theo launched himself on his first long speech. Could that be Theo's voice, so full and rich, piercing her very heart as he spoke of the woes of love? And how gracefully he moved, pacing the stage, his eager gaze raking each part of the crowded playhouse. The pit, the galleries, and finally the glittering boxes—

his eyes fixed on them each in turn, but always stopped maddeningly short of the box that held Lord Fortescue's party.

Miranda was torn between joy and disappointment. She was sure she knew why he avoided looking at her— he'd find the sight too painful. But *she* couldn't look elsewhere. This maddening separation—so tantalizingly close, and yet so far.

And then, like an answer to prayer, he turned straight toward her with a quick, vivid gesture, as if he was throwing all caution to the wind:

> *Love is a smoke rais'd with the fume of sighs;*
> *Being purg'd, a fire sparkling in lovers' eyes;*
> *Being vex'd, a sea nourished with lovers' tears:*
> *What is it else? A madness most discreet,*
> *A choking gall, and a preserving sweet.*

Discreet! Dear God, there was nothing discreet in the way he was gazing at her! The whole house would be in on the secret; he was speaking those eloquent lines to the woman he loved. He seemed to read in her eyes both her joy and her terror—joy at this proof of his love, terror inspired by the angry muttering beside her. He finished the speech with a flourish, and abruptly shifted his gaze in a safer direction, leaving her dazed and shaken.

The rest of the play swept by like a shadowy dream. From time to time she would hear Theo's voice again— that new, rich actor's voice, so full of emotion. The other players scarcely seemed to exist. The playhouse dissolved around her; no one was left in the world but herself and Theo.

She came out of her dream with a start as the curtain descended, astonished to find herself still in Fortescue's box instead of the Capulet tomb. She looked to her left and met Fortescue's sullen gaze; she looked to her right, hoping to see Sir Lucas, hoping the time had come for that *climactic scene* he had promised. With a sinking heart, she saw that his chair was still empty. What in the world was he up to? She'd waited so long for this night. How long must she go on waiting?

Fortescue's patience, too, had come to an end. He was gathering up his cloak and preparing to leave. She felt her heart plummeting. Surely Sir Lucas had asked him there for only one reason—to be part of the promised scene that would mean her rescue. "Leaving so early, my lord?" she managed to murmur. "The evening's not finished yet—there's the afterpiece—"

"I've had enough of this nonsense." Fortescue pushed his way past her to the back of the box. She moved to join him, hating each step that took her away from Theo.

"My sentiments, sir, exactly. We've had enough nonsense." A strangely familiar voice boomed out from the box's back entrance, halting them both in their tracks. A burly man in a capacious red velvet coat was standing there, blocking their exit.

"Dr. Johnson!" gasped Miranda. What was he doing here, glaring at her like an outraged Old Testament prophet?

"I see you cringe from me, madam. No doubt you thought you could keep your guilty secret forever? But that secret will out; I'm here to expose the masquerade you've been foisting on London!"

Miranda couldn't believe her ears. Was this part of Sir Lucas's promised scene? Was Dr. Johnson their ally, coming here to denounce his lordship and demand Amanda's freedom?

She looked wildly around for Sir Lucas. She couldn't find him. Astonished faces stared at her from all the surrounding boxes. Dr. Johnson was holding them spellbound with his denunciation. But he wasn't denouncing the culprit who kept her prisoner. He was denouncing *Miranda,* railing away at the victim, while the true villain stood there pretending to be her defender!

"You see that my wife is not well, sir." Undaunted

by the force of Johnson's wrath, Fortescue sounded cool and apologetic. "Could we not discuss this affair in some more private place?"

"I've chosen the best place and time we shall ever find." The nearsighted eyes seemed to blaze with a holy fire. "This cunning young woman beside you has falsely foisted herself on all of fashionable London. You, sir, as her foremost victim, should rejoice to see her nefarious scheme exposed before the very same people she's deceived so vilely."

"Dr. Johnson," Miranda cried, "if Sir Lucas has told you the truth, why are you blaming me? Surely you know it's his lordship—"

"Silence, you wicked strumpet! I know nothing of any Sir Lucas. My information comes from an irrefutable source. I've brought a witness along to confront and accuse you." He turned with a sweeping gesture to clear the way for a man who was standing behind him, a frail, parchment-skinned old man whose cloud of white hair stood out from his head like a halo. Miranda knew him at once, despite the five years since she'd seen him.

"*Maestro* MacCrae!" she cried, all her dismay dissolved in a surge of joy. She sprang toward him, arms outstretched. "If only I'd known all this time that you were in London. I thought I was friendless, alone—"

"Keep your distance, you infamous creature." There was no hint of frailness or age in the white-haired man's voice. Miranda shrank back from him, appalled by the look of contempt he was turning upon her.

"But *Maestro*—surely you know me?"

"I know you all too well, Miranda Testa. You're the child of Italian peasants. How dare you usurp your mistress's name and position? After all she has done for you, to turn on her thus so cruelly! What have you done with the real Amanda Fitton? Come, girl, give us an answer. Don't try to brazen things out. You'll have to confess in the end. Dr. Johnson and I will see that you do."

Miranda's thoughts were in a whirl of confusion. She stared in dismay at the tense, watchful faces around her. It was there in everyone's eyes, that same look of outraged contempt. Where on earth was Sir Lucas? Surely he'd come to her aid now, explain to this angry man that she was as much a victim as poor Amanda.

Then she noticed that Fortescue's face had gone rigid and staring. Her heart gave a sudden leap of exultation. He was just as frightened as she was, as terrified by that sea of unfriendly eyes around them! She'd longed for witnesses; here they were by the hundreds. The moment for truth had come; she had only to seize it.

"Yes, dear *Maestro* MacCrae, I confess it gladly." She beamed at the hostile faces, flung out her arms to them in delighted welcome. "I proclaim my fraud, here before all the world. You all thought you saw me married to this man beside me. But there never was any marriage. I'm not Lady Fortescue. I am Miranda Testa. The whole thing's been a charade from the very beginning."

She felt Fortescue grasp her arm in a steely grip. "Dr. Johnson," he muttered grimly, "I fear *you've* been gravely deceived. My wife's not herself of late. She's been babbling all sorts of madness. I must take her away from here now, put her under a doctor's care—"

Miranda used all her strength to wrest her arm out of his grasp. "I'm telling the truth!" she cried. "You know it's the truth, you monster! You've met the real Amanda. You know she looks nothing like me." She raised both hands and tore the wig from her head, dashing it to the ground, then stood there glaring at him as the glossy, black ringlets cascaded around her shoulders. "She's fair and pale-skinned. I'm dark and tawny. That's what this dear friend of my childhood will tell them all now, all the people of London you've forced me to help you deceive."

"You're raving," Fortescue shouted. "You're all of you raving. And you, Dr. Samuel Johnson, are the maddest one of the lot." He looked around the circle of watching faces as though daring anyone to dispute him. "You proclaim my wife a pretender and my marriage a fraud? I fling the lie back in your faces! I challenge you to produce the real Amanda!"

He glared at *Maestro* MacCrae and Dr. Johnson. The big man glared back at him belligerently. The smaller man looked confused, and turned appealingly to Miranda, as if to call on her once more to make a confession.

"Aha!" His lordship's voice rang out on a note of triumph. "You can't do it, you see. There's a very good reason you can't. This golden-haired Amanda simply doesn't exist."

"I believe that's my cue, sir." The voice cut through the hushed playhouse as triumphantly as had his lordship's. All the watching eyes turned to Sir Lucas Trotter, as he deftly ducked under the rail at the back of the box and made his way straight toward his glowering nephew.

"Sir Lucas!" Miranda moved eagerly toward him, then stopped halfway. The voice had been that of Sir Lucas, but this elegant man had nothing in common with that black-clothed old merchant except the familiar grin on his lined old face. Instead of the rusty black clothes of the colonial merchant, he wore the satin coat of a man of fashion. Instead of the untidy straggling hair, this man wore a gleaming wig. She'd never seen him on stage, had seen only his picture, but she instantly recognized him—and so did Dr. Johnson.

"Davy Garrick!" the portly man blared out in stentorian tones. "So you're part of this brouhaha! I must call upon you, it seems, to prove that Mr. MacCrae and myself are in our right minds."

"That's easily done," said David Garrick. He moved to the back of the box, pulled aside the curtain. "My lords and ladies; good people of London—you've seen a false bride exposed. I present you a true one. Here is the former Miss Amanda Fitton—and her new husband, Lieutenant Charles Halstead."

And there—at last—was Amanda, radiant in her lemon satin gown, her golden ringlets piled high on her head. Miranda stood there transfixed for a moment, then rushed toward her with arms outstretched. *Maestro* MacCrae was there before her, his seamed old face streaming with tears. "So it was all one of your pranks, my little Amanda! What a fool I was to blame your foster sister. You were always full of them, these sly little schemes, but this one surpasses them all."

"Please don't scold her, *Maestro* MacCrae. You don't understand the horror she's had to suffer." Miranda embraced her friend, her eyes alight with joy. "You look perfectly lovely, Amanda. No one would ever dream that you had spent those two horrible weeks in Bedlam!"

A trace of confusion furrowed Amanda's brow. Then she was smiling again, the confident sunny smile Miranda loved so. "Bedlam? Is that what the villain told you? You should have known he'd never dare do that. Not to the only daughter of Nicholas Fitton—" She stopped abruptly, a stricken look clouding her eyes, as if she'd let something slip she now regretted. The lapse—whatever it was—lasted only an instant. Then she turned gaily to Charles, looking up into his eyes with a brilliant smile. "But that's all behind us now, thanks to our gallant heroes! How exciting it was, the way you and Mr. Garrick overpowered the guards and snatched us out of that awful garret. My brave, brave Charles. Risking such danger for me!"

"A paltry risk, compared to the prize it won me." Charles gazed down at her with his heart in his eyes.

"A poor, tattered prize, I fear. My hair is quite a disaster." Amanda glanced down with a grimace at the green and white waistcoat. "And this is hardly the sort of attire I'd have chosen for my wedding. Perhaps we'll be married again, once we're back in Florence, so I can wear something a little more *à la mode*."

Miranda turned accusing eyes toward Garrick. "You

215

let me believe she'd really been sent to Bedlam! I suppose you knew all the time."

"Please, Miranda, don't scold your poor old uncle." She had to laugh at him then, at the cracked old voice emerging from all that grandeur. "Of course I won't scold you," she said. "You promised a marvelous scene, and you've certainly produced one. But how in the world did you ever find Mr. MacCrae? That was the best touch of all, even though I was terribly shocked when you had him denounce me."

"I was as shocked as you." Garrick smiled ruefully. "I promised you a grand climax, but this one surpassed my wildest expectations." He turned to the portly man beside him. "Now, my dear Sam, it's time for *your* explanation."

"Easily given, sir. I think you know my Scottish friend, Mr. James Boswell. During his younger days, he once met the late Mr. Fitton, and corresponded with him for a number of years. When I met the supposed Miss Fitton here in London"—he waved toward Miranda—"I naturally mentioned our meeting in a letter to him, described the young lady at length, and told him about her brilliant marriage."

"You described her as being dark-haired with a tawny complexion," Mr. MacCrae broke in. "Mr. Boswell's my friend and landlord up in Scotland. He brought Dr. Johnson's letter to me, feeling quite perplexed. He remembered Amanda, you see, remembered her golden curls and skin like alabaster."

"And *you* remembered me, your other pupil, the dark-haired intruder—"

Amanda gasped in dismay, and looked reproachfully at Miranda. "Oh, don't say that, my dear sister! You're not an intruder, far from it."

"I jumped to conclusions, my dear." *Maestro* MacCrae's smile was tinged with melancholy. "I'm sorry for that. I should have remembered how open and honest you were, and how much you always adored our dear Amanda. Can you ever forgive this poor dotard, exiled for years in a dour and suspicious climate?"

"Of course I forgive you, dear *Maestro*." Miranda beamed at him. "After all, it was you who finally gave me the chance to proclaim the truth."

"That's enough talk of forgiveness," Garrick cut in crisply. "I for one will never forgive you for stealing my crowning scene. But that scene's not over yet, as any playwright could tell you. We have rescued the heroines—these two charming young ladies—but the villain remains to be punished." He swung around toward the silent red-faced man whom they'd all forgotten in the excitement of greeting Amanda. He'd been edging around toward the back of the box, clearly intending to slip away unobserved.

"Please don't leave us, your lordship!" Garrick continued to smile, but his steely tone turned the request into a command.

Fortescue halted abruptly, glowering at him. "Punishment, Mr. Garrick? Surely you've gone to great lengths to do that already! You've wormed your way into my house under false pretenses, you've conspired with my household against me—"

Miranda couldn't believe her ears. The man was still trying to brazen it out, and shift part of the blame to Garrick. She looked back at the master actor, expecting to find him as indignant as she was. But he seemed not the least bit perturbed; he grinned at Fortescue blandly, with a little mock bow.

"Guilty as charged, my lord. I, too, played a fraudulent part. But like Miranda's, my fraud was inspired by friendship. I won't bore our audience now by reciting the details. Suffice it to say that my impersonation of Sir Lucas Trotter enabled that worthy man—still back in Jamaica, your lordship—to make an important decision. His letter arrived this morning, just in time to provide an epilogue to our show."

He made a fine piece of stage business of drawing the folded parchment out of his pocket and opening it with a flourish. By the time he was ready to read it, the excited hubbub in the neighboring boxes had dwindled to an expectant hush.

"*My dear friend Garrick.*" He intoned the first words grandly, then dropped his voice and murmured under his breath, "*Et cetera, et cetera, et cetera.* Ah, here's the important part!" The famous voice swelled to fill the playhouse. "*I have today given my lawyers instructions to settle the whole of my fortune on my nephew—Lieutenant Charles Halstead.*"

"Hell and damnation! You detestable mountebank!" The circle of startled eyes swung round to Lord Fortescue, now hunched like a wounded bull against the box's back curtain. "So you've destroyed that too, my only chance of escaping utter ruin. And you two pestilent bitches! Wouldn't you love to see me in debtor's prison? But you won't have that satisfaction. By tomorrow morning, I'll be where your bailiffs can't catch me."

He made a sudden plunge toward the curtained back of the box, and disappeared. Charles whipped out his sword and started after him, but a few seconds later he was hustled back into the box, complaining loudly to the two burly men who held him in their practiced grip. "What the hell are you doing, Garrick?" he shouted to the smiling actor. "I thought you were on our side. Now these bullies of yours have just kept me from scotching that viper."

Garrick smiled at him unconcernedly, an impish gleam in his eyes. "A comedy, sir, is never allowed to end in bloodshed. I propose we permit his lordship to go where he pleases. For a man who rails at such length against foreign countries, exile in France or Spain is a far worse fate than a comfortable cell in the Fleet. The courts will quickly restore Amanda's fortune."

"Oh, yes, Charles, do let him go," broke in Amanda. "As Mr. Garrick says, the courts will take care of things. Meanwhile your delightful new expectations will enable the three of us to live very comfortably, once we're back at the villa."

"The three of us?" Miranda felt a telltale flush rise to her face. "That's kind of you, Amanda, but I'm sure you and Charles would prefer to be by yourselves."

"Nonsense, my dearest Miranda. Of course you'll come with us. I've already told Charles my plan. He agrees with me; you must share the villa with us. After all you've endured for my sake, it's my evident duty to see that you're well taken care of, all the rest of your life."

And so I will be, but not, dear sister, by you. Miranda's heart began to pound wildly. Her throat felt scratchy and dry. "But—but I've learned to love living in England," she stammered. "I really don't want to go back with you to Florence."

"Ridiculous child! What on earth would you do in this barbarous country? Haven't you seen how abominably they treat their servants? No, not another word. My mind is made up. I know you don't realize fully what I mean by *my duty*." She bit her lips nervously, then looked at Charles as though seeking his guidance. "I know I've never mentioned this subject before. It— it's quite a delicate matter. But now I'm a married woman, perhaps I can manage to tell you. Miranda— you too are Nicholas Fitton's daughter!" Her determined look turned to anxious concern. "I see it's come as a terrible shock to you. But the secret had to come out, sooner or later. Now surely you'll see why I want you to share our villa. It's not out of charity; I'm merely restoring you to your proper station."

Miranda stared at her, dazed and astonished. So Amanda had known all the time! After she had been at such pains to keep that embarrassing secret!

It was very convenient for her to pretend not to know. Miranda quashed the disloyal thought on the instant. Why should she dig up the past? It was really quite handsome, this offer of restitution. A year ago, she'd have thought it the height of good fortune. But so much had happened since then. . . .

"Thank you, Amanda," she said, "for making that generous offer. But perhaps I have other ideas of my proper station. I think our dear Mr. Garrick can guess my meaning."

Garrick looked startled at first, then gave her a smile of paternal understanding. "Indeed I can, my dear. Good Lord, how remiss I've been. Mr. Moreland must think I'm a boor for waiting so long to congratulate him on his excellent Romeo. Perhaps I can deputize you to repair that omission? Or is it below your new station to speak to mere actors?"

Miranda answered him grin for impish grin. "Indeed not, Mr. Garrick. As you kindly explained to me once, we're *all* imposters, one way or another."

Epilogue

Miranda heard the raised voices minutes before she reached Theo's dressing room.

"But I will go! I must go, Mrs. Hester. Miranda is out there, I tell you. I saw her for a few moments only, but her face swam before me through all the rest of the play."

"Over my dead body, Theo Moreland! I've been plotting this happy ending for too many weeks to see you spoil it all now. Leave things to Mr. Garrick. Didn't he promise to rescue them both tonight?"

"Garrick's a cautious old man. How can he rescue Miranda? I must go, I tell you. I *will* go—"

Miranda had just raised her hand to knock on the dressing-room door when it suddenly gave way before her. She stood there face to face with a gaping Theo. They were both too astonished to speak. It was a breathless Mrs. Hester who broke the silence. "Miranda, my dear, what has happened? You look as though you ran into some kind of trouble?"

"Trouble?" echoed Miranda absently, all her senses entranced by the sight of that longed-for face. "What on earth do you mean? How could there by any trouble when I'm here with Theo?"

Her ecstatic look dispelled Mrs. Hester's fears. "It all went well, then? Thank God! When I saw that wild look on your face and your hair all in disarray, I feared Mr. Garrick's scene might have miscarried."

"My hair!" exclaimed Miranda, abruptly regaining her senses. "Good Lord! I must look a fright!" She made a few futile gestures toward smoothing her curls into a semblance of order. Theo soon put a stop to that by snatching one of her hands and covering it with kisses.

"I forbid you to touch one curl," he murmured, reaching out and pulling her to him. "This is just how my angel looked the day she descended from heaven to kneel at my bedside, the day I swore that nothing should ever part us."

A tiny shiver of fear nudged at Miranda's heart. "That promise was made to a girl named Amanda Fitton. Now that you know who I am—"

Theo groaned in exasperation. "My darling, what's in a name? It wasn't your name and fortune I fell in love with, but this woman I hold in my arms and will never part from. How can I banish that doubt from those lovely eyes? I'll swear it again, this very moment. Mrs. Hester shall be our witness."

He looked around the room in search of that amiable lady. "Where has she gone?" He stared at Miranda, astonished. "Why did she slip away without saying good-bye?"

A glint of mischief sparked in Miranda's eyes. "Oh dear," she sighed demurely, "you know how unschooled I am in your English customs. A lady alone in an actor's dressing room? I believe that's most improper. Perhaps I should leave at once?"

"Never!" said Theo firmly, and at once took appropriate action to keep her from going.

After quite a long time had elapsed, a dreamy-eyed

Miranda lifted her tousled head from Theo's shoulder. "You really don't mind that I'm not Amanda Fitton?"

"How many times must I tell you?" Theo buried his face in a cloud of ebony ringlets. "It's Miranda I fell in love with, the adorable girl whose book I picked from the mud."

"All the same, it might have been pleasant to live in a Florentine villa."

"My dearest Miranda!" A shade of exasperation crept into Theo's voice. "What have you or I to do with Italian villas? Remember your station in life, girl. You'll live in Bow Street and like it. You know I have to be close to my place of work."

Miranda tightened her arms around the silken-clad shoulders, all her qualms finally at rest. "Marvelous work, my darling. You were truly splendid tonight. That moonlit garden scene—how does it go? *It is my lady; O! it is my love—*"

Theo finished the quotation for her, accompanying the ardent words with suitable actions. When Garrick and all the rest burst into the room a few minutes later, the two young lovers were hopelessly compromised, and had to be married promptly—to the great delight of Mrs. Amelia Hester, who liked all her stories to have a happy ending.

Let COVENTRY Give You
A Little Old-Fashioned Romance